A corpse is a corpse is a corpse . . .

Lina lay there on her back, the pink satin robe foaming loose around her. The wooden handle of a cheap knife reared up from the pink nightgown under the left breast. And there was blood —crimson blood pulsing up and spilling over the pink material.

But the blood wasn't the worst part. The flowers which I had vaguely noticed on the hall table had been spilled out of the vase. They were strewn haphazard over that prostrate little body.

They were roses, of course . . . dozens of pure white roses.

I ran to Lina. I knelt at her side. I felt her wrist for the pulse that was not there. . . .

PUZZLE FOR PUPPETS

by PATRICK
• QUENTIN

AVON
PUBLISHERS OF BARD, CAMELOT AND DISCUS BOOKS

AVON BOOKS
A division of
The Hearst Corporation
959 Eighth Avenue
New York, New York 10019

Cover photograph by William Douglas King
Dress design by Anthony Muto
Hat design by Stuart Jay

First Avon Printing, February, 1980

PUZZLE FOR PUPPETS

CHAPTER I

Sailors, thousands of them, crawled up and down Market Street like a plague of blue locusts. Doubtless they brought color and racy vigor and all the other things sailors are supposed to bring to a scene. But I hadn't come to San Francisco to see sailors. After three rough-and-tumble months at a naval training camp up the Coast, I had absorbed enough maritime color and vigor to hold me indefinitely. The sailors, jostling against Iris and me as we beat our way forward, were just another of the things like overcrowded hotels and non-existent taxis that were conspiring against our week-end.

I looked through bobbing white caps for a taxi which I knew wouldn't be there. My wife, stubbornly obedient to the regulation that naval officers should keep their right hand free, had insisted upon carrying her own suitcase. She shifted it from one hand to the other. It bumped against mine. I jerked mine away, almost eviscerating a machinist's mate, second class.

In a chin-up voice, my wife said: "I could always call Eulalia."

"Eulalia who?" I said.

"Eulalia Crawford."

"Who's Eulalia Crawford?" I patiently disentangled my wife from a young ensign. The ensign didn't seem to want to be disentangled.

7

"Eulalia Crawford's a cousin. I haven't seen her since we were kids. But she lives in San Francisco. Maybe she has a spare bedroom."

"I'll be damned," I said, "if we'll spend any of our precious thirty-six hours in the spare bedroom of your sordid spinster cousin."

My wife was nettled. "Eulalia isn't a sordid spinster. She's dazzling and beautiful and disreputable. She has lovers and things."

"Spinster or strumpet," I said, "no, Eulalia."

"Such language from a lieutenant junior grade," murmured Iris, and then said: "Oops" as she ran into headlong collision with a marine sergeant.

I was a man of one simple idea. I hadn't been alone with my wife for three months. I wanted to be alone with her. Even though seventeen hotels had turned us down by telephone at the station, I believed that, war or no war, a husband still had the right to a room with his wife. A miracle had made Iris's birthday coincide with my first liberty since my temporary transference from sea duty to the training camp. Another miracle had made it possible for my wife to snatch the week-end from the picture in which Hollywood was grooming her for stardom. If miracles had any functional value, a third one would have to come along and make it possible for us to reap the benefits of the first two.

"If only we'd had time to wire ahead for reservations," sighed Iris. She came to a halt, put down her suitcase, and stared at me forlornly. "Darling, we can't just wander in a void. You got a medal for being resourceful somewhere off Truk. Be resourceful."

The stream of sailors swarmed by on either side of us. Iris was so beautiful in something slim and black with a silver-fox cape that it hurt to look at her. I had only kissed her once since our individual trains had dumped us almost simultaneously into the madhouse of the railroad station. Everything in me was yelling out for privacy where I could start to kiss her in earnest. We had reached the mouth of Stockton Street. I took her arm and guided her out of Market Street's sailors into an almost equally dense mass of harassed shoppers.

"We're just a block from the St. Francis and the St. Anton," I said. "We'll try them."

"But they've already said they're full."

"That was over the phone. We'll experiment with personal charm."

Iris slipped her free hand into mine, thereby breaking her pet regulation about the right hands of naval officers. "Whose personal charm? Yours or mine?"

"Yours," I said. "And if they don't respond to it, I'll try a blunt instrument."

As we started to climb Stockton, I sneezed. I had felt a cold coming on in the train. That was another cross I had to bear. Iris said: "Bless you." Half way up the block we passed a sign proclaiming a Turkish bath. With wild hopefulness, my wife said: "You don't suppose Turkish baths rent rooms to mixed couples—I mean, if you explain you're married?"

"It's extremely unlikely," I said and sneezed again.

I was still sniffling when we dragged ourselves into Union Square.

The St. Francis Hotel and the St. Anton Hotel stared at each other across the formal flower beds of the park like two rival and opulently upholstered dowagers at a garden party. We tried the St. Francis first. It would have none of Iris's charm or my blunt instrument. Traipsing across the little park, we pushed through the swing doors and stepped into the haughty vestibule of the St. Anton.

Although it tried to look as if it had given banquets for Mr. Sutro and the Big Four before the fire, the St. Anton had been built after the First World War. Its atmosphere, however, was studiedly Old San Francisco—gilt, red plush with pompoms, great mirrors, and chandeliers. The rush of war-time custom had somewhat frazzled its dignity. The fat chairs that had been designed for the comfortable buttocks of peacetime matrons were now occupied by service mothers with squalling infants or lean women in slacks, hot from the shipyards. The inevitable sailors, lavishly augmented by army and marine officers, lounged around the potted palms, adding a rowdy, canteen note.

We weaved through baggage and the general chaos towards the room clerk's desk. A knot of room seekers was congregated there. Since the battle was obviously to the strong, I elbowed Iris into a strategic position. Two thin-necked clerks with pince-nez were trying to cope with the situation. One of them had been corralled by a woman on Iris's left, a sordid blonde in red with a hat like a feather duster, and with a lion-taming eye, who had a swarthy Greek civilian in tow. She was gabbling at her clerk with gestures and a foreign accent and bursts of throaty laughter which possibly constituted her conception of charm.

I didn't listen to her. The second clerk, like a straw in the wind, fluttered by. I called an ominous "Hey," and Iris with superb timing threw a ravishing smile which caught him in mid-flight.

As he hesitated in front of us, she said: "Please, my husband and I want a room. It's terribly . . ."

"Sorry, madam."

"We'll take anything." While I glowered, Iris put out her hand, laying it on his sleeve. "We're just here for the week-end. I haven't seen my husband for six months. I've come such a long way. I . . ."

Another peal of lusty laughter soared from the blonde with the feather-duster hat. She must have been having success. I loathed her for it.

"I'm very sorry, madam." The clerk tried unsuccessfully to draw his sleeve from Iris's grasp.

"But you must understand." Her story was getting more pitiful and apocryphal by the minute. "My husband's going overseas any day. This is the last chance we'll have to be together. We're only just married. We've tried every hotel in town. Anything will do. A single room. A room with no bath, a bath with no room . . ."

Behind the pince-nez, the clerk's eyes softened slightly. For a mad moment I thought Iris had got away with it. Then in a this-hurts-me-more-than-you voice, he murmured: "I'm truly sorry, madam. I'd be only too glad to help you. But . . ."

Dimly I was conscious that the blonde with the hat had turned and was staring at Iris.

"Listen," I said.

"I'm sorry, sir," said the clerk.

The blonde tapped Iris on the sleeve. The cluster of feathers wobbled on the massive blonde curls.

"You want a room, yes?" she said.

Both Iris and I spun around on her.

"Yes, yes," said Iris.

"Yes," I said and sneezed.

The blonde beamed at the Greek and then beamed at us. She put both her hands on Iris's arms.

"You poor cheeldren. I hear what you say. You part from each other and you are in love. Just thees minute I come to give up my room. You shall have it."

I couldn't believe it. Iris faltered: "You mean . . .?"

The blonde turned majestically to her clerk. "Thees lovely child and her sailor husband . . . you give them my room."

The clerk looked flustered. "But, Mrs. Rose, the room is yours, yes. However, now that you intend to give it up, there is a long waiting list of people who . . ."

The blonde's eyes flashed. "Unless these two have it, I do not give up my room. I keep it."

The Greek burst into an agitated foreign monologue. The blonde paid him no mind and continued to stare at the clerk. So did Iris and I.

The clerk hesitated for a long moment and then said pettishly: "In that case, Mrs. Rose, rather than have the room vacant, I'll let your—er—friends have it."

"That is good." Mrs. Rose's boisterous laugh boomed again.

I grinned at her. I could have taken her, feathers and all, to my bosom. Iris said: "Thank you, Mrs. Rose. Thank you more than we can say."

"Oh, no. It ees nothing. My child, I see you standing there and you are so, so like a lovely girl I used to know. And I say to myself, these two poor cheeldren they are in love." Mrs. Rose's broad, friendly face was dewy with sentiment. "I too am in love." She drew forward the large, sheepish Greek. "Thees is Mr. Annapoppaulos. Tonight we get married. Thees is why I give up the room."

Mr. Annapoppaulos bowed. So did we.

Mrs. Rose winked a ribald wink and dug Mr. Annapoppaulos in the ribs. "Tonight I get married. Tonight I need no bedroom of my own, yes?"

Mr. Annapoppaulos looked even more sheepish. Bobbing the feather duster and blowing us a kiss, Mrs. Rose, that most admirable of women, turned from the desk, sweeping her bridegroom with her.

Her gusty laugh rang out again as the two of them disappeared into the milling vestibule crowd.

The clerk looked after them balefully and pushed a pad of registration slips toward us. "Sign here, please. The room is number 624."

I signed Lieutenant and Mrs. Peter Duluth with a flourish. The clerk summoned an ancient bellhop to take our suitcases.

The third miracle had crashed through, after all. I was on the top of the world again.

A gilt and gingerbread elevator took us and the ancient bellhop and dozens of other people up to the sixth floor. The bellhop tottered ahead with the suitcases and let us into Room 624 with a key. As he wheezed around, opening windows and things, Iris and I, hand in hand, surveyed the miracle.

It was quite a room. Lushly Louis Quinze, it boasted as main attractions an enormous double bed with a crimson spread, a Madame Récamier couch, and a huge mirror friezed with gilt, naked cupids. It conjured up visions of girls' garters and naughty nights in the nineties. An open door revealed glimpses of a modern tiled bathroom. I gave the bellhop fifty cents to get rid of him. He closed the door on us.

"Darling," Iris gazed around her in ecstasy. Throwing off her hat and the silver foxes, she came to me, tossing back her dark hair. "Darling, all this splendor—and a bathroom."

I took her in my arms. I kissed her. I kissed her again, letting my hands remember her. Touching her was like white bread after months in a Jap prison camp.

Keeping my lips close to hers, I said: "Honey, I love Mrs. Rose."

"Darling, I love Mr. Annapoppaulos." Her green eyes behind their smudgy lashes flickered. "Mrs. Rose said I reminded her of someone she knew. I wonder who it was."

"What difference does it make?"

"None. I just wondered. I . . . Oh, Peter, it's so good to be with you again."

I picked her up in my arms and carried her to the

regal bed. I laid her down on the crimson spread and dropped at her side. She lifted her hands to the lapels of my uniform.

"Peter, let's dress up tonight and be frightfully glamorous and have dinner and dance. And then let's come back here and never get out of bed, never till you have to leave."

I bent over her, running my hand down the curve of her cheek.

"Why not skip dinner and dancing, baby?"

My finger was on her lips. She kissed it and then pulled me down, hugging me.

"Let's skip everything," she breathed.

She rolled away, grinning up.

"Such loose thoughts I have. Something about the room makes me shameless. I think it's the cupids' bare behinds."

She lay still for a moment, gazing up at me tenderly. "Your ears. The way they fit on to your head, so flat and smooth. When you're away I dream of your ears."

I leaned over her. "When I'm away, I dream of your . . ."

"Darling!" She grimaced. "Aren't you going to say happy birthday?"

I'd almost forgotten the birthday; there were so many other things to think about. I scrambled off the bed to my suitcase and took out my reserve uniform, the ultra-special tailor-made I kept for gala occasions. Flopping it down on a chair, I pulled out a brown paper bag and tossed my wife three pairs of stockings.

"Happy birthday, baby."

Iris picked up one stocking. She stared at it. She made little cooing sounds.

"Nylons! Peter, how—how on earth did you get them?"

I kissed her ear. "By selling my body in the right places."

She threw her arms around my neck. "This is the nicest birthday of my life."

The scent of her perfume was compounded of all the things I'd missed. Iris wasn't the only one the room made shameless, and with me it wasn't the cupids' behinds.

For one long moment she relaxed in my arms and then drew away. Rather breathlessly she said: "Darling, let's be conversational for a while. How's the training camp? Nice and peaceful after the Pacific?"

"Nice and dull. And sweaty." I hesitated. "Some news, though. Just before I came away, the Commander told me that if I'm a good boy and don't get into trouble, I'll be a lieutenant s. g. soon."

Iris smiled proudly. "Marvellous. What this family needs is more gold braid."

I wished she hadn't mentioned the camp. This wasn't the moment to let her know that, if the promotion went through, it would almost certainly send me to sea again. One of the toughest things in the world is explaining to a wife just how you can love her with every part of you and still be raring to get back into battle.

To veer the subject away, I asked: "How's Hollywood?"

In the old days before I joined the navy, I'd produced plays on Broadway for a living and Iris had been making herself quite a career as a dramatic actress. When I was transferred to the Pacific, however, she had dropped everything in the East and taken up a small-time movie contract to be near me. It was an act of great renunciation because she loved the theater and hated Hollywood.

Iris crinkled her nose. "Darling, don't let's talk about Hollywood. I'm still working on the first picture. I'm the other woman. I saw some rushes last week. I photograph like Hedy Lamarr's idiot sister."

She gathered up the stockings, stroking them, got off the bed, and went towards the pseudo-French highboy. I started after her and then had a fit of sneezing.

Iris turned. "You *are* getting a cold."

"Looks that way."

Her face puckered. "Darling, you can't have a cold, not on my beautiful birthday." She glanced at her watch and looked executive. "There's only one thing to do with colds."

"What's that?" I asked doubtfully.

"A Turkish bath. It's only five. I'm going to spend hours making myself glamorous, anyway. You've got heaps of time. Why don't you run down to the Turkish bath we passed on the street?"

She put her hands on my arms. "Have a steam bath,

darling. Let a rubber pound the daylights out of you. You'll feel wonderful. Then we can go to town."

I resented the idea of a Turkish bath. Any time spent away from Iris was a dead loss. But my wife had a point. I had no right to submit her to a snivelling mate.

"O.K.," I said grudgingly. "That is—if you can trust me alone in a Turkish bath."

It was then that the phone rang. My wife scrambled on to the bed and, reaching across the crimson spread, picked up the receiver.

"For God's sake," I said, "don't make any dates."

Iris nodded. "Hello," she said into the mouthpiece. And then: "What room do you want? . . . Yes, this is Room 624. But I'm Iris Duluth, Mrs. Peter Duluth . . . Oh, maybe you want Mrs. Rose. This was her room. She's just checked out . . . What? . . . Eulalia who? . . . Eulalia Crawford?"

She tensed visibly.

"Oh, no, I'm not Eulalia Crawford. But I am her cousin. Yes, I'm told I look very like her . . . Yes, that was my husband, Lieutenant Duluth . . . No, I wrote Eulalia from Hollywood, but we're in town such a short time we won't have time to see her . . . I'd love to ask you up but . . . well, I'm—I'm in the middle of unpacking and my husband's just going down the street to a Turkish bath . . . Oh, no, don't be silly . . . Thank you. Good-bye."

She put down the receiver. A frown rippled her forehead.

"That's funny," she said.

"What on earth was it?"

"A man—downstairs in the lobby. He'd seen us come up with the bellhop. He thought I was Eulalia Crawford."

"That dreary cousin again."

"She's not dreary," and Iris. "I've already told you she's disreputable and glamorous. And I've heard she looks very much like me. Several years older, of course. But . . ." My wife was looking at me with what I call her Mary Roberts Rinehart look. "It was so odd. Even if he had thought I was Eulalia, why did he call? He said he was a friend of hers, but . . ."

My wife's insatiable curiosity constantly starts her

skittering off after imaginary mysteries. To discourage her, I said: "He probably thought he'd caught Eulalia sneaking upstairs for a little nookey with a random naval lieutenant. You said she went in for lovers and things. Maybe he was a rival lover, checking up."

"Peter, stop being nasty about Eulalia. You don't even know her." She paused. "But this man, he also said he was a great friend of Mrs. Rose's. He seemed to want to come up here. And . . . and, well, he seemed curious about whether I was going to see Eulalia. She did write me, matter of fact, a few weeks ago. She makes puppets or something crazy and she'd read about my going to Hollywood. It was a sweet letter all about how I used to put pollywogs in her drawers in Jamaica Plains when I was four. I wrote back, very cousinly, promising to look her up one day. But . . . Peter, why should that man be a friend of Eulalia's *and* Mrs. Rose's? And why was he so interested in our movements?"

"I don't know or care." I added firmly: "And neither do you."

"But, darling, I do care."

"Why?"

She paused and then said solemnly: "There was something about him, something about his voice. Peter, he had a horrid little lisp. He said: 'Yeth' and 'Of courth' and 'Mithuth Rothe.' He sounded sinister."

"Listen," I said, "if you're going into one of your clutching-hand moods, I won't go to the goddam Turkish bath. I'll just sit here and sneeze."

Iris looked stubborn. "But it was odd."

"Nonsense," I said.

That's what I said. Nonsense.

In the words of the immortal Mrs. Rinehart's immortal phrase: *Had I but known . . .*

CHAPTER II

The vestibule of the St. Anton Hotel was even more animated when I battled my way across it and through the
swing door to the street. The street was animated, too.
There's an elusive something about San Francisco that no
other city has. Maybe it's the flower stalls blossoming on
every street corner. Maybe it's the crazy gradients that
make roller-coasters out of the streetcars. Or maybe it's
just the air. But people in San Francisco doing the most
humdrum things look like people at the peak of some
enthralling adventure. Although I was sulking at being
without Iris, the zest of it all infected me as I strode down
the hill towards the Turkish bath. I bought a luscious
gardenia and gave a fairly honest-looking boy a quarter to
deliver it to my wife.

I found the Turkish bath in the next block. It was
painted a crisp white and black, but the Turkish bath itself was on the second floor and the stairs leading up to
it had that bleak, neutral atmosphere which characterizes
the approaches to Turkish baths and athletic clubs all
over the country.

A glass swing door let me into a small room almost
entirely taken up by a wire cage with a slit window. Sitting inside the cage was a bony man with a green eyeshade
who pushed a register to me and chanted:

17

"Dollar - fifty - including - alcohol - rub - sunlamp - extra - check - your - valuables - here."

I signed the book, gave him the money, and bundled my wallet, my identification papers, and my watch into the brown envelope he tossed me. He yawned, licked the flap of the envelope, stuck it down, and slid it back to me together with an indelible pencil.

"Sign - across - flap - of - envelope - countersign - when - you - come - out."

I signed. The clerk took the envelope and flicked it into one of the many pigeonholes behind him. He gestured with his thumb towards a green baize door and then slumped into a middle-aged reverie.

The green baize door opened on to the social room, or whatever it's called, of the Turkish bath. Waves of artificial heat rolled towards me. Green metal lockers stretched away in rows on the left. On the right, men in various stages of undress lolled around in wicker chairs, smoking, chatting, drinking, and reading dog-eared magazines. At a table, four solemn, executive-type gentlemen, stark naked, were playing bridge.

A colored locker-boy with a bunch of keys led me down the aisles of lockers. Those already in use were locked. The vacant ones were left ajar. The boy, using some obscure method of selection of his own, picked me a locker, swung the door open, gave me a key with an elastic wristband attached, and wandered away.

Several other men, servicemen and civilians, were undressing in that particular aisle. I paid them no attention as I threw the key down on my individual three-legged stool and started to get out of my uniform. It was disgracefully out of press after my long, crowded train trip and there was a triangular rip low on the left leg of the pants where I had caught them on a nail. I was glad I had brought my glamour uniform along for our birthday celebration that night.

The colored boy came back with another customer in tow. As he passed me, he dropped a towel for me on my stool. I hung my uniform and my shirt on the hooks inside the locker, peeled off my socks and tossed my shorts in after them. I remembered cigarettes from my uniform pocket, slung the towel over my shoulder, slammed the door so that the automatic lock snapped into place, picked up the key from the stool and slipped its elastic around my wrist. Dodging through elbows and rumps, I weaved my way past the other undressing men and out, around the nudist bridge foursome, into the baths proper.

I had not been in a Turkish bath since my days of civilian hangovers. It was a Friday evening and the warm, oozy-walled rooms were jammed with my fellow creatures. Although I had been submitted to an excess of male nakedness in the navy, the other bodies around me had at least been youthful. I had forgotten what unkind variations age can play on the theme of the masculine form. As I looked sourly around me, I reflected that nature must have a taste for paradox. So many shoulders that should have been broad were narrow, and so many hips that should have been narrow were broad. So many stomachs that should have been flat were bulging, and so many chests that should have been bulging were flat.

Feeling rather smug about my own relatively orthodox proportions, I shared a shower with a stomach and followed a bunch of hips into the sweltering hot room, where I stretched myself and my cold out on a burning wooden deck chair. I relaxed, wondering how soon I could legitimately get back to Iris and the cupids in Room 624.

The bodies around me were contentedly chatting and sweating and visiting each other, but to me they had no individuality. Men in bulk, without their clothes, lose all personal identity. As the heat seared its way through my pores, the elastic around my wrist became oppressive. I slipped the key off and put it down on the arm of my chair. A dark, lissom youth came over, perched himself on the foot support of my chair, and said hadn't he seen me at the ballet. I said he hadn't and wasn't likely to and, picking up my key, stalked off to the steam room.

I stayed five minutes or so in its stifling, anonymous mist, feeling hemmed in by the swarming, sticky bodies of the other men around me. When I couldn't stand it any more, I left, took a plunge in the ice-cold swimming pool and was ready for my rubdown.

Before the war, I had always found a rubdown something of an ordeal, but I was pleased to discover that my naval training had toughened me. Now, as the heavyweight colored masseur bent and kneaded me all over the slab, my muscles took it in their stride. By the time he was through with me and I strolled back to the lounge, I felt fresher than paint, without a sneeze in my system.

A clock on the wall above the naked bridge quartet showed that the whole business had taken me less than an hour. My mind full of Iris, I lit a cigarette and, without lingering in the creaky wicker chairs, returned to the lockers.

A couple of other men were in my own aisle, putting on their clothes. I located my locker and, pulling the key off my wrist, inserted it in the lock. I turned but nothing happened.

I wrestled with the lock for a few seconds and then decided I must have mistaken the locker. I tried the green cubicle to the right and then to the left, with no result. I was back struggling with the first lock, swearing under my breath, when the man nearest to me strolled over.

"Havin' trouble, bud?"

I looked up. He was somewhere in his late thirties, with grizzled black hair, gloomy eyes, and the sardonic mouth of a philosopher with no illusions as to his fellow men's intelligence. He was wearing nothing but a gaudily striped purple and white shirt, from below which protruded a pair of man-sized legs.

"Yeah," I said. "Can't get my locker open."

The somber black eyes watched me for a second. When I yanked the key from the reluctant lock, he held out his hand. I was flustered and mad enough to respond to his air of sour efficiency. When I passed him the key, he looked at it, looked at the locker, and then turned on me a gaze of melancholy resignation, as if I were a retarded little girl who couldn't tie the bows on my own pigtails. He tossed the key back to me.

"Key number 312. Locker number 168," he said laconically. "You're screwed up, bud."

I stared at the number on the key and then at the number on the locker. He was only too right. Feeling foolish, I said: "I'm sure this is the locker I put my clothes in. But—maybe you're right. I'll try locker 312."

Twisting my towel around my hips, I started down the other lines of cubicles, looking for the locker whose number matched the key. My neighbor gazed after me and then sauntered in pursuit, the tails of the purple and white shirt flopping around his massive thighs. I found number 312. My neighbor stood at my side, watching skeptically. It was only too plain that his low opinion of human nature in general had crystallized into a low opinion of me in particular.

"Open it, bud," he said. "You'll find you're just screwed up."

I put the key in the lock. The green metal door swung open. Inside the locker, dangling on the hooks, were a henna-brown suit, a grubby white shirt, a pair of athletic shorts, and a pair of broken-down brown brogues.

"There!" the man in the shirt said with gloomy satisfaction. "You were just screwed up. See?"

"I wasn't screwed up," I snapped. "These aren't my clothes."

At that moment the colored locker-boy came by. I grabbed him.

"This isn't my locker. You've given me the wrong key."

The boy rolled his eyes in pained surprise. "No, suh. I ain't never done give a party no wrong key, not since all the time I been here."

"Well, you've done it now." I was becoming inflamed both against the boy and the man in the purple and white shirt who was still gazing at me in his own maddeningly wiseacre fashion. "Have you got a pass-key?" I asked the boy.

He moistened full lips. "Why, yes, suh."

I gripped his arm. "Then come along and I'll show you the locker I put my clothes in. You open it for me. I want to get out of here."

The three of us returned to the original locker. My neighbor strolled back to his own quarters, grabbed a pair of fancy lavender shorts, and came back.

Staring at him belligerently, I said to the boy:"This one."

The boy opened the locker with his pass-key. My neighbor craned his neck.

"Well . . . ?" he asked.

I had nothing to say because the locker was empty. Suddenly unsure of myself, I faltered: "Well, maybe it was one of the other lockers right about here. But I know it was this row."

The boy opened the two lockers on either side of the first one. Then he opened all the lockers in the row. He revealed civilian suits of various shapes and sizes, a marine sergeant's uniform and an army captain's. But there was no sign of my clothes.

The man in the shirt thrust his legs into the shorts and buttoned them over a lean waist. "Well," he said triumphantly, "you're certainly screwed up now."

Suppressing an impulse to strangle him, I whipped round on the locker-boy.

"I'm sure that first locker you opened is the one. If you gave me the right key in the beginning, then someone's switched keys with me and run off with my uniform. Get the manager."

"Yes, suh." The boy scurried away.

While I fumed in silence, my neighbor stared into the empty interior of what had been my locker. He scratched his head.

"Guess someone really did snitch your clothes, bud."

"Big of you to admit it," I said tartly.

"Uniform, you said. You in the army?"

"Navy."

"That's tough. Losing a uniform's tough. You can get into trouble for that, can't you?"

"I probably won't be shot at dawn." I craned my neck for the manager. "But I'm not cheering about it. That uniform set me back eighty bucks."

"Tough."

"And what riles me, even if the boy did switch keys by mistake, it's deliberate theft. No civilian, however drunk, could have walked out of here in my uniform instead of that brown suit without noticing it. Thank God, I've got another one back at the hotel."

"A uniform's quite a thing to steal." My gloomy friend had taken his own pants from his locker. They were made of a loud blue check tweed with startling red suspenders dangling from them. "A guy with the cops after him, for example. A slick idea to duck in here as a civilian and come out as a sailor. Then again"—he added with ominous emphasis—"enemy agents, maybe. I figure there's plenty of uses an enemy agent could put an American navy uniform to."

Although that sounded on the melodramatic side, it added to my already exasperated uneasiness. Losing a uniform was bad enough, but if there was something more sinister behind it than simple theft, this was a hell of a time to have had it happen—with my promotion teetering in the balance.

My neighbor had put on his pants and was buttoning them. "Figure this thing straight. Granted the boy gave you the right key, then the guy from 312 switched keys with you. When could that have happened?"

I remembered that I had taken my key off for a few moments in the hot room and put it down on the arm of my chair. I thought of the dark boy who had come over to me, but I was pretty sure that what he'd been interested in had not been my key. Someone else in the hot room, however, might easily have exchanged keys without my noticing. I also recalled that I'd left the key on the stool while I undressed. Any passer-by could have taken it then. It was only too clear that an attempt to narrow things down would be hopeless.

I said: "I guess almost anyone could have switched keys on me—anyone in the place."

"That's bad." My neighbor was knotting a formidable purple and white necktie over the purple and white shirt. Now that he was dressed, his jaunty clothes, warring with the cadaverous gloom of his face, made him look like a Salvation Army captain disguised as a racing tout. He held out a rough hand and, as if he felt our relationship was now serious enough to formalize, he said: "Call me Hatch."

"O.K., Hatch," I said. "I'm Peter Duluth."

The manager came fussing up then with the locker-boy. I gave him a thoroughly bad-tempered account of what had happened. I had lost my towel at one stage of the proceedings and felt a little bizarre complaining to the management stark naked, but there was nothing else I could do. The manager was propitiating but chiefly concerned lest his other clients should be inconvenienced by any disturbance. He politely refused to accept my word that the uniform had been stolen until all the lockers had been searched. After a mild amount of confusion, the search took place.

My uniform, of course, was not discovered.

The manager murmured: "Most distressing. Most distressing, Lieutenant. The man who—er—took your uniform must obviously have left. What can I do? Nothing of this sort has ever happened here before."

"I don't care what has or hasn't happened before," I said. "You've got to do something. I want to get out of here, and if you think I'm going to walk bare-ass up Stockton Street you're out of your mind."

Hatch had been watching, his jaws moving over a piece of gum.

"Figure this thing straight," he said. "The guy who stole the Lieutenant's uniform left his suit in 312. O.K. Search the suit. Maybe it'll give you a lead. Figure this thing straight."

In spite of his exasperating habit of running a phrase into the ground, Hatch, I was beginning to realize, was on the beam. We all trooped back to locker 312. An exhaustive search of the henna suit and the underwear produced nothing. Even the maker's label was missing from inside the jacket.

Hatch's jaws worked around the gum. "Well, at least it's something for the Lieutenant to wear back to the hotel. He walks off with your uniform. You wear his suit. Better than nothing."

I was repelled by everything about that suit and the crummy white shirt, but there was nothing else for me. While the three men watched intently I scrambled into the clothes. The suit wasn't so bad as a fit. The shoes were wearable, too.

"Must have been a guy about the Lieutenant's size," ruminated Hatch. "Figure this straight." He turned to the boy. "You don't remember nothing about the guy you gave 312 to?"

The boy shook his head.

Reluctantly the manager said: "I've always tried not to associate this establishment with the police, but . . ."

"The police." Hatch's voice broke in thick with scorn. "The police'd mess around, keep the Lieutenant at the station answering questions till daybreak, but would they bother about getting a uniform back? Not them."

Although I was not in a position to be that cynical about the San Francisco police authorities, Hatch as usual had a point. Nothing, let alone a uniform, was going to make me spend Iris's birthday kicking my heels in a police station.

"No," I said. "The police are out definitely."

I'd been set back eighty bucks and I was tired of hanging around. Eventually, I would report the incident. O.K. I was ready to leave it at that.

I was telling the manager as much when Hatch put his hand on my sleeve.

"Not so fast, Lieutenant. This guy must have signed the register with the pay clerk when he came in. And he must have passed the pay clerk again as he went out. The pay clerk's the guy. He may give us a lead. Figure this thing straight."

The thought of the pay clerk brought the unnerving realization that my wallet had been left with him. It had been humiliating enough to have lost my uniform in a Turkish bath, but if my identification papers were gone too . . . The very idea sent needles up my spine.

"Let's get to that pay clerk."

I rushed out into the small vestibule with the manager and Hatch after me. The bony pay clerk was still sprawled in a chair behind his cage.

I said: "Lieutenant Duluth. My valuables."

He blinked. With an unendurable slowness, he fumbled in the pigeonholes behind him. "Lieutenant Duluth," he murmured. "Duluth. Ah . . . here you are."

He passed a brown envelope through the slit in the grille.

"Countersign," he began chanting again. "Just - like - you - signed - when - you - come - in."

He took in my civilian suit then and made a grab for the envelope.

"*Lieutenant* Duluth. You ain't a lieutenant."

"It's all right," put in the manager quickly. "There's been a little mistake."

I tore open the envelope. To my infinite relief, all my things were safely inside.

Hatch, thumbs thrust inside the scarlet suspenders, was staring at the pay clerk with his particular air of seedy authority.

"Listen," he said, "someone's stole this Lieutenant's uniform. That means some guy came here in that suit"— he pointed at me—"and left some time ago in a naval lieutenant's uniform. If you got an eye in your head, you should've noticed something like that."

The clerk stared at my brown suit and looked flustered. "I don't reckon I . . . Wait. Maybe I do. Yeah. Just now, not fifteen minutes back, a naval lieutenant come out. He kind of had a handkerchief up to his face like he had a cold or something. He comes right by me and I calls after him: *Hey, what about your valuables?* Lieutenants, they always has their passes and things with 'em—all the servicemen, they always leave valuables with me. But this guy, this lieutenant, he just calls over his shoulder: *I don't have any valuables. Just what I got with me.* And then he scrams out real fast."

Hatch said: "What did he look like?"

"I couldn't rightly tell you. As I said, he had a handkerchief up to his face like. I guess he was about the same build as the Lieutenant here and . . ."

"Didn't you notice anything about him? Not his voice? Not nothing?"

"His voice." The clerk resitated. "Yeah. Seems to me I did notice his voice. It was kind of soft and funny, like he had a lisp or something."

I was so pleased to get my wallet back that I wasn't paying any of them much attention. I turned to the manager.

"Listen, I haven't time to waste making a fuss. You know my name. I'm registered up the street at the St. Anton. Call me if anything shows up. Otherwise, forget it."

The manager looked relieved. But Hatch's gloomy gaze fixed my face.

"Not so fast," he said. "Eighty bucks is eighty bucks. I don't like to see no one get screwed like that."

"Forget it."

Hatch chewed his gum reflectively and pulled me aside. "Listen, Lieutenant, I don't normally bother myself with things like this. Chicken feed, it is to me. But right now—well, I come to this bath following up a case and I didn't get the lead I expected. I got a free evening. Just on account of I thought you were a dope and I guess you're not a dope, I'll make a stab at getting that uniform back for you."

I stared at him. "What the hell . . .?"

With a certain gloomy pride, he produced a formal printed card from his pocket and handed it to me. I read:

"HATCH" WILLIAMS AND "BILL" DAGGET
CONFIDENTIAL AGENTS

"So!" I said. "A private detective. No wonder you've been so smart."

Hatch Williams lowered his lashes modestly. "With any luck I can narrow down the names in that register. There's plenty of leads yet. I got my contacts. I got my methods. I'm not promising nothing, understand. But—well, is it a deal?"

I looked at his mournful face with its black, embittered eyes. Hatch Williams, I felt, had more than a sporting chance of getting anything if he set his mind to it.

"O.K." I said. "And, as for the fee . . ."

"There won't be no fee." Hatch forced his reluctant features into a shy grin. "I got a kid in the navy myself."

"But . . ."

"There won't be no fee. Just tell me where you're located and I'll keep in touch with you. You put it all out of your mind. Have a good time. Let me do the worrying from now on."

Mrs. Rose. Hatch Williams. San Francisco went in for a fine type of civilian. I patted his shoulder and said: "That's darn decent of you, Hatch." I told him my room number at the St. Anton and, eager to get back to Iris, hurried out into the street.

I was half way up Stockton, feeling foolish and guilty in my disreputable brown suit, when something the pay clerk had said came rushing back to me.

The clerk had said that the imposter who had run off with my uniform had spoken in a voice that was *kind of soft and funny, like he had a lisp*. A vivid memory rose of Iris as she sat on the bed, telling me about the unknown man who had called her from the hotel lobby. *There was something about his voice. He had a horrid little lisp.*

As those two reflections came together in my mind, I had the sensation of something vaguely sinister lying just beyond my grasp.

Then common sense reasserted itself with the reflection that thousands of men in San Francisco must lisp.

"Nonsense," I said to myself.

That was the second time in so many hours that I had said: Nonsense.

CHAPTER III

Back at the St. Anton, I tapped on the door of room 624 and called: "Honey, it's me."

The door opened. My wife had turned back to the rococo French vanity and was doing something exotic in the mirror. Consequently, she didn't see my entrance.

Iris is given to looking more beautiful than anyone else, but that night she was looking more beautiful than herself. She had changed into a full-skirted black evening gown which covered very little territory above the hips. Her back and bosom gleamed smooth as ivory. She was wearing absolutely no ornament—nothing but the cream-thick gardenia, attached to a black velvet ribbon which circled her throat.

"Thanks for the lovely gardenia, darling. It's just what this dress needed." She shifted the angle of the flower the fraction of an inch. "Well, lost your cold?"

"Yes," I said.

She turned then. Her eyes batted in astonishment at the monstrous civilian suit.

"Good grief!" she exclaimed. "Is the war over?"

I looked hangdog. I said: "The cold wasn't the only thing I lost at the Turkish bath."

I told her everything then—everything, that is, except the coincidental lisp of the uniform thief. With her erratic

29

passion for mystery, that lisp, tied to the lisping telephone call, would have been more than enough to send her into a frenzy of speculation. And I wasn't going to spend our week-end speculating. I was still a man of one idea.

Luckily, from the way I told it, the story merely seemed funny to Iris. She laughed rudely at the picture of me upbraiding the manager in my outraged nakedness. Then a shadow of worry passed across her face.

"Darling, you won't get into trouble, will you? There isn't any Naval Regulation, page 42, paragraph 17b, with frightful penalties for losing uniforms? With your promotion and . . ."

"So far as I know, I'm safe from court-martial. Anyhow, we've got Hatch on the job. My own private private detective."

My wife shook a drop of perfume on to her finger and rubbed it pensively behind her ear.

"Men get all the breaks," she sighed. "If I'd gone to a Turkish bath, I'd never have met anything as exciting as a naked private detective—never in a million years."

"You'll probably meet Hatch. He said he'd get in touch with me later."

"I can just picture him," said Iris dreamily. "A lovely squawking check suit and one of those mouths you talk out of the corner of and a cigar."

"I can't vouch for the cigar. Otherwise, that's Hatch."

Iris sighed. I couldn't go on looking at all that beauty without doing something about it. I slid her into my arms, kissing her below the gardenia.

"You're gorgeous, baby. You're something any private detective would be proud to meet in a Turkish bath."

"You mean that? You're not just trying to make me feel better?"

"Idiot."

"The dress, Peter. I bought it especially for your leave."

I felt along her shoulders with my lips. She gave a little contented gasp. Then she drew herself away.

"Darling, that suit! It's like being kissed by the man who reads the gas meter." She crinkled her nose. "You might have picked a better-dressed thief. Get out of it into your uniform. I hung it up in the closet."

I was only too glad to part company with that suit. I

yanked it off and the shirt and shoes after it. I tossed them all down on the floor and took a shower to wash away all memories of it. When I came back, Iris had picked up the jacket and was going through the pockets rather furtively.

"What's the idea?" I said.

"Oh, I was just looking to see whether there was anything in it. Anything to give a clue."

"We've already looked," I said.

Starting from scratch, I dressed in my own clothes. I was quite proud of my glamor uniform. In fact, when I was through, I felt I looked pretty smooth. Luckily I had new shoes and a new cap, too.

While I dressed, Iris pottered around the discarded suit. I didn't like the symptoms. I took her arm and drew her away from temptation.

"Listen, baby," I said. "Promise me something."

She looked innocent and remote. "Why, yes, darling."

"Don't get a brilliant idea for catching uniform thieves."

Iris looked even more innocent. "But, of course. How absurd. Why on earth would I want to chase around after a uniform?"

"Swear?"

Her fingers went up caressing the insignia of my lapels. "Gee, but you're sharp." She twisted away and bent down, catching her skirt in both hands and lifting it to her hips. "Look, Lieutenant, nylons."

I said, staring: "Do you want any dinner?"

"I'm simply starved."

"Then drop that skirt or we'll never get out of here."

Meekly, my wife let the folds of black taffeta slide down to the floor. She put her hand through my arm and we started towards the door.

On the threshold she paused, throwing a glance over her bare shoulder at the gilt frieze around the mirror.

"Don't worry," she murmured to the cupids. "We'll be back."

We had cocktails at a table by the dance floor in the dining room of the hotel. If possible, the St. Anton dining room with its Jacobean panelling and its huge crystal chandeliers was even more Old San Francisco than the vestibule. It made a gesture to the twentieth century, however, in the form of a rumba orchestra. It was a good one, too. Iris and I danced between cocktails and, every now and then, during a meal consisting of all the most wicked and expensive things we could order. Quite a lot of other people were there, eating and dancing, but I didn't notice any of them, except maybe to feel sorry for them for not having Iris. We had brandy with our coffee. Then we were back dancing again.

"Happy birthday?" I asked, veering Iris past a dowager who should never have been rumbaing in the first place.

"Ecstatic," she said. "Darling, we do a mean rumba, don't we?"

"Very mean."

"Twenty-six," murmured Iris. She glanced at me suddenly. The scent of the gardenia seemed to come from her smudgy lashes. "Peter, do I look twenty-six?"

"Twenty-seven, isn't it?"

"Beast." Iris slid close against me and our rumba became intimate.

It was then that I saw the Beard.

I saw him over Iris's shoulder. He was sitting alone at a table close to the dance floor, a massive, imperial gentleman dressed in elegant grey with a red carnation in his lapel. His Jovian dignity was enough in itself to attract attention, but his principal feature by far was a black curly beard which sprouted with magnificent vigor above the red carnation.

At his side on the white tablecloth was an empty champagne bottle. He looked as if it hadn't been the first champagne bottle that had been there that evening. He was gazing at it with high solemnity while weaving slightly in his chair. Iris and I had a friend in New York who was a sober and distinguished psychiatrist. This man might have been Dr. Lenz's reprobate brother.

We were only a couple of feet away from him when he looked up from the champagne bottle and saw us. At least it was Iris he saw. Naturally. Somewhere above the beard, his eyes lit up. The beard waggled in a roguish satyr smile. One heavy lid lowered at Iris in a ponderous wink.

The maze of dancers forced us even closer to him. He was still peering at Iris. Suddenly the goatist leer left his face. Another expression took its place, a kind of astonishment, as if something about Iris had shocked him into momentary sobriety.

"You . . .!" he said.

The tone of his voice made us pause in front of him. I looked at him. Iris looked at him.

Ready to be belligerent, I said: "Iris, do you know this unattractive gentleman?"

Iris peered deep into the whiskers. "Not unless the beard's false and it's Mr. Finklestein." She beamed at him. "Are you Mr. Finklestein of Magnificent Studios in disguise?"

He either ignored or was unable to grasp this remark. He tried to get up, sank back, and then did get up. He leaned across the table towards us. A large finger, hovering precariously over the empty champagne bottle, pointed at Iris. Very slowly, he said: "Are you mad being out toni' of all ni's—with your picture ri' there in the *Chronicle?* I warned you on page eighty-four. Warned you, l'il fool."

That was an odd thing for a complete stranger—even a completely drunk stranger—to say. He was obviously up to the gills in champagne and a right-thinking and clean-living husband should have rumbaed his wife away then. But I didn't. There was something about him. I think it was the Ancient Mariner quality of the burgeoning black bead and the hypnotic stare.

He swayed slightly. The beard bobbed in a defined little hiccup. With immense effort, he managed: "The white rose! The red rose!" He paused. "The roses mean—blood."

The music went: Pomtipomtipom*pom*pom. The dancers writhed by us. No one seemed to be paying any attention. The Beard was still staring at Iris. She stared back, her eyes fascinated.

Tentatively, she said: "The white rose and the red rose mean blood. I'm sure that's terribly nice for them. Go on."

"The whi' rose." The Beard clutched for his empty champagne glass and lifted it to his lips. I don't think he realized it was empty. "The whi' rose and the red rose—out. They're out. You know they're out. Warned you."

He dropped the glass and raised one of his large hands. The gesture practically toppled him forward into the champagne bottle. Pointing his ambassadorial finger again, he said: "Life or death for you, li'l lady. Musht realize that. Life or death." He weaved. "You've forgotten. The elephant hasn't forgotten. Never—th'elephant."

Riddles are awfully entertaining. The Sphinx got a long way on a couple of them. But I was beginning to realize just what effect this maudlin old man was going to have on my wife in her current mood. A mysterious telephone call and a stolen uniform were nothing to this. I tried to rumba Iris away, but I was too late. Agog, she broke away from me and crossed to the Beard.

"The red rose and the white rose mean blood," she said. "And the elephant never forgets. Whose elephant?"

The Beard looked vague. "Life or death."

"Life or death for me?" asked Iris. "Or life or death for the elephant?"

The Beard looked vaguer. "Life or death," he muttered. "Mushn't die, young lady. Too buriful to die."

Slowly, like a hillside settling down after an earth tremor, he sank back into his chair. His eyes went far away and sad. He hiccuped again, daintily.

"Tell me." Iris's voice was pleading now. "What is it? What are you trying to tell me?"

The Beard tittuped up and down. One eye, opening craftily like a basilisk's, stared at her with a look of complete non-recognition. He had obviously forgotten us.

I seized my opportunity. Grabbing Iris, I pushed her out on to the dance floor and steered her away from the Beard through a marine lieutenant and a blonde and an army major and a brunette.

For a moment she let me lead her without objecting. I held her close, trying to remember that it was her birthday and we were having a wonderful time. But somehow that filthy old man with the beard had tarnished the magic.

Suddenly Iris said: "I know what you're thinking."

"What?"

"You're thinking that I know that man."

"Do you?"

"Of course I don't. What on earth would I be doing with a beard like that in my past? He must have mistaken me for someone else." Iris's green eyes were aglow now with an unholy light. "Peter! *The red rose and the white rose mean blood. I warned you on page eighty-four. The elephant hasn't forgotten. Life or death.* Isn't it wonderful? It's the sort of movie I'd love to play in. Darling, let's go back and get some more."

"No," I said.

"But, Peter, darling, please . . ."

I held her closer. "No beard, no roses." The scent of her gardenia was wonderful. "Tonight you belong to me. Remember? Besides, it was all a lot of drunken gibberish."

Iris shook her head at that. "He was tight, darling. Of course he was. He was stinking. But it wasn't just the champagne. You could tell that. It all meant something. I'm sure of it. Life or death."

"Stop saying life or death," I said pettishly.

"I certainly shan't stop if I don't want to," said my wife.

I tried another approach. "There you go again," I said. "You're always the same. Just as soon as any man makes a pass at you . . ."

"A pass! Who made a pass at me, I'd like to know?"

"That old goat."

"A pass, indeed!"

"Well, that's what it was. He thought you were the whimsy type. He thought that's the way to make a pass at a whimsy girl. And apparently he's right."

With extreme hauteur, Iris said: "I won't even demean myself to discuss it any longer."

For some moments we rumbaed in icy silence. Gradually the gleam returned to her eyes.

"The white rose and the red rose," she murmured. And then sharply: "Roses. Mrs. Rose!"

"What about Mrs. Rose?"

"The woman who gave us her room. Mrs. Rose. She was wearing red."

"So what?"

"Oh, I don't know. I'm just wondering."

The music pounded untiringly. Iris, apparently, went on wondering.

At length she said: "He said my picture was in the *Chronicle.*"

"Yes."

"Maybe that's the key. My picture might be in the

paper. The studio's started releasing publicity stills." She glanced at me cozeningly. "Peter."

"Yes?"

"Peter, darling, even if we don't go back and talk to the Beard, can't we at least go out and buy a *Chronicle*— just to see?"

Dismally I saw the evening I had planned vanishing into thin air. I made a futile attempt to grab at its skirts.

"Iris, baby . . ."

"Darling, don't be so tweed-coat-and-pipeish. Come on."

"O.K."

Triumphantly, Iris slipped her hand through mine and drew me off the dance floor.

With a hatred for all beards smoldering in me, I accompanied my wife down thickly carpeted corridors to the vestibule. The lighted chandeliers and the drawn red plush curtains had done something to mellow the raucous atmosphere of the afternoon, but the place was still as crowded and active as ever. Indifferent to a barrage of masculine glances as outspoken as whistles, Iris led the way through the potted palms to the magazine stand which lurked in a corner.

A frayed blonde was scuttling around behind the counter, dispensing magazines and cigarettes. Iris grabbed a copy of the San Francisco *Chronicle,* leaving me to deposit a resentful nickel.

My wife had started to turn the pages of the newspaper when a hand tapped my shoulder.

"How's tricks, Lieutenant?"

I turned to see Hatch Williams standing behind me. He was wearing the same check suit and, to make Iris's imaginary portrait of him complete, a fat, unlit cigar drooped from his lips. In this festive setting he looked even more melancholy than he had at the Turkish bath.

"I just called your room and got no answer, Lieutenant. Figured you'd be down in the dining room eating. Then I saw you."

Iris had stopped looking at the paper and was watching Hatch. He was staring back at her with an expression which, for him, indicated rapturous appreciation.

I said: "Iris, this is Hatch Williams, the guy who was

so kind about my uniform. Hatch, this is my wife."

Iris held out her hand. "I've been dying to meet you."

Hatch's rough fingers folded over hers. "If I'd known what to expect, lady, I'd have reciprocated." He threw me one of his sardonic glances. "No wonder you were so hot to get back to the hotel."

I said: "Any news on the uniform?"

"Not so fast, Lieutenant. I'm no lightning valet service. I've narrowed things down to a couple of names in the register and I'm going to follow 'em up. I've got my partner, Bill Dagget, interested too. He's got a kid brother in the navy. But Dagget's the guy for detail, always was. He won't touch it until you give us something what you might call distinctive about your uniform—something that can prove positive identification."

I told him the tailor's name in the jacket. I also told him about the triangular tear in the left leg of the pants. He took it all down methodically in a little book.

"That's for Dagget. Must have the facts down on paper. Me, I don't bother with notes. Keep it in my head."

Iris gushed: "You're being awfully sweet about my husband's uniform."

He shrugged. "Ain't nothing, lady. The case we've been working on came to what you might call a dead end at the Turkish bath. We had a free evening. Neither Bill nor me's one that likes lazing around." He looked wise. "Besides, to tell the truth, in our racket, you never know. Something that looks like nothing—if you follow it up, maybe you get on to something big." He grinned at me. "Maybe you're puttin' us on to something big, Lieutenant, without knowing it."

I hoped I wasn't.

Iris seemed to be struggling with some inner decision. I didn't get what was on her mind until she blurted: "Hatch, if—if you do have a free evening, maybe you would help us. I don't mean the uniform. I mean something else— something that really might be something big."

I felt a flood of embarrassment for her gall. "Iris," I said sternly, "Hatch is a professional. You can't expect him to bother with your girlish . . ."

Hatch held up a hand to check me in a gesture of gloomy authority. "What's on your mind, lady?"

"It's just some crazy thing that happened a couple of minutes back," I said. "Some old drunk who said a lot of crazy things."

"I don't think they're crazy," said Iris. "Hatch, listen. What do you think?"

My wife gave him an accurate if enthusiastic account of the Beard episode. At second hand it sounded even more lunatic than when it had actually happened. Hatch watched her face while he listened, his eyes slowly widening. When she was through, he knocked back his hat, scratched his head, and chewed the unlit cigar.

"Lady," he said very slowly, "are you kidding me?"

"No, no, of course I'm not. That's what he said, isn't it, Peter?"

I nodded. "But he was tight."

"Tight." Hatch laughed then. His laugh was about as cheerful as the interior of the Capulet tomb. He nudged me in the ribs, winking a wiseacre wink. "An old drunk gives her some double talk and right away she's in the middle of a Nazi plot. That's women. They're all the same. Every time."

He rocked back and forth on his heels, guffawing. I could have embraced him for not encouraging her. But Iris, still clutching the *Chronicle,* was obviously pained by his skepticism.

"All right, all right. Laugh at me. I don't care. I'm going to find that picture."

Peevishly, she started to leaf through the paper. Hatch and I watched. She stopped at a page. She gave a gasp.

"Peter."

I was at her side instantly, looking at the paper over her shoulder. She had come to the social page. At the head of a short column of newsprint was a photograph of a very beautiful woman—a woman whom anyone except a husband might easily have taken for Iris. Dark, with the same amazing, slightly slanted eyes and the finely etched bone structure.

In fact, for a second, I thought myself that it was a picture of Iris until I read underneath it the two words: *Eulalia Crawford.*

"Eulalia Crawford." Iris looked at me triumphantly.

"That's the explanation. The Beard mistook me for Eulalia."

Hatch queried, "Eulalia—what?"

"She's my cousin," explained Iris. "She lives here in San Francisco. She's fairly well known. Only this afternoon someone mistook me for her."

While she told him about the telephone incident, I read the newspaper paragraph under the photograph. It was nothing much. It just announced that Miss Eulalia Crawford, "the distinguished puppeteer," had consented to give some sort of show for some sort of relief benefit.

Iris was winding up: "You see, Hatch? The man with the beard wasn't just making passes at me. He thought I was Eulalia. He knows there's danger for her and he'd warned her to stay home. When he saw me, he thought she'd come out in spite of his warning."

Hatch stroked his lean jaw. "Sounds pretty screwed up to me."

"Of course it's screwed up," I said.

Iris flared: "Oh, I'm bored with both of you. Here's the most exciting thing that's ever happened to me and you stand around like a couple of dreary old owls. Don't you see there's terrible danger for Eulalia?"

"Danger from what?" I said.

Iris's lips tightened. "From the red rose and the white rose . . ."

". . .and page eighty-four and the elephant," I cut in derisively.

"Go on." My wife's cheeks were flushed. "Go on, both of you. That's right. Laugh. Don't lift a little finger with my poor cousin Eulalia in danger of being killed or—or worse."

"Killed?" echoed Hatch. "Not so fast, lady. Not so . . ."

"Oh, shut up." Iris turned on me. "As for you . . ."

People had started to stare. Iris knew that I squirm from any kind of public scene and took shameless advantage of it.

With a sigh of resignation, I gave in. "O.K., baby, if you're set on making a mystery of it, we'll go back and make the old wolf explain himself. He's probably under the table by now."

My capitulation had mollified her. But she shook her

head. "Possibly," she announced, "that drunkenness was just an act, something he put on. But it's no use going back to him. He only spoke to me because he thought I was Eulalia. Once he knew I wasn't Eulalia, he'd shut up like a clam."

"Very well. Then what are you going to do?"

"The only right and proper thing. I'm going to telephone to Cousin Eulalia."

I liked that Cousin Eulalia business. She hadn't even seen the woman since she'd dropped pollywogs in her drawers during her charming Jamaica Plains childhood.

Since her outburst, Hatch was watching my wife with a certain amount of awe, as if she were a beautiful beast of prey to be admired but also to be handled cautiously.

"Excuse me, lady. You say this Eulalia's in danger and you say this guy with the beard has warned her. O.K. Why do you want to warn her all over again? What are you going to say?"

Iris withered that extremely sensible remark with a glance. "I," she said haughtily, "am going to tell her about the white rose and the red rose and page eighty-four and the elephant and life or death."

She swept away from us towards a lighted sign saying TELEPHONES. Hatch and I looked at each other and shrugged in mutual masculine understanding. Then we started through the vestibule after her.

She wasn't gone long. When she came out of the booth, her whole body, the very way she walked, exuded determination.

"Well," I said, "did you get Cousin Eulalia?"

"No." Iris fingered the gardenia at her throat. "A man answered the phone. He said she'd just stepped out but would be back any minute. He knew my name. He said Eulalia had just been talking about us. He said she was very eager to see us—that she wanted us to go over right away." She paused. "I said all right. I said we'd come."

"Go to Eulalia's?" I snarled. "We break our necks trying to get a hotel room to be alone and away from your revolting Cousin Eulalia. And now you want to drag me . . ."

Iris didn't smile. "We've got to go. I don't know what

it's all about any more than you or Hatch do—but something's wrong."

"Why?" I asked.

"The man, Peter. The man who answered the telephone. His voice was soft and funny and he had a lisp."

She stared me straight in the face.

"He's the same man who called me from the hotel lobby this afternoon."

CHAPTER IV

Both Hatch and I were watching my wife. For the first time, I was getting a little worried. Not for Eulalia. I didn't give a hoot what happened to Eulalia and her elephant and her roses. I was thinking about the one detail of the Turkish bath episode which I had kept from my wife, the fact that the man who had stolen my uniform had also lisped. I considered telling her now, but I decided against it. Her deductive fires had more than enough fuel already.

Hatch had received Iris's dramatic news phlegmatically, which was reassuring. Legs apart, thumbs under the lapels of his blue check jacket, he surveyed my wife with paternal indulgence.

"I'm not saying there isn't trouble," he said. "Maybe there is. But figure this straight. You're worried because the guy who's with your cousin now's the same guy who mistook you for her here in the lobby. Right?"

"Of course." Iris was clearly impatient with his Socratic method.

"Now don't you think you're just a bit screwed up? This guy said he was a friend of hers. What more natural than he should be visiting her? What more natural than he'd tell her about mistaking you for her? What more natural than she'd want to see her own cousin?"

Even Iris quailed before the solid common sense of that remark.

"I suppose," she faltered, "when you put it like that . . . but, well, it's not just the man with the lisp. It's everything. The roses, the elephant. . ."

She wasn't going to let her Dick Tracy dream fizzle out without a struggle. She turned to me, her eyes pleading. "Peter, please come to Eulalia's. She lives right here on Nob Hill—on California Street. It isn't far. Oh, I know you hate the whole idea. I know I'm just the sort of a wife a serviceman on leave shouldn't have. But—darling, I swear we'll just drop in, make sure she's all right, and then leave. It isn't ten yet. It's early."

Partly because refusing her would have been like stealing a little girl's doll, partly because a bug of uneasiness still stirred in the back of my mind, I said: "O.K., baby."

"Thank you, darling."

"But no lingering around. No girlhood reminiscing."

"No, no, of course not." Iris turned radiantly to Hatch. "And, Hatch, I'm sorry I was rude just now. Won't you come, too?"

Hatch looked uncomfortable. "Don't you think it would look kind of funny calling on your cousin after all these years with a private dick in tow?" His face cleared: "Tell you what I will do, though. If this Eulalia's part of a Nazi plot"—he lowered an eyelid at me—"then you won't want to lose sight of this guy with a beard, will you? I'll stick around here until you come back and keep an eye on him."

"Wonderful."

"You'll have to point him out, though."

"Oh, you can't miss him. He's the only beard in the whole dining room. A black curly beard. A grey suit. A red carnation in his buttonhole. You're so very, very sweet."

Hatch smirked almost coyly. "Think nothing of it. It's a pleasure to help out some people."

Impulsively Iris leaned forward and kissed his gloomy ear. "Come on, Peter. I'd better get my wrap from the room."

As we headed for the elevator, Hatch strolled away towards the dining room. He was waiting for us a few minutes later when we came down again into the lobby, the unlit cigar limp in his mouth.

"The old guy's still there," he announced. "He's picked up a redhead. He's dancing—if you call it dancing." He grinned. "His line don't pay dividends with a brunette, so he settles for a redhead. Guess she's getting the roses now."

Iris drew the silver-fox cape around her shoulders. "You still think I'm a fool, don't you?"

"In my set-up, lady, I don't think no one's a fool until they've proved it. Maybe, when you come back, you'll have the laugh on me."

He moved away, headed towards his post. I noticed that, sensibly, he was approaching the dining room by way of the bar.

Since it was impossible to get a taxi, Iris and I decided to walk up Stockton and take the cable car over on California. The warm night air seemed to quiver with a promise of excitement. San Francisco was still being San Francisco and the passers-by still seemed to be following their own individual adventures. We passed through a long dark tunnel and, as we emerged at the other end, we were in another city where unreadable hieroglyphics took the place of names on the stores and the faces around us had lost their Anglo-Saxon features and were slant-eyed and Oriental.

Iris, watching the Chinese men and women moving past, made a little crooning sound. Already, I could tell, she was in a world more exotic than this real Chinatown. A world peopled with roses and beards and elephants and . . . life or death.

We waited on the precipitous corner of California Street. Soon the cable car bucketed down the hill and ground to a last-minute, breathless stop. We boarded it. Iris chose places in the open section under the shadow of the giant brake lever. We sat there on the absurd benches which faced out towards the sidewalk.

That cross-town ride, lurching up hills and zooming down hills, added the final touch of insanity to our mission. Iris, clinging to an iron pole like a pole on a merry-go-round, kept her own counsel. Once, as we wheezed up to the great bulk of the Mark Hopkins Hotel, she murmured caressingly: "The white rose and the red rose mean blood."

Cutting into her sanguinary thoughts, I said: "Since I'm stuck with Eulalia, I might as well know something about her. What else is there besides the pollywogs and the puppets?"

Iris started and said: "What, dear?"

I repeated the question.

"Oh, really nothing. She's my mother's sister's only daughter. She's about five years older than I am, and when I was just a tot her mother quarrelled with my mother—and there was no trafficking with each other after that."

"What's all this about her being disreputable and having lovers?"

"I don't know the details. She got into some scandal with an Italian or something and came West. It's very vague. It all came through a poisonous spinster cousin of Mother's. It's probably exaggerated just because Eulalia's artistic and beautiful and . . ."

The great brake lever behind us ground down for the eleventh or twelfth time. Iris got up suddenly.

"This is where we get off."

We were out of Chinatown, in a residential district of apartment houses. The streets were dark and almost deserted. As the cable car rattled away, Iris started to inspect numbers. We walked a short distance and then with a "This is it," she turned in under an awning of a smallish, Georgian apartment house.

I followed her into a dressed-up, modernistic foyer. An old doorman in plum livery with shaggy white hair and thick bifocals was sitting in an upholstered chair, peering at a newspaper. He jumped to his feet as we entered.

Iris walked up to him. "Miss Eulalia Crawford, please."

His eyes blinked at her cautiously behind the bifocals. "What name, ma'am?"

"Lieutenant and Mrs. Duluth."

His face relaxed. "Oh, yes, Mrs. Duluth, Miss Crawford's expectin' you." He grinned, showing an occasional tooth. "Have to be careful with Miss Crawford. As much as my job's worth to let anyone up unless she phones down special that she's expectin' 'em."

There was a small, self-propelling elevator in the corner. Iris started toward it. The doorman shambled along, chattering. I followed.

"Yes, ma'am," the doorman was saying. "Never can tell with a woman. Now Miss Crawford, she's normally one for society. People streaming in and out every minute of the day. Then all of a sudden last night—no one's to go up, not even a telegraph boy, she says."

Iris reached the elevator. I joined her. It was only then that I came into the restricted visual sphere of the doorman. When he saw me, he exhibited the few teeth again.

"Want me to take you up, Lieutenant Duluth?"

"No. We'll manage ourselves, thank you," said Iris. She opened the door of the little elevator and stepped inside. I edged in next to her. "What floor is Miss Crawford on?"

"Why, the top floor, ma'am. Your husband will show you the way." The doorman laughed a cackle of a laugh. "Didn't take you long to come back, did it, Lieutenant? Don't forget to take care of that cold of yours. Frisco's mean on a cold if your blood isn't thicked up for it. Yes, sir."

I opened my mouth to speak, but at that moment Iris closed the elevator door and pressed the button for the top floor.

As the cramped elevator started upwards, I said: "What's all this about my coming back? And how in Hades did he know I had a cold?"

Absorbed with more tantalizing problems, my wife gave this real and alarming one scant attention.

"Oh, he's obviously blind as a bat. He probably mistook you for someone else."

There was altogether too much of this mistaking people for other people.

The mobile coffin came to a jolting halt at the top floor. We stepped out into a small foyer. There was only one door. Apparently, Eulalia had the entire floor to herself. We moved to the door. A formal card, slipped into a metal slot on the panelling, announced: *Miss Eulalia Crawford.*

Iris pressed the buzzer. I could hear it ringing inside the apartment. We waited. Nothing happened. Iris pressed the white button again. Once again the buzzer whined inside. Once again there was no answer.

Iris's face clouded. "Surely the doorman would have told us if she'd gone out."

Impulsively her hand went to the door-knob. She turned it, and surprisingly the door opened inward on to a lighted hall.

"The door's open and the lights are on. She must be in."

I wanted to be done with the whole business. "Iris, we can't go barging in . . ."

"We're not barging," said my wife primly. "We've been invited. Probably Eulalia's visiting in one of the other apartments. That's why she left the door open." She stepped into the hall, calling: "Eulalia. Eulalia Crawford."

Embarrassed and uneasy, I joined her. If my wife was determined upon housebreaking, the least I could do was to give her moral support.

A half-open door ahead led into a lighted inner room.

"Eulalia," called Iris again. This time her voice tilted with anxiety. "Eulalia."

No sound came from the apartment beyond. Gripping my hand, Iris pushed through the door into the inner room. We took one step across the soft carpet and then stopped dead.

At a first glance, that large, studio-like room seemed to be crowded with people—weird, silent people in fancy dress who were lounging over chairs and sofas in postures of abandon. For a moment I thought we had plunged into some satanic orgy. Then, as I saw string trailing from floppy arms and grotesquely sprawled legs, I realized that we were merely looking at the "distinguished puppeteer's" distinguished puppets.

And they were indeed distinguished. Large as life, all of them had an uncanny aura of vitality. For the most part, they were carnival or circus figures, a parade of gaudy clowns, a blond equestrienne in a stiff ballet skirt, a black and white ringmaster, a harlequin, and a giant of a trapeze artist in purple tights.

There seemed no rhyme or reason for their being tossed in such a haphazard fashion around that deserted room.

Eulalia, I supposed, must be in the process of preparing them for her relief benefit next week.

"Eulalia," called Iris again with an urgency that made the silence seem even more intense.

No answer came.

My wife turned to me. "She must be in the building somewhere. The man on the phone, the man with the lisp, he said she'd be expecting us."

We looked at each other bleakly. The huge, staring puppets with their corpse stillness were getting on my nerves.

Irritably, I said: "It was a crazy idea to come, anyway. Let's get out of here."

"No, Peter. We must search everywhere and wait."

There was another door at the far end of the room. In front of it stretched a massive George Washington desk on which an empty flower vase lay on its side across a pile of papers.

From behind the desk a silver-slippered foot protruded.

As we moved towards the inner door, that slippered foot hypnotised me. Somehow, with the rest of the body invisible behind the desk, it seemed more human than the other puppets.

We passed a gypsy in the lascivious embrace of a clown. But my gaze remained fixed on the silver slipper.

Iris was a little ahead of me. She reached the desk first. She glanced down at the floor behind it and, as she did so, her face became contorted into a white mask of terror.

"Peter! . . ."

I ran to her side. I stared down at what was behind the desk.

A female figure lay there on her back, with her arms flung puppetlike above her head. The skirt of her lemon-yellow dress was bizarrely askew and beneath it her slender legs tapered to the silver slippers.

I noticed these little things automatically as the blinding realization came that this woman was not a doll on strings. This woman was real.

Or rather, she had been real.

For she was dead—obviously.

The wooden handle of a knife stuck out of the yellow dress just above the left breast. There were two other crimson-stained gashes in the material where the knife had struck before.

Her face, staring up from blank, open eyes, was terrible to me—terrible because, even travestied as it was by death, it was dark, beautiful, and shudderingly familiar.

If Iris hadn't been standing at my side, I would have sworn that it was she lying there stabbed in the breast— murdered.

"Eulalia." My wife said the name in a stifled whimper. "Eulalia Crawford."

But the nightmare did not end there. A trickle of water fell on Eulalia's legs, drop by drop, from the overturned vase on the desk. And strewn across the corpse, as if plucked from the vase and thrown there by the idiot fingers of some Ophelia, were roses, dozens of dark-red roses.

Iris fumbled for my hand. Her eyes came up to meet mine, dilated with horror.

"Roses," she breathed. "The red rose and the white rose. The roses mean—blood."

CHAPTER V

That phrase, which until then had seemed senseless as a child's jungle, was now terrifyingly, obscenely fraught with significance. I gazed down at the rose-scattered body of the unknown woman whose name had hounded us ever since our arrival in San Francisco. I suppose I felt pity for Iris's dead cousin, but my chief emotion was indignation—howling, personal indignation against a fate which could do this to me. In those first seconds I wasn't capable of detailed thinking. Everything seemed as simple as it was terrible.

Iris and I had found a body. We would have to do something about it. All hope for a quiet, domestic weekend had gone for good.

My wife had been gazing down at the funeral canopy of red roses. Slowly she lifted her gaze and looked across the long, brilliant room with its flaunting company of puppets. Their painted, simpering faces stared back at her as if they were watching, passing silent judgment.

Iris's face showed the shock of brutal reality crashing through her frivolous dreams of adventure. Here was adventure with no holds barred, and she wasn't liking it any better than I was.

"Somehow I never thought . . . Peter, it is real. There was danger for Eulalia. Life or death."

"Not life or death," I said grimly. "Just death."

The uncanny resemblance of the corpse to Iris was the worst part. I stepped back from the desk so that I didn't have to see the face.

Iris went on huskily: "It can't have been done long. That vase . . . He must have done it—the man with the lisp, the man who called me from the hotel lobby and then answered the phone here."

"I guess so." What did it matter who'd done it or why? It was done.

"He must already have murdered Eulalia when I talked to him from the phone booth." Iris turned to me, her cheeks gaunt. "And he told us to come here. He told me Eulalia wanted to see us. And when we came, the door was open. He deliberately got us to come here. Why?"

Why? When she said that, my brain started functioning for the first time. Like a galloping horse, a thought thundered into my mind.

I said: "There's something I never told you, baby. I guess it's rather late to tell you now. The man who stole my uniform at the Turkish bath had a lisp. The clerk said so."

"Peter!" she gasped. "Then that's why the doorman . . ."

"Exactly. That's why the doorman thought I'd already been here. The man with the lisp came here to murder Eulalia tonight in *my* uniform."

Iris said passionately: "Why, why didn't you tell me about the lisp before?"

Why hadn't I? My motives had seemed perfectly adequate at the time. But now . . .

"I guess I was scared you'd tie everything up together and get excited about a mystery and—and spoil our evening."

"Spoil the evening!" She gave a bleak laugh. "That's funny."

"There's something else. We know now why the doorman asked about my cold. The pay clerk at the Turkish bath also said that the man who stole my uniform kept a handkerchief up to his face as if he had a cold."

We stared at each other. The walls of that bright, puppet-strewn room seemed to be closing in on us.

Iris must have been feeling the same thing. She took a

quick step towards me. She wanted to be near me.

As she passed the corner of the desk, her elbow brushed against a pile of papers. A printed circular on top half-slid off, revealing part of some paper with writing on it, which had been lying beneath.

I was far too jittery to have noticed that piece of paper, except for one thing. There is one word which the eye picks up almost automatically and that word is one's own name.

Written on the paper, I saw *Lieutenant Peter Duluth*.

I drew the paper out of the pile. It was the first paragraphs of an unfinished letter on a piece of formal stationery with Eulalia's address at the top. The writing was small and so mannered as to be legible only with difficulty. The ink was recent and the letter was dated Friday evening. It must have been written within the last few hours.

Iris, at my elbow, said: "It's Eulalia's writing. I remember it from the letter she wrote me."

Puzzling with the words, I read:

> Dear Lina,
> I've been desperately wondering how to get in touch with you. I can't come to see you. I don't dare leave the apartment. Even the slightest sound at the door brings my heart to my mouth. But, thank heaven, I have an opportunity at last. The husband of a cousin of mine, a Lieutenant Peter Duluth, has just telephoned me. He's in town and he and his wife are coming around to visit me. He can't have anything to do with this terrible thing. I can trust him. I'm going to tell him everything and ask him to go to you immediately. I am expecting him at any minute . . .

There was more, but I couldn't get beyond that point. Evasive and hysterical as the paragraph was, it was plain enough to make me realize just how hopelessly deep into a quagmire Iris and I had been lured.

I looked at my wife over the letter. The thing that had happened to us was so utterly unanticipated that I still needed time to take it in.

Iris was faltering stupidly: "Eulalia says you called her.
You didn't call her."

"Of course I didn't. *He* did."

My wife gave a weak nod. "The man with the lisp."

"He stole my uniform. He called Eulalia, pretending to
be me, and asked to come around. Eulalia told the doorman to let up a Lieutenant Duluth. He came. He told the
doorman he was Lieutenant Duluth. He came up. The
uniform tricked Eulalia into letting him in. He killed her."

"And then I telephoned from the hotel, Peter. I made
it perfect for him. He told us to come over. He went
downstairs. He told the doorman he was going to come
back with his wife and he—he escaped. He kept a handkerchief to his face. The doorman's almost blind." She
clutched my arm. "When he hears Eulalia's dead, the
doorman's going to swear you were the only person who
came here tonight. He's going to swear you're the only
person in the world who could have murdered her."

"Exactly. I've been framed." I said it then, that cheap
jargony phrase that until then had had no reality for me.
"Baby, that's what's happened to us. I've been framed
by a man I've never seen for the murder of a woman I
never knew."

Now that I'd faced the truth squarely, I felt a little
steadier. Ever since we'd arrived in San Francisco we had
been watched by invisible, scheming eyes. Everything
that had happened had been part of a secret design building up to—this.

Iris was moaning: "It's all my fault. It was all my crazy
idea to come here and . . ."

"No, baby. None of that." I went to her, steadying her.
"We've got to keep calm and figure out just where we
stand."

I took out a packet of cigarettes, lit two, and gave one
to Iris. She took a deep pull on it. It seemed to make her
feel better.

I could hear the faint plop of water drops still falling
from the upset vase on the desk. That tiny sound was
more fraying to the nerves than a naval broadside.

When you find a corpse, you call the police. But, as
Iris had pointed out, if I called the police in this case,
they'd have to be idiot fringe to believe me against the

statement of the doorman. I had witnesses, of course, to prove that my uniform had been stolen at the Turkish bath. Eventually I would be able to prove I was not a cousin-in-law murderer. But a great many unpleasant things could happen before that "eventually."

The anger which had been banking up inside me burst out now and I was as mad as a bull. Until we arrived at Eulalia's, my only idea for the week-end had been to be alone with Iris. Now I was a man with another single idea. I was going to get my own back on this murderer for playing on me one of the dirtiest tricks ever played. I was going to get my own back even if I had to start another earthquake in San Francisco.

Iris's distracted voice came into my thoughts. "Peter, if we call the police, they'll be sure you did it."

"Exactly."

"And what can we say for ourselves? That your uniform was stolen in a Turkish bath, that we were lured here by a man with a lisp, that a drunk with a black beard babbled about roses and elephants. It'll sound like jabberwocky."

"Sure."

She faltered: "In the end they'll have to realize you're innocent. But before that, the scandal, the publicity. Peter, your promotion—it's shot to hell and it's all my fault."

Suddenly it came to me what we would have to do. I looked down at Eulalia's unfinished letter, which I still held in my hand and which was packed with dynamite for me. Feeling almost casual, I folded it, still half unread, and slipped it into my pocket.

"Just in case the police do show up here tonight," I explained. "We can't risk their finding it—not yet."

"But, Peter, you mean . . . ?"

"I mean we aren't going to call the police," I said. "We're going to walk out on Cousin Eulalia. We're going to leave her here by herself—dead."

Iris stared. "But we can't just walk out and pretend it didn't happen. The doorman knows your name. When you're in the navy, you can't possibly hide. The moment the police come, the whole city will be searching for Lieutenant Duluth."

"When the police come, yes." I took her arm. "Listen,

baby, we can't afford to be messed up with the police now. You see that. We'll never get anywhere using up our week-end jabbering about beards and roses. If only we had some idea what was behind all this craziness, it'd be different. But we don't. There's one person, however, who does."

Understanding dawned on her face. "The Beard?"

"Exactly. We don't know his name. We don't know where he lives. We don't know anything about him. But he must know the truth about who killed Eulalia and why. Not only that. He's the only one who can prove why we came here. If we let ourselves be held now, we may never be able to locate him again."

"Hatch promised to watch him," broke in Iris excitedly. "If we go back to the hotel, Hatch will be able to take us to him. We can shake him sober, make him tell us the truth. Then we can take him with us to the police."

I nodded. "That's it. We'll go to the police all right, but we're going with that goddam Beard safely tucked under our arm."

Iris hesitated. "But what—what if they discover the body before we can get the Beard? We'll be in a far worse position than we are now."

"That's a chance we have to take. And it's a pretty good one. We know Eulalia's been warned about this, probably by the Beard. She's been barricading herself in up here. She's given the doorman orders to let no one up unless she calls down to say she's expecting them. That means, even if some friend does drop in to see her, he'll never get past the doorman. It's a hundred to one she won't be discovered until tomorrow—and long before tomorrow we'll be at police headquarters with the Beard."

Iris looked around the room. Her gaze rested on the pitiful silver slipper.

"It seems rather awful walking out on Eulalia."

"Eulalia's dead," I said grimly. "We're alive. And, if I have anything to say about it, we'll stay alive and kicking —kicking straight into the lisping teeth of her murderer."

I went around the room just to make sure there was nothing we had missed. The puppets stared at me from their painted, moron faces. Let them stare. They didn't bother me any more.

I took Iris out of the apartment into the little foyer and closed the door on Eulalia Crawford's corpse. Iris's face was still paper pale. I put my hand under her chin and kissed her.

"Chin up, baby. And smile. Don't let that doorman start suspecting things."

We went down to the first floor in the elevator. The doorman was back in his chair, reading the newspaper. As we passed him, arm in arm, trying to look casual, he rose.

"Going so soon, Lieutenant?"

"Yes," I said.

He took a half step towards us. "Miss Crawford send me down any message?"

Iris's arm in mine was quivering.

"No," I said.

"Then I guess she won't be needing anything more tonight."

"No," I said, "Miss Crawford won't be needing anything more tonight."

The door seemed miles away. But we made it. We hurried through it out into the street.

CHAPTER VI

I am a law-abiding man by nature. Even if I hadn't been, two and a half years of navy discipline would have made me so. Although I had convinced myself we were justified in walking out on Eulalia, I felt almost as guilty as if I actually had murdered her. With every step we took away from that apartment building, I expected an accusatory shout from the darkness behind us.

Iris looked as guilty as I felt. I would have given anything for a taxi, something to rush us to the hotel, to the Beard, and ultimately to police headquarters. But there weren't any taxis. Arm in arm, trying to act like a naval lieutenant and his girl out for a stroll, we walked to the street corner and waited there for the cable car.

That wait was most unpleasant. My mind filled it with images of Eulalia Crawford's face as a knife stabbed once, twice, three times, into her breast—a knife gripped in the hand of a man wearing my uniform and calling himself Lieutenant Duluth.

At last the cable car swooped down on us, clattering to a halt. I no longer thought of it as something quaint and picturesque and exciting. It was just a means of escape.

This time, by tacit agreement, we avoided the conspicuous seats and sat in the small, boxed-in section. While we took our places, I had the absurd sensation that guilt

57

must be scrawled on our faces for all the world to see. But our few fellow passengers were encouragingly uninterested in us. They went on reading their papers or staring into space without so much as casting us a casual glance.

As the car rattled on, I began to feel more secure. Iris gave me a pale little smile. I grinned back reassuringly and squeezed her hand. Everything would be all right, I told myself. Once we found the Beard, we could go to the police and legalize ourselves again. We might even have a little peace and quiet together. That's what I told myself.

For a time I tried to make some sense of the hocus-pocus of roses, lisps, warnings, and puppets which lay behind Eulalia's murder. Perhaps it was all part of some international espionage drama. Or perhaps it was the closing act of some complicated personal tragedy. If this had happened to me as a civilian. I'd have been like a bloodhound on the scent. Both Iris and I had worked on some pretty mysterious affairs back East and this would have been right up our alley. But now I was a naval officer, I couldn't go around playing amateur sleuth. As we blundered up and down hills, I concentrated completely on our own predicament.

Although the basic facts were only too clear, I hadn't had an opportunity to figure out just how it had all come about. As I looked back, however, I saw exactly how the pieces fitted together.

For some reason, the man with the lisp, who was planning to murder Eulalia, had been in the St. Anton lobby that afternoon when Iris and I had played out our little comedy with Mrs. Rose. He had glimpsed Iris going up in the elevator with me and the bellhop and, naturally enough, had mistaken her for Eulalia. Presumably, he thought he might have a chance to kill her there—a chill settled on my spine as I reflected what might have happened—but, either to make sure that Iris was Eulalia or for some other motive, he called up on the house telephone before doing anything. Over the phone he learned that he had been mistaken and that Iris wasn't Eulalia Crawford.

But that wasn't all he learned. In an attempt to be polite to what she thought was a friend of Eulalia's, Iris had played straight into his hand. She had told him she was Iris Duluth, Eulalia's cousin; she had told him we had too little time in Frisco to visit Eulalia. She had even told him I was going down the street to the Turkish bath.

Obviously, the murderer knew that Eulalia had been warned of danger and had shut herself up in her apartment. He knew he had no chance of getting into that closely guarded fortress—as himself. But, thanks to Iris, he realized Eulalia might well let the doorman admit her own cousin-in-law, Peter Duluth.

A little quick thinking was all he needed. He'd seen me with Iris. He knew what I looked like. It was easy for him to get to the Turkish bath ahead of me and, later, to switch his key with mine and walk off with my uniform. If he'd dared, he would probably have taken my identification papers too.

Since Iris had told him we weren't planning to get in touch with Eulalia, there was no risk of our barging into the picture at the wrong moment. All he had to do was to carry through his brash impersonation of me. He did, and it worked. Once he was in Eulalia's apartment, she was at his mercy.

I saw then that our involvement might have ended there if it hadn't been for Iris's telephone call from the St. Anton. That had given him the golden opportunity of elaborating what had started merely as a trick to gain access to Eulalia's apartment into an ingenious plan for throwing the guilt on me.

It had all been as simple as that. Two innocent little telephone calls had brought me as near to arrest for murder as any blameless citizen was ever likely to be.

At last the cable car dumped us at Stockton Street. We could have waited for another car to take us the four blocks to the hotel, but we decided to walk. We had hardly spoken since we left Eulalia's. Even now, as we hurried through the gay crowds on the sidewalk, we maintained the same uneasy silence.

That afternoon, I had been envying the San Franciscans for looking as if they were all at the peak of some personal adventure. Now I could only hope for their sakes that their adventures didn't match up to ours.

We reached the St. Anton and pushed through the

swing doors. The familiar, animated lobby with its chandeliers and red plush curtains seemed quite unreal, a memory from some almost forgotten past when our only worry had been whether or not we could get a room.

Anxiously we surveyed the motley throng for a glimpse of Hatch.

Iris said: "Peter, it'll be awful if Hatch let the Beard go."

A truer word was never spoken. We moved through the milling servicemen and civilians. There was no sign of Hatch. I went to the desk to see if a message had been left for us. It hadn't.

"He's probably in the dining room," I said. "After all, if the Beard's still here, that's where he'd be."

We sped down the corridor to the dining room. The strains of a rumba filtered towards us. It seemed impossible that the same orchestra could still be playing the same rumbas for the same people. We started through the tables. A headwaiter came up.

"A table, sir?"

"No. We're just looking for someone."

We weaved our way down one side of the dance floor and up the other. Neither Hatch nor the Beard was there.

We moved out again into the corridor.

"We should have expected it," Iris said gloomily. "Hatch is a professional detective. He's got his own work to do. Why should he waste an evening watching an old drunk with a beard just because a dizzy female asked him to?" She gave a peaked smile. "Well, darling, we've lost the Beard. We'll never find him again."

I thought of Hatch's sardonic face. Somehow I felt he was too loyal and too cagey to have walked out on us. I took Iris's arm.

"If I know Hatch," I said, "he's in the bar."

And he was.

To my immense relief, I saw his massive, blue-check torso perched on a stool amid a flurry of sailors and marines.

He saw our entrance and, elbowing through the servicemen, came towards us, drink in hand.

"Well," he drawled, "how'd you make out with Eulalia?"

Iris gripped his arm. "Hatch, where's the Beard?"

He turned on her a pair of black, quizzical eyes. "Oh, he's left."

"Left!"

"Yeah. The redhead gave him the air. Left about a half-hour ago. Feeling no pain."

Iris and I exchanged a wild glance. Iris said: "You mean you let him go, Hatch? You let him walk out of here and didn't do anything to . . ."

"Hey, not so fast, lady." Hatch winked at me. "Didn't I promise to keep an eye on him? O.K. So I followed him."

I was getting familiar with Hatch's exasperating weakness for creating suspense. There was no way of hurrying him. While Iris fidgeted, I said: "Where is he now?"

"Up at the Green Kimono. That's a dive in Chinatown. He's got him a blonde now. Pouring champagne into her. Quite a guy, he is."

Iris spun round to me. "Peter, he may be leaving any minute. Come on. Quick."

"What's the hurry?" Hatch patted her shoulder paternally. "Think I'd quit? I said I'd be here when you come back. O.K. So I called my partner Dagget from the Green Kimono. Dagget's up there keeping an eye on your Beard. Dagget's a dependable guy, bulldog style. Not flighty like me." He grinned. "That Beard's not going to shake Dagget off. No, sir."

Iris's face relaxed into a radiant smile. For a moment I thought she was going to kiss him again.

Hatch had been so intent upon impressing us with his own efficiency that I don't think he'd looked at us until then. Now, as he glanced from one to the other of us, his eyes came suddenly alert.

"Hey," he said. "What's the trouble? This Eulalia hasn't put you on to anything, has she?"

Until then, I hadn't decided exactly what to do about Hatch. It was risky taking anyone into our confidence right then, but, knowing as much as he did, it would be difficult to stall him off. Besides, Hatch could be very useful to us, at least as a witness of the uniform theft, at most as an outright ally. There was something about that sour face of his. He didn't look the type that would recoil in horror from a couple of reluctant lawbreakers. I took the plunge.

I said: "We're in one hell of a spot, Hatch. And we need your help." I glanced around the thronged, noisy bar. "Since Dagget's covering the Beard, we've got time to explain. Come on up to the room. We'll tell you."

Still staring at us, Hatch tilted the hat a little farther back on his grizzled head.

"O.K. You're the boss."

He drained his drink and, edging between a couple of marines, put the empty glass down on the bar.

"Let's go."

The gingerbread elevator took us upstairs. I let Hatch and Iris into Room 624 and turned on a light. The crimson spread still gleamed invitingly on the huge bed. Around the mirror, the gilt cupids still stuck out their erotic behinds. They made me painfully conscious of our change in status. This room was to have been our love nest.

What was it now?

Hatch didn't take off the hat. He sat down on a corner of the Madame Récamier couch and watched us.

"O.K. Let's hear it."

I told him then. I told him the whole works. As he listened, he sat up straighter and straighter on the Récamier couch until I expected him to topple forward like one of Eulalia's puppets. When I'd finished, he gave a low whistle.

"Geez," he said. "So you walked out on a body."

"What else could we have done?" asked Iris passionately. "If we hadn't, Peter would have been arrested by now and we'd never have found the Beard."

"Now, now, lady." Hatch held up his hand. "I ain't criticizing. I figure you did the smartest thing. Needed some sharp thinking too." A sudden, unexpected smile spread across his face. "Geez, a murder."

Iris snapped: "You needn't be so pleased about it."

"I ain't pleased." Hatch looked indignant and then confidential. "You see. it's just that—well, me and Dagget's been doing O.K. I've no complaints. More work than we can handle. But it's always been smalltime work, see? We've always needed something big, something like a murder to put us on the map. Now it's come. And don't you worry. From now on you've got Williams and Dagget back of you solid."

It was irritating to have him gloat over our misfortunes with such professional relish, but I was glad that I'd told him. There were worse things than having two private detectives rooting for you when you're working outside the law.

Hatch seemed to take it for granted that he was officially in charge from now on. He had disposed of the cigar in our absence. He took out a cigarette and lit it ponderously.

"You're in a spot all right, a real spot, and I guess you're right. Our best bet is to get hold of this guy with a beard. We've got to handle him with kid gloves, though. We can't just kidnap him and rush him off to the cops. This is a free country. If he doesn't feel like playing ball, if we get his back up and he denies knowing anything about Eulalia—well, that'll be too bad." He looked at me gloomily. "As I figure you, you're an impetuous guy. You'd just barge in and get things screwed up. We've got to watch out for you."

Maybe he had something there. It had been my plan to jump on that drunken old goat and grab him off to police headquarters by the beard. I saw now just how fatal that might have been.

"Yeah," Hatch was saying, "we got to figure out a plan. And first we got to figure where we are." He looked at Iris. "You're this Eulalia's cousin. Seems to me you ought to know something about this roses and elephants racket."

Iris shook her head. "I hadn't seen her since we were kids. All I know is that she was in some sort of scandal with an Italian. I don't know what it was all about or where or when or anything."

"An Italian, eh?" Hatch pondered. "What is it again the guy with a beard said? The white rose . . ."

"The white rose and the red rose mean blood," put in Iris. "Then he said: 'I warned you on page eighty-four.' "

Hatch grimaced. "We're not going to get any place with that stuff." He glanced at me. "Show me that letter you snitched, Lieutenant. That was a risky thing you did—stealing material evidence. You could get into real trouble for that. But we got it, so O.K., let's see if it can help us."

I'd almost forgotten that unfinished letter of Eulalia's. As I pulled it out of my pocket, I remembered that there was still a paragraph we had not read.

I sat down next to Hatch on the Récamier couch. Iris dropped at my side. Both of them craned over my elbows as I smoothed the letter out.

Hatch read the inscription. "Lina," he said. "Who's Lina?"

"Some friend of hers," I said. "Eulalia was planning to send me around to her. I guess she figured this Lina could help her somehow."

We read through the first paragraph which Iris and I had already seen at Eulalia's apartment—that paragraph with its undercurrent of hysterical terror and its ironical eagerness for "Lieutenant Duluth's" arrival.

We came to the second paragraph which, in the stress of the moment, Iris and I had not read.

> This is my one chance of getting in touch with you in time. I only hope and pray that you've been warned too. If you haven't been warned, for God's sake take care. Stay in the house. Don't let anyone in—anyone. There's danger, Lina, terrible danger for all of us. The red rose and the white rose are out and the . . . .

At this point there were only three more words, but Eulalia's pen had been shaking so violently that they were almost illegible. We all peered down, trying to decipher the crabbed scrawl.

"*The red rose and the white rose are out,*" said Iris, "*and the . . .* the something *is opening.* Those are the last two words, Peter. *Is opening.*"

I saw she was right. I struggled with the third word from the end. It began with a *c*.

"Crocus!" Iris and I said the word simultaneously.

All three of us stared at each other.

"*The red rose and the white rose are out and the crocus is opening,*" said Iris.

There it was again, that crazy fairy-tale gibberish which the Beard had used. Only now it was even crazier. The red rose—the white rose—the opening crocus . . . I thought of the blood-red roses scattered so bizarrely over Eulalia's body. What could there be about those innocent flowers to inspire so much mortal terror in Eulalia Crawford?

The red rose—the white rose—the opening crocus. It was something out of a florist's nightmare.

Iris's voice broke sharply into my thoughts. "So Lina isn't just a friend. The man or the gang or whatever it is that murdered Eulalia is going to murder Lina too. She's in as much danger as Eulalia was."

Of course I saw that. And I felt an icy rush of panic. I'd walked out on Eulalia. That was all right. She was dead. Nothing could have helped her. But, in walking out on Eulalia, I'd walked out on Lina too. And not only that, I had walked out with the one piece of evidence to prove that Lina was in danger. In failing to report Eulalia's murder to the police and losing them valuable time, I might unwittingly have signed this unknown Lina's death warrant.

Fate, it seemed, was not through with me yet. Having delivered one straight left to the jaw, it had suddenly come up with this second, smashing punch.

I stared at Iris and Hatch. "See what it means? If this Lina gets killed, we'll have her death on our hands. We can't carry this thing through any longer. We've got to go to the police."

Iris was hovering distractedly. Hatch seemed the only one to be taking this new development in his stride.

"OK.," he said. "So you throw in your hand and go to the cops. What happens? If this Lina's in danger, she's in danger right this minute—now. How long d'you suppose it'll take you to explain all this crazy setup to the cops? First they'll go to Eulalia's and discover the body. Second they'll talk to the doorman. Third, they'll think you killed Eulalia. Fourth—" he shrugged. "The cops, they got to do things by the book. By the time they get around to Lina, these guys could have bumped her off a dozen times over."

"Hatch is right," said Iris.

Of course Hatch was right.

"Somehow," went on my wife, "we've got to get Lina ourselves."

"Lina," I said. "Lina, U.S.A. She's going to be a cinch to locate."

"At least we know she's in San Francisco, Peter. Eulalia was going to have you take the letter to her. She must live here somewhere."

"I stand corrected," I said. "Lina—San Francisco."

Hatch had risen. He knocked the hat forward over his eyes. He looked very dour and very efficient.

"Pretty straightforward to me," he said. "We want to locate this Lina. O.K. Who knows her name and where she lives? This guy with the beard. If he knows about the setup with Eulalia, then he knows the setup with Lina. What are we waiting for? Let's get to the Green Kimono."

"Yes, of course," said Iris. "The Beard."

I folded the letter back into my pocket. I grabbed up my hat. Iris and I got too excited. That was our trouble. Hatch's stolidity was worth its weight in—roses.

"Come on," I said. "To the Green Kimono."

To the Green Kimono. It sounded like something from an old-time Chinese melodrama with booming gongs. Somewhere behind the Panzer division of anxieties that was plaguing me, a vestige of humor stirred. To think that I, a one-time figure in Broadway's theater world, should be sweeping out of a hotel room with a corny exit line like that.

To the Green Kimono.

CHAPTER VII

It was exactly eleven-fifteen when we turned down the dark alley off Columbus Avenue which led to the Green Kimono. We had had to walk, but it had not been far. The Beard, as restricted as we by transport problems, had been forced to pursue his champagne orgy in a limited area.

Even in wartime, Chinatown managed to keep some of its mystery. The shadowy figures who slipped by us in the alley moved with supple grace which, in spite of their mundane Western clothes, marked them as a race apart. An occasional tinkle of Chinese chatter trailed out from behind closed shutters. Somewhere a phonograph was playing reedy, jangled music. Its rhythm, pulsing on the night air, dissolved reality into a dreamlike illusion of old Shanghai.

Somehow there was glamour and I found myself reacting to it. The tawdriness, the acute personal danger seemed to fade from our predicament, giving way to a specious sense of adventure and romance.

Iris's arm was through mine. I squeezed it encouragingly and she returned the squeeze.

A grimy green lantern glowed dimly in the darkness ahead. As we approached it, I could see that it hung over a heavy door protected by a sheet of metal from which stood out the bas-relief figure of a Chinese girl in a kimono.

Hatch opened the door and a shaft of light cut into the darkness of the alley. The quiet throb of American jazz from a jukebox inside broke the spell.

Nothing can be done about making a bar Oriental. This one, definitely Occidental, with carved mahogany and mirrors, stretched down one side of the room. A sprinkling of low divans and pallid Chinese murals did what they could to reinforce the desired atmosphere. At the rear, a curtained arch screened off an inner room, hinting at darker mysteries beyond.

As we entered, I let my glance move along the handful of customers at the bar. Rather uneasily I saw that the Beard was not one of them. A couple of very young sailors were drinking Coca-Colas and trying to look wicked. A small Chinese man crouched over a beer. A blonde with an air of faded gentility sat sipping a highball with a woe-begone Chihuahua perched on a stool at her side. There was another man, a man in a dark-blue suit, who sat nearest to the door, with his massive back to us.

Hatch led us to the broad back and tapped it on the shoulder. The man swung round irascibly and then, seeing Hatch, broke into a slow smile.

Hatch gestured to him with some pride. "Meet my partner. This is Dagget. Bill Dagget. Bill to you."

Iris and I shook hands with the second half of Williams and Dagget, Confidential Agents. Bill Dagget looked like a handsome, sulky ox. He was younger than Hatch; his dark eyes were large and placid, and his broad mouth, working over a piece of gum, had the stubborn patience of a cow chewing the cud. There was nothing gentle about his stolidity, however. He was, I felt, an ox that could very quickly change into a rampant bull when roused. I approved of his muscles. They were as solid as Hatch's common sense.

Bill Dagget seemed to be a man of few words and fewer curiosities. Although his partner had dumped him there to watch the Beard, he was taking it all merely as something that came in a day's work. He jerked his head towards the curtain that screened off the inner room.

"The guy with the beard," he said in deep, telegraphic monosyllables. "In there. Been there all the time. I've kept here out of the way. Didn't want him to know I'm tailing him."

Iris took a step towards the curtain, but Hatch threw out a hand to restrain her. He glanced swiftly around at the straggle of other customers. None of them, not even the Chihuahua, was paying us any attention.

"Listen." His voice was low and conspiratorial, as if he were giving signals to a football team. "We don't want to fuss him with me. He's seen you two before. You've got a better chance to handle this alone. I'll stay out here with Bill and give him the setup. O.K.?"

I nodded.

Hatch's hand was still on Iris's arm. "And for Pete's sake, be careful. Don't scare him. Drunks can be sly as women. Try and get the whole story. But whatever else you don't do—get this Lina's address. That's the big thing right now."

"Sure," I said.

Hatch released Iris's arm then. Feigning a complete indifference to us, he slumped on to the stool next to Bill Dagget and called out to the Chinese barman to bring him a bourbon with water chaser.

The jukebox had groaned and clattered into a jive version of "Wait Till the Sun Shines, Nellie." Trying not to look conspiratorial, Iris and I started down the bar towards the curtain. As we passed the Chihuahua, it stretched its scraggly little neck out, almost toppling off the stool, to lick Iris's hand. Its blonde mistress hiccuped over her drink and, pulling a pink handkerchief from her purse, brought it genteelly to her lips. The Chinese man was lost in some profound reverie of his own. One of the two very young sailors glanced at Iris and looked as if he wondered whether he dared to whistle his appreciation. Then he saw my uniform. He didn't dare.

We reached the curtain. I pushed it aside. I had half expected a den of unmentionable vice. Instead we were confronted by a tepid little room divided into booths where a few couples, Chinese and Occidental, sat at tables covered in five-and-dime-store chintz spreads. The atmosphere of tame respectability was heightened by thin vases of artificial flowers which stood on the tables. This room, presumably, was provided for those who preferred to drink in private. You either picked the bar and semi-Chinese atmosphere or privacy and no Chinese atmosphere.

A less colorful locale for our crucial meeting with the Beard would have been hard to find. Why he came here I couldn't imagine, unless he liked the brand of champagne they served.

The room was dimly lit, and cigarette smoke further blurred the picture. We glanced around the booths. In an extreme rear corner, we saw the Beard.

We started towards him. Luckily, he was alone. The blonde with whom Hatch had last seen him, apparently, like the redhead before her, decided that free champagne was not sufficient compensation for his satyrish attentions. He was sitting up very straight with his back to the wall. One empty and one half-empty champagne bottle stood by the artificial flowers on the table in front of him. By that time, he must have been ninety-nine per cent pure champagne, but he looked sober as a judge. He was even more magnificent than my memories of him. Words could not do justice to the beard. It sprouted with the crispness of a fat head of lettuce. Even the red carnation in his buttonhole looked as fresh as ever.

As we weaved through the tables towards him, I felt a tingle of excitement. The Beard had become an almost legendary figure. We didn't know his name. We didn't know where he came from or where he was going. We hadn't the slightest idea how he figured in the mad pattern.

And yet my own future and the very life of the shadowy Lina rested precariously in the palm of his hand.

Remembering his goatish propensities, I whispered to Iris: "You do the talking, baby. He likes girls. I'll keep in the background."

My wife, looking beautiful and intense, nodded.

We reached the Beard's booth. Iris was not an actress for nothing. Arranging her face in a scintillating smile, she leaned into the booth, caught the Beard's eyes, and said: "Hello."

Slowly, little by little, he moved his noble head.

Slowly, as he peered at her, his face lit up in a leer worthy of Priapus himself.

"Buriful girl," he said.

Iris slipped into the booth, sitting down across from him. The champagne bottles and a spindly spray of artificial narcissi made a barricade between them. I hovered at my wife's side.

Iris leaned into the narcissi. "You remember me, don't you? We met at the St. Anton this evening. You mistook me for Eulalia Crawford."

Behind the curtain, the jukebox was giving like mad to "Wait Till the Sun Shines Nellie." While I watched the Beard, suspense was like a fox at my vitals. He clutched at the stem of his champagne glass and loomed towards Iris. The smile had got into the beard and stretched it.

"Y're not Eulalia Cr'wford," he muttered. "Much more buriful th'n Eulalia. Younger. Much more buriful." His ponderous hand unclasped from the glass and, weaving past the narcissi, fell—flop—on my wife's. "Buriful girl."

Such superb drunkenness seemed to nonplus even Iris.

"You must remember me," she said lamely. "You told me about the white rose and the red rose."

The Beard's hand left Iris's. He giggled. Then, suddenly, he brandished his arm at a Chinese waiter who was slipping by. "Drink!" he said. "Drink for the buriful girl. Champagne."

As the waiter glided away, the Beard's aimless gaze settled for the first time on me. He half rose.

"Who'sh tha'?"

Iris said: "Oh, he—he's just with me."

The beard came closer and closer. It was almost in my mouth. Above it, his eyes, screwed up around the corners in a fury of concentration, examined my face. "Nasty man," he said. "Nasty man. Go away. Go away." The beard bobbed up and then down. "Boo-oo!"

That was startling, to say the least. Iris was looking wild-eyed now. She said: "You've got to understand. Please. This is terribly important for us. It's—it's life or death. The elephant never forgets. You mustn't forget. Page eighty-four. You've got to help us."

"Nasty man. Buriful girl." The Beard sank back into his chair. He looked at me sideways with the coy craftiness of a little boy. "Nasty man. Go away. Won't have you here. *My* booth."

Iris gave a sickly smile. She glanced up at me and breathed: "It's no use, darling. He just doesn't like you. But he likes me. Maybe, if you go away, I can get something out of him."

Even as she spoke, the Beard's large hand trundled forward and closed again affectionately over hers. He liked her, all right.

"Go back to Hatch and Bill," she whispered. "Wait for me at the bar. I'll try to get him to talk."

I didn't like the idea of leaving my wife alone with that horrible old man, but in a public place she was relatively safe from being ravished. I darted the Beard one long, dirty look and started back towards the curtain.

"Wait Till the Sun Shines, Nellie" had come to an end. As I stepped through the curtain into the bar, the jukebox broke into a polka, its thumping German rhythm doing awful things to the Chinese atmosphere. Hatch and Bill were still sitting at the end of the bar. I joined them.

Bill Dagget, his massive buttocks bulging over his stool, turned on me a blank, uninterested stare.

Hatch said: "I told Bill the setup. He's in with us."

Dagget nodded sulkily. "Yeah."

Alert as a hound-dog, Hatch asked: "Well, Lieutenant, what's the payoff?"

"He won't talk with me around, the old goat. Iris is trying to handle him alone."

"She'll work it." Hatch patted my shoulder approvingly. "Treat him easy. That's the ticket."

He beckoned the Chinese barman over and bought me a bourbon and water. The three of us sat there in silence while the jukebox clog-danced its way through the polka.

As the minutes ticked by, I felt more and more tense. Hatch's philosophic remark about drunks had been justified. The Beard was as sly as a mongoose. I was sure he knew everything that we needed so desperately to know. I was also sure that it was some clouded cunning born of the champagne rather than actual sogginess that had kept him from telling us. What if Iris didn't succeed? Every hour that delayed my going to the police would make my future that much darker. I'd already kissed my promotion goodbye. Now even gloomier visions scudded through my mind—visions of permanent disgrace and court-martial.

But that wasn't the worst part. Lina was the worst part. I had become obsessed with my own responsibility for Lina's safety.

A woman was in mortal danger. Because I had failed to go to the police, I had made that danger even graver. I was never going to have an easy moment if somehow I didn't get to Lina and save her from this lunatic menace of roses and crocuses.

For what seemed like hours, we sat there. In actual fact, the clock above the bar showed me it was only a matter of minutes. Even so, the hands now pointed to eleven-fifty. In ten minutes the wartime curfew would bundle us all out of the place. And once we left the Green Kimono, it would be a lot tougher for us to keep contact with the Beard.

And then, just as the barman started dipping the lights to signal the curfew, Iris came hurrying through the curtains towards us. My wife looked dazed but faintly triumphant.

As she joined us, we all spun round on her, even the phlegmatic Bill Dagget.

"Well?" I asked.

Iris made a little grimace. "He's crazy about me. *Buriful girl*. He knows another dive where they serve champagne after hours. He wants me to go with him. What a man!" She paused. "But I've got Lina."

I felt my pulses racing. "You've got Lina?"

"Yes, I know her name, where she lives. Nothing more than that. But at least I know that." Iris was breathless. "He's canny, Peter, terribly canny. He knows something frightfully important, but he also knows he's drunk and he's not letting himself admit a thing. I tricked him into telling about Lina just because he thinks it's funny. The address makes a sort of jingle. He chanted it as if it were a nursery rhyme and giggled into his beard."

"What is it?"

My wife chanted: 'Lina Oliver Wendell Holmes Brown, three-eight-six-two, Wa-wo-na.'"

"Lina Oliver Wendell Holmes Brown," I exclaimed. "That can't be a real name. It's a gag."

Iris shook her head emphatically. "I'm sure it's right. I could tell by the way he caught himself up after he'd said it as if it had slipped out without his meaning it to."

"Wawona," put in Hatch sharply. "That's Wawona Avenue, way off, down by the zoo."

There was a phone booth behind me. I jotted down the address, hurried to the booth and leafed it open at the Browns. There was no Oliver Wendell Holmes Brown listed.

As I rejoined the others, the barman blinked the lights again. Iris and I looked at each other bleakly. It was then that Hatch showed his real qualities of leadership. He got up, tilting the hat on the back of his head.

"O.K.," he said. "All of you. Out of here."

"But the Beard . . ." began Iris.

"Out of here."

Hatch started for the door, with Dagget trundling obediently after him. Iris glanced back at the curtain and then with a shrug slipped her hand into mine. We followed the two men into the darkness of the alley.

Hatch grouped us all around him in a huddle.

"We got to figure quickly." The words came firm and low. "We know what we got to do. First there's Lina. Someone's got to get to Lina right away."

"That's me," I said.

"Yeah. You're the best bet for Lina. O.K. Then Mrs. Duluth, she's in well with the Beard. He wants her to go on to this other dive. We can't afford to lose him. When he's sober, we can get the whole story from him. O.K., from now on, Mrs. Duluth sticks with the Beard."

"But . . ." I expostulated.

"Don't worry." Hatch gave a faint chuckle. "We're not throwing her to the wolf. Bill here goes along with 'em. Not so the Beard knows. Just tailing 'em. O.K., Bill?"

Bill Daggett shrugged his massive shoulders. "O.K."

Hatch had taken Iris's arm. "Listen, honey. Give him the works. You've got one job to do and you've got to do it. You've got to get this guy with the beard back to your room in the St. Anton before he passes out." He chuckled again. "And don't worry about your virtue. Bill here'll take care of that. All right?"

Iris's whisper came out of the darkness. "All right."

"Then go straight back in. Catch up with him again before they throw him out."

Iris moved back to me. Slipping her arm around me, she reached up and kissed me on the mouth. I wished she hadn't kissed me. It reminded me of all the things I was missing.

"Don't worry, darling." The scent of the gardenia was bitterly sweet in my nostrils. "By the time you get back from Lina, I'll have that Beard twisted around my little finger."

She moved away and under the dim green lantern back into the Green Kimono. Seeing her go like that was the thing I hated most about that whole hateful evening.

Hatch was talking to Dagget. "O.K., Bill. You hang around out here. Tail 'em. But easy now. The old guy's smart. If he finds out he's being tailed, anything may happen."

"O.K." Bill Dagget strolled away deeper into the shadows. For all his oxlike bulk he moved lightly as a doe.

Hatch took hold of my arm and started leading me down the dark alley towards the street.

"Got a gun?"

I shook my head.

"Too bad. But if you ain't, you ain't. Now you'll never get a taxi, so you'll have to take the trolley. But step on it. Get out to Wawona as fast as you can and when you get there—handle this Lina." He stopped in the alley. "You got to understand that. You got to go just as easy with her as with the old guy. Now maybe she's been warned the way Eulalia was. If so—good. Only that means you'll have a heck of a time getting her to listen to you. You got Eulalia's letter, haven't you?"

"Yes."

"Fine. Show Lina that. It should make her see you're O.K. But, as I said, handle her. Don't get her scared and above all, don't tell her Eulalia's dead or she'll probably go screaming to the cops. Remember, she knows as much as Eulalia did. If she's handled right, she can clear you just as easy as the Beard can. So this is what you've got to do. You've got to somehow persuade her to come back to the hotel with you. Then we'll have Lina and the Beard. That's when we can go to the cops. And, if I know anything, once we got the two of them, we'll have your reputation just as sweet as a baby's by morning."

His optimism was as encouraging as his efficiency. He gave me detailed instructions as to the layout of Wawona Avenue and the right trolley to take. Then, as we emerged from the black alley into the subdued street lighting of Columbus Avenue, he concluded: "Just one thing more. You got that civilian suit back at the hotel. You have to pass that way, anyhow. What you'd better do is change into that civilian suit right away and duck that uniform."

"Civilian suit!" I echoed. "You're crazy if you think I'm going to wander around San Francisco in civilian clothes. If I was caught out of uniform, I'd get into all kinds of trouble."

"So you'd get into trouble." Hatch looked patient. "And what you think you're in now? Figure this straight, guy. We're hoping the cops won't discover Eulalia till to-morrow. O.K. But maybe they will, see? And if they do, they'll be screaming all over town for a naval lieutenant. We can't risk having you picked up before you get to Lina. What's naval regulations stacked up against Lina's life? Phooey."

As usual, Hatch was on the beam.

"O.K.," I said. "You're the boss."

Hatch grinned. "That's the boy. Then you're all set. Know your way back to the St. Anton?"

I nodded.

"Fine." Hatch paused. "As for me, I got a little job of my own. I know the cops in this town. I'm going down to headquarters an' do a little tactful snooping. If they have found Eulalia, I'll know soon enough. And if they have, somehow I'll stall 'em until you've had time to get Lina. If all's quiet when I get there, then there's a good chance we're safe till morning. In that case, I'll be back at the hotel, waiting for you."

He stood on the dowdy street corner, watching me from shrewd black eyes as if he were mentally weighing my assets against my liabilities for such a responsible job.

"Remember," he said. "Handle her. None of that ranting around you go in for. Kid gloves."

"Yes," I said meekly.

"O.K." He turned away and hurried back into the alley where, presumably, he was going to make sure that Iris and Dagget were fulfilling their allotted tasks.

Quite a little Napoleon, Hatch.

I stared after him. Then I turned into Stockton with its rowdy sailors, its silent Chinese, and its lighted, junky curio stores.

I was on my own now.

CHAPTER VIII

It took me less than ten minutes to get back to the St. Anton. Once out of the spell of Hatch's dour optimism, a sense of urgency was riding me like a band of Furies. It was all right for Hatch to talk glibly about bringing Lina back to the hotel. Time was the crucial factor. Already at least three hours had elapsed since Eulalia's murder. Already the menace of the roses and crocuses had been given three precious hours in which to shift its attack to Lina. At any minute, some shadowy figure with murder in his heart might be ringing the doorbell of that impossibly named Lina Oliver Wendell Holmes Brown at 3862 Wawona Avenue.

I was scared of the trolley. After midnight trolleys are infrequent. They are always maddeningly slow, and Wawona Avenue, huddled close to the Pacific on the fringes of the Fleishhacker Zoo, was maddeningly remote.

A dim fear that the police might have found Eulalia's body and be waiting for me proved groundless. No one paid me any attention as I hurried through the lobby, which was settling now into a post-midnight somnolence. An incurious elevator man took me to the sixth floor. Back in Room 624 I tore off my uniform and scrambled into the white shirt and the brown suit. With a twinge of revulsion, I realized I was putting on a murderer's clothes. But my anxiety to get to Lina kept me from worrying about a little thing like that. In a matter of minutes, I had sloughed off my naval identity for an inconspicuous civilian seediness. I glanced at my unfamiliar reflection, framed by the cupids' behinds, and slipped out of the room, locking it after me.

Afraid that the elevator man would notice my startling transformation, I took the stairs down—six flights of them at the double. Iris might well get back to the hotel with the Beard ahead of me. Making myself as unobtrusive as possible, I edged over to the desk and slipped the room key into the key slit. Then I ducked out of the hotel through the side door on to Geary.

I had to walk to Market to reach the trolley. I hesitated under the lighted awning of the St. Anton, glancing up and down the unending stream of sailors. I had taken my first step towards Market when a voice behind me startled me by calling: "Hey, Peter. Peter Duluth."

A panicky impulse to escape gripped me. But it was too late. I felt a hand on my arm and once again the voice came.

"Peter, fancy meeting you of all people."

I turned. Standing by the open door of a parked car was a dapper little man in a tuxedo with a pinkish moustache and pale, watery eyes. With an effort, I managed to recognize him as a small-time actor who had worked with me in a couple of plays back East. Grey. Archie, Cyril, Cecil. That was it. Cecil Grey. A nasty, slippery little number. They say that sooner or later you meet everyone you've ever known in San Francisco. This was one hell of a time to have it happen to me.

While I fidgeted, Grey's eyes, avid with curiosity, slid up and down the civilian suit. "Well, well. I read in the papers you were being one of our brave boys in the Pacific." He giggled. "What's the score? Did the navy get tired of you?"

I didn't know what to say, but, luckily, he said it for me. An expression of understanding passing over his face, he breathed: "So that's it. Intelligence, eh?"

I looked at the parked car behind him. I saw that Cecil Grey might turn out to be a blessing in disguise.

"That your car?" I asked.

He said: "Why, sure. I'm up from Hollywood for the week-end." He tittered. "Gas isn't a problem if you have the right contacts."

"Fine," I said. "I've got to get somewhere. And I've got to get in a hurry." I gave him a meaning look. "I can't say anything. But it's important. Understand?"

Cecil Grey's puffy mouth spread in a fascinated smirk. "Why, sure. Sure. Get right in." He winked. "Secret work, eh? Wait till they hear about Grey, the espionage agent, back in Hollywood."

"You won't tell anyone," I said, making it tough out of the corner of my mouth. "Get it?"

He looked even more fascinated. "O.K. Sure. Anything you say."

He got into the car. I piled in after him, shutting the door.

"Where to?" he said.

"You know San Francisco?"

"Why, sure. I was raised here."

I had enough sense not to give him the actual address. "Dump me at the intersection of Sunset Boulevard and Sloat. And make it snappy."

"Sunset and Sloat it is." Cecil Grey nosed the car out into the traffic. He tittered again. "That's the zoo. So that's the idea, eh? One of the giraffes is a Jap agent."

He laughed at that. He thought it was terribly amusing. He was still laughing as he swung into Market and along it to MacAllister, headed for the Golden Gate Park. He could laugh himself blue in the face for all I cared. I had my transportation. Priceless minutes were being saved in my obstacle race towards Lina Oliver Wendell Holmes Brown.

Once you're out of the main arteries, San Francisco can be a lonely place. There was hardly a person on the street as we raced past the old houses of MacAllister and reached the shadowy purlieus of Golden Gate Park. The actor in Cecil Grey was responding to the drama of the situation. As he hurtled the car past the park and swung it into the broad lanes of Sunset Boulevard, his face had assumed the grim, tight-lipped expression of a B-feature movie hero. In almost no time, it seemed, he jerked the car to a halt at the end of the boulevard.

"Thanks," I said and jumped out.

For a moment he sat behind the wheel, watching me as if plucking up his courage to ask me whether I needed a grim, tight-lipped assistant in my secret undertakings. Luckily, he didn't have the nerve. With a little sigh, he swerved the car around and roared away up the boulevard into the night.

I had left myself quite a few blocks to walk. I rather wished I hadn't been so cagey with Grey, but I didn't trust him. Even now, although he had brought me to my destination far more quickly than the trolley, I realized that Cecil Grey was yet another menace I had built up for the future. The moment Eulalia's body was discovered and the newspapers flaunted my name, he would be the first to go to the police and let them know that I was wandering around San Francisco in guilty civilian disguise. Each step I had taken since we left Eulalia's apartment house had led me that much deeper into a morass. Everything was gambled now on Lina and the Beard.

I headed down Sloat towards the sea. I had never been in this district by night. It was desolate beyond words. A few houses straggled on my right. On my left, the bleak edge of the Lake Merced park stretched away into the darkness. As I hurried on, the street curved into the park itself and there was nothing but the darkness and the gaunt skeletons of trees. From the great zoo ahead of me, the lonely yowling of wild beasts rose every now and then, intensifying the silence. I quickened my pace until I was out of the park again and had turned right into Wawona Avenue itself.

I was in a section of small, Spanish-style villas. The newness of the houses and the damp night air, drifting in from the ocean, made for an atmosphere of raw gloom. I located number 3862. It was on a corner, across the street from a dark drugstore which was closed for the night. Larger than the other houses and obviously older, number 3862 was built of red brick. An iron railing fenced in an old-fashioned basement and a flight of stone steps led up to a dingy front door. It looked like a broken-down, once solitary private residence caught up to by a new building project and converted into apartments.

I went up the steps. There was a double front door: a glass one outside which led into a small, drably lit porch, and a wooden one beyond the porch, leading into the house proper. I moved into the porch, where a series of buzzers marked with names showed that the place was an apartment house. I scanned the names on the buzzers. There was no Oliver Wendell Holmes Brown.

For one bleak moment I envisaged my whole expedition as a gigantic hoax played on us by the drunken Beard. Lina Oliver Wendell Holmes Brown was only a figment of his crafty champagne dreams and 3862 Wawona Avenue was an address attached at random.

Then I remembered the basement. I ran down the steps to the street and, tugging open a little iron door in the railings, descended the twisting stairway to the basement door. No light was visible in this subterranean apartment. Beside the door, a tall window, protected against burglars with iron bars, exhibited a pair of white curtains.

A card was pinned to the door. I had to strike a match to read it. As the spurt of light flickered, I felt a surge of relief.

On the card was written: *Sgt. and Mrs. O. W. H. Brown.*

I pressed the metal buzzer. It's shrill whine, echoing beyond the door, brought sudden jittery recollections of Eulalia Crawford's buzzer. The whining faded. I rang again. I thought I could hear faint, scuffling footsteps. Then I was sure of it. They came pattering towards me. Then they stopped and a light went on in the room behind the window.

The footsteps came to the door and then stopped again. For a long, strange moment nothing happened. Then, instead of the door opening, a woman's voice, high and frightened and with a foreign accent, called from inside: "Who ees it, pliz?"

I said: "Is that Mrs. Brown? Mrs. Lina Brown?"

"Yes, yes. Who ees it, pliz?"

Those two little "yesses" sent a shiver of excitement through me. So much for the darkest of my forebodings. Lina Oliver Wendell Holmes Brown was at least alive.

Putting my mouth close to the door, I said: "I'm Lieutenant Duluth. Please let me in. It's very important. I've come from Eulalia Crawford."

"Oh, yes, yes." The voice had lost some of its quavering uncertainty. "One moment, pliz."

There was a rattle of metal as if she had slid a chain into place. Then the door opened about six inches and a face peered around its edge. There was no light in the hall except for a faint radiance coming from the room beyond. I could distinguish no features in that small, white face.

For a moment, Mrs. Lina Brown stared at me. Then her head bobbed back behind the shelter of the door.

"You are not Lieutenant Duluth." The words tumbled out breathlessly. "Lieutenant Duluth, he ees a sailor. He wear a uniform like a sailor."

I had overlooked the fact that the civilian suit might alarm her. The door wavered while she was making up her mind whether or not to slam it in my face.

Quickly I said: "I am Lieutenant Duluth, Eulalia's cousin's husband. It's just that my uniform has been stolen. Here, I can show you my identifications."

Grudgingly, the face appeared around the edge of the door. I took my dog tags out of my pocket and held them to her. She grabbed them from me with a small hand like a bird's claw and slammed the door. I heard her pattering inside, presumably taking the dog tags to the light. In a few moments, she was back. This time the chain clattered off the door and she opened it wide.

"O.K. I read the leetle tags. I see there Lieutenant Duluth."

I stepped into the hall. She scurried round me and shut the door, slipping the chain in place. I had known from her voice that she was afraid, but now, alone with her in that cramped dark hall, I could sense the fear in her almost as if it were some invisible third person hovering at our side.

"Come." She squeezed past me towards an open door which led to the lighted room. "Come, Lieutenant Duluth."

I followed past a shadowy table on which vague white flowers gleamed in a vase. A few steps took me after her into the room. It was a small parlor full of threadbare furniture arranged with a rather pathetic neatness.

For the first time I could see Lina Oliver Wendell Holmes Brown. She was somewhere in her thirties—a tiny Italian thing with big black eyes and a fading prettiness. She must have been asleep or at least in bed when I rang, for she wore a little pink satin wrap over a little pink nightgown.

We stared at each other. The dread in her eyes was so marked that I was afraid to say anything, afraid that the wrong phrases or the wrong intonation might send her skittering away like a flushed phoebe bird. Hatch was right. I would have to handle this terrified little woman with infinite caution and gentleness if I was to persuade her to accompany me to the St. Anton.

"So!" The word came from her in a thin peep. "Eulalia Crawford send you, Lieutenant Duluth?"

"Yes," I said warily. "I'm her cousin's husband. She sent me to warn you."

"Yes, yes." The black eyes never left my face. I felt she was already beginning to wish she hadn't let me in.

"She wants you to know—" I paused. "She wants you to know that the red rose and the white rose are out."

Her hands gripped each other convulsively. The fear in her seemed to be an actual physical pain like a cancer.

"Yes, yes. I know. I keep myself here all the time shut up. The cat warn me."

The cat! The white rose, the red rose, the elephant, the crocus—and now the cat. That's what I liked about this case. It had so much natural history in it.

I wondered whether the cat was her name for the Beard. He was the obvious one to have warned her. And yet, what was catlike about him?

She was still staring. She wasn't going to help the conversation along.

I said on a hazard: "Have you seen the cat recently?"

Lina shook her head.

"But he told you about the roses?"

"I already say." The eyes flickered. "Why you ask these questions? What ees it that Eulalia want?"

"She thinks you'd both be safer if you kept together. She's sent me to take you to her," I lied. "She's at the St. Anton. Here." I felt in my breast pocket and brought out Eulalia's letter. I handed it to her. "She wrote this."

Lina took the letter and stared at it. Something was wrong. Instead of lulling her suspicions, the letter seemed to have sharpened them still more. She looked up, fixing her gaze on my face.

"It ees not finished, thees letter."

I hadn't thought about that. "No."

"Why?"

I couldn't tell her that Eulalia had been murdered before she finished the letter. I could not risk having her run out into the street for the nearest policeman. I said: "Eulalia just wanted you to see some of her handwriting so that you would know you could trust me."

"I see." She added sharply: "And Eulalia ees at the St. Anton Hotel?"

"Yes."

"Why is she there when she has an apartment that ees her own?"

That stopped me for a moment. "Because—because she thinks it's safer at a hotel."

"I see."

Slowly, step by step, she began to back away from me towards the door.

"You do trust me, don't you, Lina? I've come here to help you."

"Yes, yes. You help me." She was still moving backwards, watching me as if I were a poisonous snake.

"You're not afraid of me?"

"Why should I be? I expect you. I get your message. They bring it from the drugstore just before they close."

"My message! But . . ." I stopped myself in time.

Lina had reached the door. The terror in her eyes was quite out of control now. She gave a wild smile.

"My glasses!" she faltered. "To read thees letter from Eulalia, I must get my glasses from bedroom. One moment, pliz."

With that, she ducked out of the room, closing the door behind her.

My pulses were pounding. *I get your message. I expect you.* That's what she had said. I saw then exactly what was happening. Eulalia's death had been foreshadowed by a telephone message from "Lieutenant Duluth." And now Lina, though she had no telephone, had received a similar message from "Lieutenant Duluth"—sent over from the drugstore across the street. The man with the lisp had called to say he was coming from Eulalia, and Lina had trusted the message. And the ironical part was that she had let me in simply because she thought I was the "Lieutenant Duluth" who had called.

The whole murder pattern was being played out again. Only this time, thanks to Cecil Grey and a kindly providence, I had arrived in time.

My first impulse was to follow Lina into the bedroom to warn her that at that very moment the roses, whatever they were, were on their way to murder her. I took a step to the door. Then I stopped. Lina was frightened enough already. If I suddenly appeared in the bedroom with news like that, she might well tilt over into panic and run out for police help. The front door was safely locked and chained. So long as we were both inside the apartment, nothing could happen to her. And if I played my cards right, I might be able to catch Eulalia's murderer myself. So far as my own anomalous position was concerned, that would be worth a thousand drunken Beards.

The thing to do was to wait, to be ready for anything and smart enough to cope with whatever anything showed up. Hatch hadn't much faith in my tact. To him I was a bull in a china shop. This was one moment when the china shop could do with a good bull.

I felt almost elated.

To keep myself occupied while Lina was gone, I started to stroll around the parlor. On the mantelpiece was a photograph of a cheerful young man in an army sergeant's uniform. Scrawled in the corner was the message:

> *Till I come home,*
> *love,*
> *Ollie.*

So Sergeant Oliver Wendell Holmes Brown was off a-soldiering.

A book with a blue cover lay on the arm of an over-stuffed chair as if Lina had recently been reading it. I picked it up and glanced idly at its title: *Crimes of Our Times,* edited by John L. Weatherby. I opened it at random to a learned essay on the Hall-Mills case. A study of true murders seemed a strange sedative for Lina's fear-jangled nerves. I started to turn the pages, then I let the book drop back on the chair because I saw another photograph on a table by the chair.

At first as I looked at that photograph, I hardly believed my eyes. And yet there was no mistaking that friendly blonde face with its beaming smile.

Staring out of a silver frame in the parlor of Lina Oliver Wendell Holmes Brown was the likeness of Mrs. Rose—the woman who had given up her room to Iris and me at the St. Anton that afternoon.

As I gazed at it, making no sort of sense of it, I was dimly conscious of the throb of an approaching automobile in the lonely silence outside. Mrs. Rose. Everything else that had happened to us in Frisco had managed to link up with this insane intrigue, but I had never thought seriously of Mrs. Rose's being implicated, too. I remembered our benefactress's bobbing feather-duster hat and her bursts of laughter. That laughter had sounded as innocent as a gusty breeze from the sea.

It didn't sound innocent any more.

The automobile had stopped somewhere quite close outside. There was no sound of Lina's return from the bedroom. That beaming photograph of Mrs. Rose was tantalizing, exasperating. I started to get worried about Lina. Why should it take her so long to find her glasses?

I went to the door to the hall which stood cater-cornered from the barred window facing out to the street. After a moment's hesitation, my hand moved to the door-knob. I turned it. Nothing happened. I turned again. It was only too clear what Lina had done.

She had locked me in the parlor.

As I stood staring at the door, I saw at once what must have gone on in her mind. She had let me in because she thought I was the "Lieutenant Duluth" who had telephoned, but my lack of uniform, coupled with my blundering remarks, had made her suspicious. Her increasingly sharp questions had indicated that. Finally the fact that Eulalia's letter was unfinished and my limp reason for her being at the St. Anton had sunk the scales against me.

Lina had locked me in here because she had decided that I was merely impersonating the genuine Lieutenant Duluth, and that I was either one of her floral enemies or their agent commissioned to lure her to their headquarters.

I couldn't think about the irony of it. I was too worried. Lina thought she had locked her potential murderer in the parlor, while I was in fact her friend and, if I was right, the man with a lisp, masquerading as me, was going to put in his deadly appearance at any minute.

I shook the handle of the parlor door. As I did so, I heard a sound that stirred the hairs at the back of my neck. Someone was coming, softly and swiftly, down the iron stairway from the street. Surely, Lina would be receiving no ordinary callers at this hour of the night.

Had it happened even more quickly than I had expected?

Was "Lieutenant Duluth" already arriving?

I stood quite still, without moving a muscle, remembering the car that had just stopped outside. The footsteps paused at the front door. There was a brief moment of silence. Then the urgent shrill of the buzzer rang through the apartment.

I started to beat with my fists on the locked parlor door. Outside the passage, I heard Lina's footsteps hurrying from the bedroom.

I shouted: "Don't let him in, Lina. For God's sake, don't let him in."

The buzzer sounded again. Lina's footsteps tapped steadily on towards the front door.

"Lina, don't let him in."

But, even as I called, I realized that nothing I said would affect her. I was the villain of the piece. She was running from me to the unknown man outside the door, who, to her, was her savior.

Desperate, I took a lunge at the parlor door, crashing my shoulders against it. The wood was heavy and old. The door shivered and stood firm.

I heard the safety chain on the front door slide out of its socket and Lina's voice crying: "Lieutenant Duluth, it ees you? You have come at last? Queeck. Queeck. I have him locked. A man from the roses. A man who pretends to be you."

"Lina!" I shouted hopelessly. "Don't let him in. They killed Eulalia. They'll kill you."

My words, muffled in that lonely basement, sounded futile and hollow. I threw myself at the door again. Once again it shivered and held its ground.

From the hall I heard a creak as Lina swung the front door open.

"Queeck . . ." Her voice sounded high with excitement. Then at what must have been the instant when she actually saw the man on the threshold, her voice toppled into a reedy cry. *"You! . . ."*

A man's voice replied, soft, husky.

"Yes, Lina, it's me."

I heard that *yes* and that *it's* clearly enough to know that this new arrival did not lisp. I felt a sudden kindling hope.

There was silence. Then, out of the silence came a small wail that turned into a hissing sigh. A sigh—and a subdued noise as of a little body crumpling to the floor.

I hurled myself a third time against the door. The lock gave a wrenching groan but did not yield. And, as I paused, panting, I heard the front door slam shut and footsteps clatter away again up the iron stairs to the street.

The window was close at my side. Its top was at street level and the area between it and the street was so narrow that the light from the room illuminated the strip of sidewalk like a theater spotlight. Out of the corner of my eye I caught sight of something moving past the window. I swung round. A pair of legs, visible only halfway up the calf, were speeding past. They were so near that, had the window been open, I could have reached through the bars and touched them.

Those legs were wearing a pair of naval lieutenant's trousers. And in the brief second before they passed from my vision, I distinctly saw low down on the left leg a small triangular tear.

That man, who had come and who had not lisped, was wearing my stolen uniform.

Recklessly I threw myself again and again at the door. Farther up the street, I heard a car start with a grinding of gears and roar away. A last, vicious attack split the door from the lock and sent it swinging open.

My shoulder raw and smarting, I dashed out into the hall. I knew what I was going to see, knew it with such nightmare certainty that I hardly had the courage to look.

Light splayed out through the broken parlor door behind me. It filtered across the dark hall towards the closed front door.

Lina lay there on her back, the pink satin robe foaming loose around her. The wooden handle of a cheap knife reared up from the pink nightgown under the left breast. And there was blood—crimson blood pulsing up and spilling over the pink material.

But the blood wasn't the worst part. The flowers which I had vaguely noticed on the hall table had been spilled out of the vase. They were strewn haphazard over that prostrate little body.

They were roses, of course. But this time, they were not red. They were white—dozens of pure white roses.

I ran to Lina. I knelt at her side. I felt her wrist for the pulse that was not there.

The scent of the roses wafted to me. Lina's big black eyes looked up, quite stupid, set in a glazed stare of terror. Her tiny wrist, under my shaking fingers, was warm.

But she was dead. I had seen enough dead people in the Pacific to be sure of that.

I stayed crouching there. What had been my plan? To save Lina and to catch Eulalia's murderer red-handed. I felt weary, spent, and utterly useless.

The red rose and the white rose mean blood.

They meant blood, all right.

CHAPTER IX

I squatted in that drab hallway beside the dead body of Lina Brown. The scent from the white roses gave the atmosphere the nauseous sweetness of a funeral parlor.

Red roses for Eulalia. White roses for Lina. A murderer with a lisp for Eulalia. A murderer without a lisp for Lina. So there were two murderers at least. And both of them had worn my uniform.

My thoughts blundered on. Surely, no mission had ever met with such dismal failure. I had been unable to prevent Lina from running straight into the arms of death. I had let her be murdered with only the thickness of a door between me and her murderer. The drugstore would remember "Lieutenant Duluth's" message. When Lina was found, "Lieutenant Duluth" would be the first name the police would hear. And this time I had no sort of alibi, for I had actually been on the scene of the crime. I had fallen into a second trap far more deadly than the one set for me at Eulalia's apartment.

With a mixture of indignation and despair, I saw that Lina's murder dealt me another body blow. Lina had known the secret of the roses. Apart from the Beard, she was the only person who, by telling the truth, could have convinced the police that I was not a psychopathic liar. Now she was dead, and there was nothing but that crafty drunken old man between me and—the deluge.

While those reflections spun in my head, my body had been instinctively on the alert for any sound from the apartment above or the street outside to warn me that my battle with the door or Lina's wailing cry had aroused the neighborhood. As the seconds ticked by nothing disturbed the silence of the night. I was getting one break, it seemed. Having failed to catch the murderer red-handed, I was at least going to be spared the discomfort of being caught red-handed myself.

As I crouched there, I became conscious of something I hadn't noticed before. Lina's right hand was half covered by the tangled folds of her bathrobe. But something was clutched in it. The edge of a piece of paper was just visible, poking out from the pink satin. Eulalia's letter, of course. I shivered to think what might happen if it was found there.

I eased it from the dead grip of the fingers. I smoothed it out before folding it and, as I did so, my eye fell on one particular line:

> There's danger, Lina, terrible, terrible danger for all of us.

For all of us! That phrase burned through me like a flame through paper. Why hadn't Hatch or Iris or I noticed that "all of us" before? It could mean only one thing. It meant that Eulalia and Lina were not the only two in danger. There were still others, men or women, who were marked for death by this impossible rose and crocus team.

I was almost at the end of my tether then. Was an infinite succession of Lieutenant Duluths going to prowl murderously through the streets of San Francisco? Was this thing never going to end?

And, as if things weren't bad enough, another thought came. Before Lina's death my position had been embarrassing enough, but there was always the comforting thought that the witnessed theft of my uniform at the Turkish bath was something definite and provable to back up my story. But now that I was so much more deeply involved, I realized with alarming clarity that even this prop could be pushed from under me. What if the police thought I had staged the whole uniform theft episode as a very elaborate dust-throwing act? The dozing door clerk had not noticed me come in as a lieutenant. I could easily have arrived at the bath as a civilian and complained of the loss of a perfectly imaginary uniform.

If the police did think that, nothing human or inhuman could stop them from arresting me as a crafty and maniacal double murderer.

I was really on the spot now.

I stood up, putting Eulalia's letter into my breast pocket. I managed to steady myself. It wasn't easy. The Beard had known about Lina. All right. The Beard would know about these other people. I hadn't put my hand to this plow. I'd had my hand chained to it. The time for turning back was long since past.

I looked down at Lina. I was getting used to thinking like a criminal. Cynically I reflected that she had been living alone as a war wife. That meant there was a good chance that she, like Eulalia, would not be found at least until morning. I would have to walk out on her, of course. There had never been any question about that. But with luck we still had a certain amount of time.

Perhaps, when I returned to the hotel, Iris would already be in Room 624, and the Beard would have told all. Perhaps I would still be able to get to the police with some halfway plausible story before the murders were discovered.

Perhaps.

I threw a last glance down at Lina, poor little Lina whose caution had killed her. She looked as limp and unreal as one of Eulalia's puppets. Sorry as I was for myself, I felt sorrier for her. That was a bad way to die, alone, with a knife in her heart and no Oliver Wendell Holmes Brown to comfort her.

I opened the front door. I peered up into the darkness of the street. There was no sound of human stirring. I closed the door behind me. I tiptoed up the iron stairs on to the deserted sidewalk.

I was a fugitive from two murders now.

I walked the few desolate blocks to the zoo terminal

of the trolley line. All my worse moments were associated with trolleys. I would never be able to face one again with equanimity. An empty car was waiting at the end of the tracks, less than a hundred yards from the endless expanse of the Pacific Ocean. I was the sole passenger at first, and by the time the car bolted forward I had only two sleepy soldiers as travelling companions.

At least my exit from Wawona Avenue had been inconspicuous.

But as the trolley rattled along its interminable journey to the center of the city, I began to feel the delayed effects of shock. Lina's big black eyes and her fluttering hands haunted me. The colossal failure of my expedition plagued me. The beaming face of Mrs. Rose, sinister now, swam through my mind.

Mrs. Rose . . . The roses. My thoughts stuck there. Over and over again, they churned out that meaningless jingle.

The red rose . . . the white rose . . . the crocus . . . the red rose . . . the white rose . . . the crocus . . .

It was exactly a quarter to three when I reached the St. Anton. Before I went in, I paused outside the Geary entrance where Cecil Grey had accosted me, trying to make a plan. If my wife had been successful, she should have been able to lure the Beard back to our room by now. Even if she hadn't returned, I didn't dare ask for the room key in my guilty civilian suit. My safest move was to sneak up the stairs to the sixth floor and, if Iris wasn't in the room, to wait outside in the corridor.

Apart from a scattering of soldiers and sailors asleep in the overstuffed chairs, the vestibule was empty. No one saw me, I was fairly sure, as I slipped in and up the stairs. I climbed to the sixth floor and hurried down the deserted corridors to Room 624. Dispiritedly, I saw that no light showed through the transom. I tried the door. It was locked. I tapped on it. But there was no answer.

Neither Iris nor Hatch and Bill had come back yet.

Although I had made such a hopeless mess of my own assignment, I had been pathetically sure that Iris would be successful with hers. Anxiety for my wife flooded through me now. What if the Beard, instead of being on our side, was on the side of the roses and had somehow managed to give Bill Dagget the slip and whisk Iris away? That thought had a double sting to it—the sting of losing our last possible ally and the even sharper sting of danger for Iris.

I paced up and down the corridor until fear of awakening some of the other guests sent me in humiliating retreat into a communal men's bathroom across the passage from Room 624. I had spent twenty jittery minutes there when I heard footsteps outside and the incalculably welcome sound of my wife's voice. It was soft and coaxing and, oddly enough, she was crooning: "Come, Pussy. This way, Pussy. That's a good Pussy."

I stepped out of the bathroom to be confronted with a sight worthy of a laudanum hallucination. My wife, tired and pale, was opening the door of Room 624. And the Beard was with her. He still progressed with the dignity of a Supreme Court justice, but, defying every normal law of locomotion, he was progressing on all fours. While Iris made a traffic-cop gesture, he proceeded into the room, one large hand padding forward and then the other, as his substantial rump followed soberly behind.

Iris saw me and her face relaxed. "Peter, darling, thank God you're here."

She grabbed my hand and, pulling me into the room after the Beard, closed the door behind us.

She turned on the light. The Beard maneuvered into reverse and stared up at me. The solemn face with its majestic black outcrop of whiskers looked unutterably wrong weaving there six inches above the carpet.

I gulped and said: "What's this?"

Iris shrugged wearily. "He's been this way ever since we came out of the elevator. He thinks he's a pussycat."

Pussycat . . . the cat! I remembered what Lina had said. "At least you've got him. That's the important part. Where have you been?"

"All over Chinatown from one dive to another. Champagne, champagne, champagne." Iris wrung her hands. "Peter, what can we do with him?"

"Haven't you got anything out of him?"

"Nothing. Absolutely nothing. It's hopeless. I don't even know his name. He—he just says to call him Pussy!"

"Pussy!" said the Beard gravely and started a laborious attempt to sit up on his haunches. Fantastically, although I had never seen a more drunken man, he had not lost one particle of his ambassadorial aplomb.

"Where's Dagget?" I said.

"Oh, he followed along faithfully." Iris gestured at the Beard. "Pussy never caught on. Bill's in the lobby now. I think he's going to wait down there for Hatch. Then they'll both be up." Her eyes changed their expression. "Lina isn't here. That—that means you couldn't find her?"

I hated doing this to her after all she'd been through.

"Lina," I said, "is dead."

"Dead!" Iris gasped. "You mean you found her dead like—like Eulalia?"

"She was alive when I got there. They killed her right under my nose."

Iris's face was without hope. "And the—the roses?"

"Of course, the roses. Only this time they were white. White roses."

"Peter!"

The Beard, who had been squatting beside us, suddenly sat down with a thud on the floor.

"We'd better get him on the bed out of the way," I snapped. "I can't stand beards all over the carpet."

Between us, we managed to haul and push him on to the crimson bedspread. He seemed to like it. He nestled back against the pillows with a sigh and closed his eyes.

Iris turned to me, taking both my hands. "Now, darling, tell me everything. Don't worry. I can't feel worse than I do."

I told her the whole miserable saga of Wawona Avenue, bringing in Mrs. Rose's picture and everything. My wife listened intently. When I was through, she said: "So there are two murderers."

"At least two. Probably a dozen or a score or a gross." She put her arms around me.

"You mustn't feel bad, Peter. You did all you could."

"I did fine," I said gloomily. "Lina's dead. I'm compromised worse with the police. And that's not all. There are other people in danger too, not just Eulalia and Lina."

We both stared at the Beard.

"He's our only hope now," said Iris.

Ponderous lids still covered his eyes. He lay luxuriously back against the crimson spread, his arms limp at his sides, his mouth half open.

"To hell with kid gloves," said Iris suddenly.

She leaned over, grabbed his shoulders, and started to shake him with an exasperation which must have been building up ever since they left the Green Kimono together.

His eyes popped open.

"You've got to listen." Iris was still shaking him passionately. "Lina's dead. Eulalia's dead. The red rose and the white rose. Someone's murdered Eulalia Crawford and Lina Oliver Wendell Holmes Brown."

The Beard looked intelligent. His eyes cleared. His whiskers took upon themselves all the gravity in the world. He opened his mouth.

Iris let her hands drop from his shoulders. We leaned over him tensely.

"Yes, yes," breathed Iris. "Say it."

He pushed his face even closer to ours. His mouth opened even wider.

"Miaow," he said.

He giggled then—a girlish giggle.

Iris stamped her foot. "You've got to help us. Eulalia and Lina are murdered."

"Eulalia," repeated the Beard. "Lina."

"Go on. Eulalia. Lina."

"Eulalia, Lina—Zelide, Edwina," he said. "Eulalia, Lina—Zelide and Edwina."

"Yes, yes," exclaimed Iris. "Go on. Is there danger for Zelide and Edwina, too?"

"Eulalia, Lina—Zelide, Edwina."

Iris glanced at me triumphantly. "Who is Zelide, Pussy?" she said. "Who—is—Zelide?"

The Beard stared. "Zelide? A bird."

"A bird," moaned Iris. "Edwina, then. Who is Edwina?"

" 'N'elephant," said the Beard promptly.

He shut his eyes again. He sighed. He gave a voluptuous yawn. He stretched both his arms and then with a grunt of contentment rolled over on to his side, curled up his legs, and started to snore.

I grabbed his shoulders and started to shake him again.

"Pussy," I said. "Pussy. Mr. Pussy. Cat. Mr. Cat."

It was like trying to shake sense into a sack of flour. The snores from the bed swelled in undisturbed crescendo. The Beard's capacity for sleep seemed as Gargantuan as his capacity for champagne.

The drunken oracle had obviously said his last say until morning.

"Zelide and Edwina," repeated Iris.

"A bird and an elephant," I snarled.

"There must be danger for Zelide and Edwina, Peter. Whenever he says anything, it always turn out to be true."

"Damn Zelide and Edwina." I didn't care any more. I just didn't care. It wasn't as if the mystery ever got nearer to being solved. The red rose, the white rose, the crocus, the cat, the bird, the elephant. It was just a succession of doors, one door leading to another door leading to another door leading in an endless chain to the madhouse. "Damn the bird and the elephant and the rose and the crocus. Let them all kill each other. Let a howling mob string me up on the nearest lamp-post as a mass murderer. I'm through."

Iris, in a voice that tried to be encouraging, said: "Darling, we can't give up now. We can't."

"I can," I said. I was suddenly remembering all the things that I'd wanted to happen that evening, all the exciting intimate, peaceable things that a husband on leave with his wife deserves.

My indignation which had been simmering so long seethed over when I looked down at the Beard snoring his head off on the bed—*our* bed. That was the ultimate insult.

"And beyond all others," I said, "damn this evil bearded old man."

I grabbed the sleeping Beard by the shoulders and dragged him off the bed. I looked around, and, half carrying, half pushing him, staggered with him to the bathroom. I lifted him full off the ground and tilted him into the tub.

He came to rest on his back and, with a slow, sleep-drunk stirring, folded his big arms over his stomach. He looked like a corpse laid out on a marble slab.

But he seemed to approve of the bathtub. The snores continued their symphonic rhapsody. Some satyrish dream twitched the beard in a shameless smile.

I slammed the bathroom door on him. It did something to deaden his snores. Wearily, Iris was hanging her silver-fox wrap on the back of a chair. The gardenia at her throat had gone brown around the edges. She tugged it off and threw it into the scrapbasket.

"Peter," she said, "if you ever grow a beard, I'll kill you."

I went to her and took her in my arms. She looked up at me from dark, mournful eyes.

"What are we going to do?" she breathed. "Peter, what are we going to do?"

I kissed her. Knowing she was so near the breaking point made me tough and aggressive again. I was hopelessly involved in two murders. O.K. There was still enough kick in me to fight back.

"We'll get out of it somehow, honey," I said. "If you think we'll let a bunch of flowers and animals lick us, you're crazy."

Puny as that challenge to fate was, it seemed to satisfy her. She grinned.

"Yes," she said. A faraway look came into her eyes. Softly she chanted: *"May the rain splash and the winds blow, we'll rout the bloody bastards. Ho!"*

I stared. "Have you taken leave of your senses?"

She shook her head. "Darling, it's something I read in a book when I was a child. It used to fascinate me. Eulalia and I spent one whole summer reciting it in the hay barn out at Grandfather's farm." She gave a wry grimace. "Poor Eulalia, the bloody bastards got her, ho, didn't they?"

A tap sounded at the door and I heard Hatch's voice in a husky: "Hey, Lieutenant."

I went to the door and opened it. Hatch came in, followed by the silent, patient bulk of Bill Dagget. In spite

of the bad report I had to turn in, it was a great relief to
see the boss. Hatch, for him, looked almost happy.

"Well," he said, "I spent a session at police headquarters. Not a word come in on Eulalia yet. That means
we're safe till morning at least." He turned to Iris. "Bill
here tells me you got the Beard. Good work, lady." He
glanced around the room. "Where is he?"

Iris gestured to the bathroom. "Listen," she said.
"He's passed out in the tub."

"Get any more dope out of him?"

My wife shook her head. "Not until just now. Then he
said two more names. Zelide, Edwina. Hatch, I think
they're in danger too."

"Two more, eh?" Hatch's face was grave. He turned
quickly to me. "Where's Lina? Couldn't you get her to
come?"

"No," I said. "I couldn't find a handy hearse."

I'd become used to telling that Lina Oliver Wendell
Holmes Brown story now. I rolled it off to Hatch. Both
he and Bill Dagget listened with expressions of stunned
incredulity.

When I was through, Hatch sat down on the edge of
the bed and pushed the hat on to the back of his head.

"Geez," he said. "Geez, but this puts you in a spot."

"Don't worry," I said. "I'm hardened to anything now.
When they get me on to the hot seat, I won't even burn."

Iris was watching Hatch with eagernesss, as if she
had great faith in his ability to cope with hopeless situa-
tions. "Hatch, what do you think about Mrs. Rose being
mixed up in this?"

Hatch sat a moment in silence. Then he threw out his
hands in a gesture denoting bafflement. "You got me
there, lady."

"And Zelide and Edwina? How are we going to find
out who they are? How can we try and save them?"

"You got me there too." Hatch leaned forward, prop-
ping his jaw on his fists. "Let's face it," he said. "I've
been a flop. I came in on this with you. I did my best.
I figured what we did was the thing to do. But now . . ."
He shrugged. "Two more dames in danger. Lina dead.
The Beard passed out. The Lieutenant here framed in

another murder. Lady, I guess I better go back to the small time. I guess I'm just not up to murder."

He looked so forlorn that Iris went to him and put her hand on his arm. "Don't feel bad about it, Hatch. You did everything you could."

"Yeah. And look where it's got us."

Even the Napoleons of this world, it seemed, have their moments of uncertainty. Hatch's was short-lived, however. His mouth forming into a grim line, he got up from the bed. He stood in his favorite football-coach stance, legs apart, hands on his lapels.

"Listen," he said, "so we're in a spot. So we face up to it. This Zelide, this Edwina, maybe they are two other dames in danger or maybe they're just something the old drunk cooked up. Whichever it is, we're not going to be able to do anything about them. O.K. Forget them. Concentrate on us. We've got the Beard. In a couple of hours, when he's slept off the champagne, he'll be sober enough to talk. There's four of us, me and Bill and you and the Lieutenant. O.K. We all stick together. We back each other up. We take the Beard down to headquarters. We tell everything. We still got a pretty good chance to get the Lieutenant out of serious trouble." He looked around. "How about that?"

Just how far out of serious trouble it would get me I wasn't prepared to say. But there was nothing else to do. Having failed in our maximum objective, we would have to fall back on a less ambitious plan. As for Zelide and Edwina—since I seemed incapable of saving damsels in distress, I could at least abandon my habit of hanging around and watching them get stabbed.

"O.K.," I said. "I guess that's the best bet."

Hatch glanced at his watch. "Four-fifteen," he murmured. "With any luck, neither body'll be discovered before nine at the earliest and the Beard needs a couple of hours to sleep it off. O.K. Bill and I have a shakedown around the corner. We're all going to want some rest. You two get into that bed and get some shut-eye. Bill and I'll be back here by eight. We'll wake the Beard up. Then we go to the cops."

"Fine," I said.

Hatch patted my arm. He gave me a grudging grin of

appreciation. "At least you can take it, Lieutenant," he said.

With a gloomy nod to Iris, he went out into the passage. Bill Dagget went after him.

I shut the door on them and turned back to Iris. Snores still soared from the bathroom.

"At least there's something to be said for this birthday," I remarked. "We're never going to forget it."

"Nor will anyone else," sighed Iris. "It'll go ringing down the centuries."

I was so tired that even the modest prospect of four hours' sleep was immeasurably pleasant. Iris yawned and started to slip out of her black evening gown. I peeled off the jacket of my ill-starred civilian suit and threw it on the floor. I stepped out of the pants, inwardly cursing the red rose and the white rose and the crocus for electing to commit their murders in my uniform. I threw the pants on the floor too. Then, just because the navy had trained me that way, I picked the suit up again and took it to the closet.

I pulled open the door. I raised my hand for a hanger. I blinked. I blinked again. Then the whole world seemed to come tumbling down around my ears.

My fancy uniform was hanging where I had left it when I changed into the civilian suit. But it wasn't hanging alone. Next to it, dangling neatly from the crossbar, was another naval lieutenant's uniform.

My hand as unsteady as a brandy drunk's, I pulled that second uniform out of the closet. I grabbed for the pants and examined the left leg.

Just about six inches from the bottom, I saw the familiar small triangular tear.

It was mad. It was quite impossible. But there it was.

Like a most unwelcome chicken, my stolen uniform had come home to roost.

CHAPTER X

Iris glanced at me standing there with the uniform in my hand. She joined me, looked in the closet, and saw the other uniform hanging inside.

"It can't be," she exclaimed.

"It is," I said. "A guy knows his own uniform."

"But it's just not possible."

I held up the pants, showing her the tear. On a hunch I examined the right sleeve of the jacket. A dark stain, still not completely dry, smeared the cuff. That clinched it.

"There's even blood on the sleeve," I said.

Iris peered at the stain. She was still having trouble speaking. I didn't blame her. "But, Peter, you saw Lina's murderer wearing it."

"He had a car. There was plenty of time for him to go home, wherever that is, change and bring the uniform up here before I got back on the trolley."

"But—but how could he get in here?"

I had figured that out too. "There was a key to the room in the pocket. I'd forgotten about it. We had two keys to begin with. I took one to the Turkish bath. I didn't bother to check it with my valuables. It was in the uniform when the man with a lisp stole it."

I started to search the pockets of the uniform. The key was not there.

Iris said: "Then they've got a key to our room. They can come in whenever they want to."

I crossed to the door. There was a knob that worked a safety catch. I turned it. At least I could prevent our being murdered in our sleep.

I watched my wife soberly. The roses and crocuses weren't satisfied with pinning their murder on me. They were brazen enough to come and go in our room as if they owned us body and soul. Our every move seemed to be supervised by these mysterious murderers. They could jerk us at will like puppets—like those great, sprawling puppets which Eulalia had fashioned and worked so expertly.

I said: "You see what this does to us, don't you? Our story was incredible enough already. Now we've got to sell the police on two murderers we've never seen who both wore my uniform and then calmly hung it up in our closet again when they were through with it." I groaned. "Can you see them believing that?"

"No," said Iris.

I was too tired to be able to whip up a great deal of emotion. Things were so bad, they might as well be this much worse. I put the bloodstained uniform back in the closet. I yawned. Iris was climbing into bed. I followed her.

The last thing I saw before I turned out the lights were the cupids' behinds. They didn't look provocative any more. The last thing I heard before I collapsed into exhausted sleep were the Beard's resonant snores issuing from the bathroom.

So much for our man-and-wife reunion.

I was awakened eventually by a tap on the door. I sat up in bed. It was daylight. Iris stirred, opened her eyes and then sat up too. The tap came again and with it Hatch's voice calling softly: "Lieutenant Duluth."

I looked at my watch. It said eight o'clock. Suddenly I remembered everything. So did Iris. She reached out of bed for her bathrobe and wrapped it around her shoulders. I got out of bed, padded to the door, and let Hatch in.

"Morning, Lieutenant."

Hatch wore the same blue-check suit, the same purple

and white shirt. He looked as if he hadn't had much sleep.

"Bill's waiting downstairs," he said. He gave a funereal grin. "At least we're O.K. so far. I looked at the papers. No news broken on the murders yet."

While Iris, looking miserable, huddled in the robe, I told Hatch about the return of the uniform and showed it to him. He whistled and pushed the hat back on his head.

"Geez," he said. And then, as if trying to comfort us: "Don't let it get you down, Lieutenant. At least we've got the Beard there in the bathroom. With him telling the whole story, you ain't got nothing to worry about with the police."

I only hoped he was right.

Iris had risen from the bed and was pushing her feet into white feathery mules.

Hatch said: "The old goat should have slept it off by now. Let's wake him up."

The three of us went to the bathroom. I opened the door. We all stepped inside. We all stared down at the tub.

There it was—a perfectly good tub. But it was just a tub.

No one was in it.

I had been so slugged around by fate that I should have been able to take that. But I couldn't take it. Neither could Iris.

We both exploded in a simultaneous moaning cry: "The Beard's gone."

Hatch was speechless. He glanced around the empty bathroom and then turned into the bedroom and began searching hopelessly under the bed and in the closet.

"They had a key," he said at last. "They must have come in when you were asleep and kidnapped him."

"I turned the safety catch on the door," I said. "No one could have come in from outside." Then I remembered. When I had let Hatch in a few moments before, the door had opened without my having to unlock the safety catch. I said: "He must have left under his own steam. He came to, didn't like the looks of our bathroom, and walked out."

Hatch turned on me. I had never seen him angry before. He was really mad now. "You mean you didn't have the sense to lock him in?"

I faltered: "We—we didn't think. He'd passed out. I never dreamed he'd sober up for hours."

"And when he'd passed out, you didn't search him to get his address or anything?"

Even more feebly I said: "We didn't think."

"So you didn't think," snarled Hatch. "So where are you now? You're much worse off than if you'd called the cops when you first found Eulalia. You're framed for Eulalia's murder. You're framed for Lina's murder. You're in so deep even your ears don't stick out. And you did all that just on a gamble to get this Beard. You got him. You let him go." He gave a despairing shrug. "Now, going to the cops'd be like shaving your own head and slitting your own pants. My first murder," he groaned. "And I have to pick clients like you."

There was no point in trying to justify ourselves. He was right.

I said: "O.K. There's only one thing to do. We've got to catch up with the Beard again."

"Yes, yes," said Iris. "He can't have gone long. Maybe if we ask people in the lobby, they'll have seen him. Come on, Peter. Quick. We've got to get dressed."

She started to pull off her bathrobe. Hatch put a hand on her arm.

"Hey, hold it, lady." He stared from her to me, his face very grim. "We got to get the Beard back, yeah. That's so obvious you don't have to say it. But any minute now they're going to find one of the two corpses. Any minute now they're going to be screaming all over the city for you two. You can't go running around in broad daylight looking for the Beard. We got to get him, sure. But Bill and me's the ones who're going to do it."

"But . . ." I said.

"But nothing. You two can't stay here either. You're registered as Lieutenant and Mrs. Duluth. The management will call the police the moment the news breaks. You're just about as safe here as if you were already in the city jail. Tell you what you got to do." He pulled a key out of his pocket. "Me and Dagget's got an apartment

over on Fillmore." He gave me the address and tossed
me the key. "You two get dressed, check out of here right
away, and get over to the apartment. Stick there. Don't
go out on the street. Don't do nothing. Stay there till we
come for you."

"But . . ." I began, but Iris broke in again.

"Yes, he's right, Peter."

Hatch grunted. "Better make it snappy too. If we get
a lead on the Beard, we'll keep you posted. But none of
this fancy business you go in for, Lieutenant. Stick right
there in the apartment, and for pity's sake don't try to
be smart. You've done enough damage already."

I grinned weakly.

Hatch made for the door. "Me and Bill's got to get on
the job right away." His opinion of me had dropped so
low that he added to Iris: "Lady, you got some sense. You
understand, don't you? Don't let the Lieutenant screw
things up again."

Iris said: "We'll go to your apartment, Hatch, and we'll
stay there."

"O.K."

Hatch hurried out of the room, slamming the door behind him.

In chastened silence, Iris and I dressed and packed our
bags. I put on my new uniform and packed the murderous
one. I put the civilian clothes in the bag, too. At least they
were something to show the police. In a few moments we
left forever the room that the anomalous Mrs. Rose had
been so kind as to bequeath us and which had brought
us nothing but catastrophe.

It is quite a sensation to know that the police are going
to be on your heels at any moment and yet not to know
when that moment is going to come. To me, our fellow
passengers on the elevator were all potential plainclothes-
men. Even the most casual glance that followed us across
the lobby brought uneasy suspense. I expected anything
from the cashier when I checked out. All I got was a mechanical smile and a mechanical: "I hope you enjoyed
your stay, Lieutenant."

I gulped and joined Iris. There were no signs of Hatch
or Bill in the lobby. They must already be out on their
desperate Beard hunt. Finding an unknown black beard

in San Francisco was going to be no simple matter. I tried
not to think what would happen if they failed.

Fugitives or no, Iris and I had to eat. We chose a
crowded cafeteria where we snatched an unobtrusive
breakfast of eggs and coffee. All around us, on stools and
in booths, people were reading newspapers. I had never
been so aware of other people's newspapers before. In
spite of Hatch's assurance that they contained no news, as
yet, of the murders, I expected each gulp of coffee to be
my last as a free man.

Nothing happened in the cafeteria, though. And nothing happened on our walk to the unprepossessing Fillmore Street. Unmolested, we reached the drab little
two-room apartment in the drab little house where Hatch
and Bill led their modest and presumably bachelor exist-
ence.

I locked the door on the inside. I followed Iris into the
living room, which was as lugubrious as Hatch's face.
There were a telephone on a rickety table, a brown studio
couch, a rocking chair, and a spattering of *True Confession* magazines. Iris dropped down on the studio couch.
I got the rocking chair. She sat. I rocked. We waited.

The most difficult thing to do in a crisis is to do nothing, and there was nothing for Iris and me to do. There
was nothing even to talk about. The situation was so simple. Either Hatch and Bill would locate the Beard or they
wouldn't. It was a waste of time and mental anguish to
speculate about the mystery that lay behind our dilemma.
Even now, after as hysterically active a night as anyone
had ever put in, we knew less than nothing about this
murderous faction which had chosen me as their scapegoat.

The red rose . . . the white rose . . . the crocus . . . the
elephant . . . the bird . . . the cat. That was all we knew.
Short of chanting the refrain to each other, there was
nothing for us to say.

Once, after she had plowed her way through two old
copies of *True Confessions*, my wife said tentatively:
"Peter, if they don't find the Beard, we might still be able
to locate Zelide or Edwina."

A grunt from me was more than enough to snuff out

her flicker of optimism. She lapsed back into the *True
Confessions*.

It was about eleven o'clock when Hatch called. His
voice sounded sardonically surprised that we had been
smart enough to reach the apartment without mishap. His
news, however, was hardly encouraging. They had managed to trace someone who answered to the Beard's de-
scription from the hotel to the ferry building. At the ferry
building, they had found someone who had seen this same
individual boarding a ferry for Oakland. Hatch wasn't at
all sanguine about their being on the right track, but they
were planning to take the next ferry to Oakland. After
exhorting me to stay under cover and not to get impatient,
he rang off.

In a solitary bookshelf hanging on the wall I found an
old atlas. The atlas told me that the population of San
Francisco was 634,536, while the population of Oakland
was a mere 302,163.

I squeezed what comfort I could from the statistics.

By one o'clock, Iris had collapsed into an apathetic
torpor. Having rocked myself dizzy, I was pacing up and
down the room, smoking an endless chain of cigarettes.

At last I said: "Honey, there must be a new edition of
the paper out by now. Hatch or no Hatch, I'm going out
to get one."

My wife sat up on the couch. "No, darling. You'll be
the one with all the publicity. It's much more sensible
for me to go."

She refused to argue and walked out, returning shortly
with a *Chronicle*.

"Well?" I said.

"I haven't looked at it, darling. Somehow, it seemed too
guilty. Here."

She spread the paper out on the studio couch. We both
sat down and stared at the front page. All sorts of things
of disastrous importance to the human race were going
on, but we skipped them. There was nothing about any
murders. With a relaxing of tension, we turned to the
second page and so right on through the funnies. Dick
Tracy was in an awful jam.

It was nice to be reminded that other people had their
troubles, too.

I got up from the couch and began pacing again. Iris sat there, listlessly, brooding over the paper. She took a cigarette out of her purse and lit it.

"Edwina," she murmured, half to herself. "Edwina, the elephant. The elephant!" She repeated the word excitedly. She swung back to the paper and started leafing through it. "Peter, I think I've got it."

"Got what?"

I crossed to her side.

"I noticed the ad when we were going through it just now. I never realized." She had found a certain page in the newspaper. She pointed down triumphantly.

"Look. It was Edwina the elephant that gave me the idea."

I looked. Staring up from a large advertisement were the likenesses of three prancing elephants.

"See, Peter? Eulalia's letter to Lina—we read it wrong. Eulalia's writing was so shaky. We thought she said: 'The *crocus* is opening.' She didn't. What she must have said was: 'The *circus* is opening.'"

Above the elephants, in bold, black letters, were the words:

MADDEN'S CIRCUS IS IN TOWN
GALA OPENING TODAY
THE LAWRENCE STADIUM

"The red rose and the white rose are out and the circus is opening," quoted Iris. "I'm sure that's it, Peter. I'm sure the clue to everything must be in the circus."

I was getting excited myself. "Eulalia had all those circus puppets. Maybe there is a tie-up. Maybe Edwina is one of the elephants in the circus. How a circus elephant fits in I can't imagine, but . . ."

"Look, Peter." Iris's finger had come to rest on a column at one side of the advertisement which listed the principal attractions of the show. Heading the column was: *Edwina, the oldest elephant in captivity.*

And that wasn't all. My eyes travelled down the column and fixed on another attraction near the end of the list. For once we were getting a break.

There, under Merlino the Magician, was the announcement: *Madame Zelide, World-famous aerialist, with her amazing Bird Ballet.*

"Zelide—the bird," I said.

Iris looked up from the paper, her eyes shining. "It doesn't matter now whether Hatch and Bill get the Beard or not. Zelide will be able to tell us the truth."

"If she's still alive," I said shortly. I hated to douse her enthusiasm. But, since Zelide seemed to be on the same murder schedule as Eulalia and Lina, the world-famous aerialist's hopes of being alive seemed on the slim side.

"She must be alive." Iris got up from the couch and ran to the telephone. She fiddled around with the phone book and then gave the mouthpiece a number.

"What are you doing?" I said.

"Calling the Lawrence Stadium, of course."

She got her number and talked to it. It was the wrong number for contacting performers. She was given another. She dialled it. After innumerable conversations that got her nowhere, I heard her say: "Yes, yes. She's not there? Well, do you know where she's staying? . . . She . . . What? . . . I see . . . Oh."

She dropped the receiver on to its stand. She turned to me, her face drawn.

"Well?" I said.

"Zelide isn't there. They're expecting her for the opening this afternoon. But she isn't there yet."

"Did they know where she's staying?"

Iris nodded. "Madame Zelide left her address with the management. She's staying at the St. Anton."

"The St. Anton."

"And that's not all. Zelide's just her professional name. She's staying at the St. Anton under her real name. And her real name is . . ."

"What?"

"Zelide's real name is Mrs. Zelide Rose."

CHAPTER XI

"Mrs. Rose!" I repeated. "Then Mrs. Rose isn't a menace, after all. She's another victim."

"Peter, it all ties up now. Mrs. Rose was a friend of Lina's. We know that because Lina had her photograph. And then Mrs. Rose told me I reminded her of someone she used to know. She must have meant Eulalia. All the three women are linked together. Eulalia—Lina—Zelide."

"That explains what the man with a lisp was doing in the St. Anton lobby when we arrived. He was hanging around Zelide."

"But she checked out to marry Mr. Annapoppaulos and the man with the lisp got sidetracked to me, thinking I was Eulalia. They'd have a time trying to murder a bride on her wedding night. With any luck, Zelide is still alive and, if she is, she's bound to show up for the gala opening of the circus." Iris looked radiant. I never thought I would see her look that way again. "All we have to do is to get to the Lawrence Stadium before the performance starts. Zelide will be able to clear us just as well as the Beard."

"When does the show start?"

"Two-thirty. It's one-thirty now. We'll have to hurry."

Hatch had repeatedly warned us against leaving the

apartment and trying to be clever. But this, I felt, was no time to worry about his forebodings. It wasn't just a question of getting Zelide to clear us. If the Beard's drunken word could be relied upon, Mrs. Rose Annapoppaulos was in as great danger as Eulalia and Lina had been. I had liked Zelide with her gusty laugh and her Greek bridegroom. She wasn't going to end up with a knife in her breast—not if I could help it.

"Let's go," I said.

Iris picked up her silver-fox wrap. "Perhaps we'll even find the Beard at the Stadium. Don't they have bearded men in circuses?"

"Bearded ladies," I said. "Maybe that's the payoff. Maybe the Beard's a lady."

Iris snuggled her shoulders into the wrap. "The Beard is not a lady, Peter. You can take my word for that."

I said: "We'd better leave a note for Hatch telling him where we are in case they get back from Oakland."

I found a piece of paper and a pencil by the telephone. I wrote that Zelide was at the circus and that we had gone to find her.

"Ready," I said.

Iris looked at me. "Hadn't you better change into the civilian suit?"

"Darn the civilian suit. I'm tired of masquerading. If we find Zelide, O.K. If we don't, then I want to go down with all flags flying."

"Hatch'd be cross." Iris grinned and then kissed me. "But you're right. I'd much rather have you arrested in the uniform. You'd look so much nicer in the line-up."

She slipped her hand through my arm. We went to the door.

"I'm so happy," she said. "Everything's going to be all right. I feel it in my bones."

I hoped Iris's bones were better prophets than mine.

The Lawrence Stadium was somewhere along Market Street. Iris and I walked down Fillmore. The sun was shining crisply. Even the somber houses and the indeterminate passers-by were transformed by it. I could feel the festive pulse of San Francisco in the sunshine, in the air, but we were no part of it. It was all like somebody else's birthday.

We reached Market. It was too early for the tidal wave of sailors, but the street was crowded enough. On the corner, a news vendor was standing by a lamp-post with a pile of papers on a wooden stool in front of him. I bought one.

Iris said: "We'd better take a trolley. Oh, there's one now."

She hurried towards a car which had just stopped at the corner. I went after her, tucking the paper under my arm.

The car was only half full. We sat side by side near the driver with the sun slanting in from the window behind us. Two little girls with spindly knees were sitting opposite us quarrelling over an all-day sucker. There was a colored woman with a basket, and there was an old man with a pipe. The car had an intimate atmosphere, as if everyone knew everyone else and San Francisco was a small town.

The car rattled forward. Iris was looking very fresh and beautiful. I took the paper from under my arm. It was an afternoon paper. I spread it open, looking at the front page.

Above a column at the bottom of the page I read the headlines:

TWO WOMEN SLAIN, NAVAL
LIEUTENANT BEING SOUGHT

Underneath, the column said more or less what we had expected it to say. Lina had been found by a milkman. Eulalia had been found by the doorman. The doorman had told his story about Lieutenant Duluth. The owner of the drugstore opposite Lina had told his story about Lieutenant Duluth. The roses were mentioned as a macaber touch. There was a little about Eulalia being a distinguished puppet maker. There was next to nothing about Lina's private life. The final paragraph concluded with the ominous sentence:

The police have inaugurated a city-wide search for Lieutenant Duluth and a woman believed to be his wife.

As I finished the column, I was suddenly afraid. I don't remember being really afraid before—not like that. I had been scared dozens of times in the Pacific when a Zero dived or when a torpedo came plunging toward us through the water. But everyone feels that way. This was different —the way a fox feels with a pack after him. It was bad while it lasted, but luckily it didn't last long.

We were going to Zelide. She would be able to tell the truth. Everything was going to be all right.

Iris saw the column then. She leaned across me, staring at it. Her mouth set in a tight line. She looked up at me quickly and put her hand on my sleeve.

"Well," she said, "the hunt is up."

There didn't seem to be much point in making any other comment.

My wife started to gaze abstractedly out of the window. After a moment she pointed across Market Street.

"Look, Peter, there's Hatch and Bill's office."

As the car lumbered on, I was just in time to see *Williams and Dagget, Confidential Agents* written in gold letters across a couple of upstairs windows in an office building. There was something about those words that helped to keep me steady. After all, we weren't entirely on our own. Two, at least, of San Francisco's well-established citizens were rooting for us.

The little girls across from us were saying: " 'Tisn't so. 'Tis, too." The colored woman stared into space over her basket, and the sunlight streamed in on the old man's pipe. Soon the trolley came to a stop.

"Here's where we get off," said Iris.

And we got off.

The Lawrence Stadium reared on the other side of the street. It was one of those big random buildings that get put up in cities and then have to be used for something. As we started across the street toward it, I began to realize that since I had read the newspaper column everything had changed. Although I wasn't frightened any longer, I was much more aware. It was as if danger had heightened the acuity of all my senses. I noticed a policeman in the crowd, a thing I would not normally have done, and in the same second I noticed that he had glanced at us and turned disinterestedly away. My ears broke down the generalized hum of the street into individual sounds and voices. Even my feet were alert, ready to sweep into action the instant my eyes or ears sent out a warning.

We started through the throng up the stone steps toward the entrance to the Stadium.

I said: "How d'you get backstage at a circus? I guess you just buy tickets and snoop around."

People were jostling each other in the vestibule. There were children everywhere—small children with dolls, children with wonder in their eyes, children clinging onto their mothers' hands, children without mothers, noisy children, good children and babies, solemn, on their parents' arms.

From beyond the swinging doors, voices were calling: "Peanuts, hot roasted peanuts" and "Orangeade, cool, refreshing orangeade." There was an indefinable circus smell of sawdust and animals and an indefinable rowdy excitement. It doesn't matter where a circus is. It makes every place the same. We might have been in New York or Baltimore or Dubuque, Iowa. We were just at the circus.

Something in me responded to the thrill of it as if I were still in knee-pants. I always felt that way at a circus. Even now, with the police after us and a murderer after Zelide, it was the same thrill.

I bought ringside seats at the ticket office. I needn't have bought such expensive ones. Heaven knows, our chances of actually seeing the circus were slim. But the circus mood was on me.

We pushed with the others through the turnstiles. Children bumped against the back of our knees and shouted their desire for peanuts and candy. Everyone was gay and expectant. There were dozens of newspapers around, but they were mostly tucked under the arm. I realized that, unintentionally, we had picked the perfect place for anonymity. Everyone had his mind crowded with innocent things like clowns and acrobats and elephants. No one was wondering about murderers or Lieutenant Duluth with the police on his heels.

It was twenty minutes past two. In ten minutes the greatest show on earth would begin. Ahead of us was one of the doorways which led into the arena proper. White-coated peanut vendors were mingling with the throng. People were selling programs, too.

I bought one. I raced through it, looking for Zelide's act. To my relief I saw that the Bird Ballet climaxed the second half of the show. There was still time.

Iris said: "What shall we do?"

A stone staircase to our left led down to a basement. Nailed to the wall above it was a sign saying: SIDESHOWS.

I guided my wife against the stream toward it. "They'll have the animals and things down there. We can probably find a way backstage."

We had the stairs to ourselves. With the circus performance so soon to begin, everyone was pouring into the Arena. As we clattered downward, the screams of parrots and the din of animal voices rose from the basement below. We reached the basement.

The first long room was lined with various booths, announcing the Wonders of the World, the fat lady, the tallest man, the snake woman, the mermaid. Beyond, through an open arch, I could see the animals.

We started past the booths. Except for two small boys, we were the only patrons, and the Wonders of the World were snatching these moments for social relaxation. The tallest man lounged outside his booth, eating ham sandwiches and drinking beer with the tattooed lady. Strolling toward us, smoking cigarettes and talking intensely, were the fat lady and a tiny golden-haired midget.

"That goddam snake woman," the midget was saying. "Each time we draw a crowd she has to barge out of her booth and start wriggling her butt."

I went up to them. I asked: "Can you tell us where to find Madame Zelide, please?"

The fat lady blew an indifferent smoke ring and shrugged. The midget tossed her golden ringlets and gave me an arch smile.

"Zelide? Go back past the animals. Turn left by the elephants. There's a passage leads to the dressing rooms. Ask when you get there."

They strolled on, resuming their own conversation. I heard the fat lady murmuring: "She's slipping, my dear, that's the trouble. Ain't as snaky as she used to be, not by a half."

We hurried on. The tattooed lady, bored with the tallest man, turned to watch curiously as we passed. She was wearing swimming trunks and a bra to expose as much tattooing as possible. As she turned, she revealed her stomach. Blazing across it in red and blue, between an anchor and a bleeding heart was the legend: BUY WAR BONDS.

Surely, no other artiste had risen to her country's emergency with such selfless nobility.

We passed the booth of the unethical snake lady and through an arch into the menagerie.

Animals were dumped everywhere with complete disregard for the niceties of zoological cataloging. Flamboyant macaws were screaming and flapping in a cage next to a stall where llamas from South America mingled in aristocratic gloom with zebras from Africa. A moth-eaten heron and a decrepit vulture confronted each other in a wired-in cubicle. The Largest Alligator in the World lolled beside a shallow tank. They all looked as if they had had a tough night travelling.

Iris pointed ahead. "There are the elephant pens."

We hurried under another arch to find ourselves completely surrounded with elephants. They were crowded into open stalls and stood there, shoulder to shoulder, huge and patient. Some of them sniffed with their trunks at the straw on the floor. Others merely stood. Their bored apathy reminded me of chorus girls waiting in the wings for the first production number.

There was one elephant who was obviously the star, for it had a stall of its own. As we came up to it, Iris gave a little exclamation. Attached to the stall was a notice which read:

EDWINA, THE OLDEST ELEPHANT
IN CAPTIVITY

"Edwina, the elephant."

We paused in front of the animal which had figured so mysteriously in our lives. She was vastly regal with her tree-trunk legs, her wrinkled face, and her small, watchful eyes. Around her neck had been tied an immense pink ribbon. It did nothing to impair her dignity.

"If we understood the Beard properly," breathed Iris. "Edwina's in danger too. Why on earth should an elephant be in danger?"

I looked Edwina in the eye. "The red rose, Edwina, and the white rose."

Edwina lifted her trunk in an s-bend, flicked her ears above the pink ribbon, and whistled.

As I watched her, I was overcome with exasperation. Eulalia was dead. Lina was dead. The Beard was drunk. Zelide was missing. Now, when at last we had found one of the chief actors in the drama who was both alive and sober, it had to be an elephant.

"The white rose, Edwina," said Iris coaxingly. "And the red rose."

From the distant arena a crash of cymbals blared.

The circus had begun.

The effect of that cymbal crash on the elephants was instantaneous. Edwina whistled again and flapped her ribbon. Her cohorts, shaking off their lethargy, broke into bustling animation. Some of them started to weave their great heads rhythmically, others lumbered into clumsy dance steps, others looped their trunks around their neighbors' tails. The trouper in them was asserting itself.

They were ready for their public.

I pulled Iris away from Edwina. "Come on, baby, we've got to get to Zelide."

There was a passage leading to the left, as the midget had said. We hurried down it and found ourselves approaching one of the vast entrances to the arena itself. Wild activity was under way as the opening parade started out for its triumphal procession into the red, white, and blue sawdust of the ring. Clowns and tumblers in gaudy costumes were racing and somersaulting past us. Behind them came an array of horses, stepping high and tossing proud manes. Huge balloon figures bobbed back and forth, mingling with men on stilts and men wearing bizarre papier-mâché animal heads. Beyond us, in the ring, the brass band was pounding out a march, while applause thundered back from the packed tiers of spectators. A dog, dressed in an apron, moved gingerly past me on its hind legs, carrying a coffee cup and saucer in its mouth.

We weaved through the bedlam. I grabbed a tumbler. "Where's Zelide's room?"

He pointed backward. "Down the corridor, first to the left, then to the right—the third room."

Fighting against the parade, we pressed down the passage, turned to the left into a deserted corridor with doors on each side, turned right again, and paused before the third room.

I knocked on the closed door. There was no sound from inside. I knocked again.

Iris said agitatedly: "Oh, Peter, you don't think . . . ?"

"She's still probably being Mr. Annapoppaulos' bride," I said. "After all, her act doesn't come on for a long time yet."

I pushed the door open and together we stepped into Madame Zelide's dressing room.

It was a makeshift affair. A portable dressing table and mirror stood against the wall. Around it, dozens of beaming photographs of Mrs. Zelide Rose herself spoke for her hearty narcissism. A closet, with its curtains half drawn, revealed a display of pink, lavender, and yellow tights bedizened with spangles and dyed feathers. There was a stale smell of disuse and make-up.

I noticed all the details mechanically. The thing that riveted my attention was a vase on a corner table in which was arranged a large bunch of blood-red roses.

"Roses for Zelide too," exclaimed Iris.

We hurried to the flowers. The box in which they had come was lying next to them on the table. Attached to the stem of one of the blooms was a florist's card. Written on it in a neat, pedantic hand were the words:

Remember Gino Forelli. This is to warn you.
    Emmanuel Catt.

CHAPTER XII

Iris and I looked at each other.

"Emmanuel Catt," exclaimed Iris. "The cat. Pussy." And then: "Gino Forelli. Who's Gino Forelli?"

I didn't know, of course. I stared at the card. If Emmanuel Catt was the name of the Beard, and I was almost sure by now that it was, the roses had been sent to the three women by the Beard. Why? To remind them of Gino Forelli. Why did he want to remind them of Gino Forelli? Were Mr. Catt and his roses part of the murderous league which seemed to be banded together to exterminate Eulalia, Lina, and Zelide? Or was he some friendly outsider who knew of their danger and had chosen this altruistic, though eccentric, means of warning them? And why were the roses red for Eulalia, white for Lina, and now red again for Zelide?

The red rose . . . the white rose . . .

I glanced at the box that had contained the flowers. It had come from a San Francisco florist. It did not help.

"I don't think Zelide's been here," I said. "If she'd arranged the flowers herself, she'd have taken off the card and thrown the box away. Someone must have dumped the roses in water just to keep them alive until she showed up."

"Then that means she hasn't got her warning," said Iris

tensely. "She won't have been on her guard. All this time, she hasn't known anything about the terrible danger she's in."

Iris was right, of course. The papers that carried the deaths of Eulalia and Lina had made no mention of disaster to Zelide. Even so, I shied off thinking what might already have happened to Madame Zelide Rose Annapoppaulos' wedding night.

I turned to the mirror with its frieze of plump, smiling Zelides. If she was alive, she would show up for the Bird Ballet. I was sure of that. And, if she was coming, she would have to come soon.

The sound of her gusty laughter outside in the passage would be the sweetest sound my ears could hear.

Under the mirror on the dressing table, I noticed a brown paper package, balanced precariously between jars of cold cream. I crossed and picked it up. It was addressed to *Mrs. Z. Rose, Lawrence Stadium, San Francisco.* There was a plastering of stamps and the message: *Urgent, Rush, Special Delivery.* There was also a return address on the left-hand top corner. That address was: *Emmanuel Catt, c/o Continental Studios, Hollywood, Cal.*

"Open it," urged Iris.

Regardless of postal regulations, I tore off the brown paper. As the object emerged from its wrappings, Iris said:

"Oh, it's only a book."

I let the paper drop on the floor and looked at the book. It was called: *Crimes of Our Times,* edited by John L. Weatherby.

That was not the first time I had seen that book. There had been a copy of it in Lina's parlor. Lina's copy had had no dust cover. This one did. Under the title was written: *An Anthology of Real-Life Murder Studies by the World's Foremost Criminologists.* I turned the book over. Both Iris and I gave a grunt.

The entire back of the dust cover was taken up by eight photographs. They were the portraits of the foremost criminologists who had contributed the various articles. Each author had his or her name typed under his or her photograph. But only one of those foremost criminologists interested us.

Between the likenesses of Miss Janet Flanner and Mr. William Bolitho, there gazed up at us a face of monumental sobriety, a face decorated by a majestic burgeoning of black beard. And under this face was printed: *Emmanuel Catt.*

"Then the Beard *is* the cat is Mr. Emmanuel Catt is America's foremost drunken criminologist," said Iris in unconscious Steinese. "That's what he is—a criminologist."

I opened the book to the flyleaf. Written across it in the same pedantic hand which had written the message on the card was the startling inscription:

> Madam: I send you this to warn you that Ludwig and Bruno Rose are out of prison and in San Francisco. I do not have to convince you that they are out for blood . . . your blood, Lina's blood, Eulalia's blood, even Edwina's blood. There is great danger. Be on your guard. Turn to page eighty-four. E. C.

As I read that, I felt a tingle of excitement. At last we were teetering on the brink of the truth. *The red rose and the white rose are out.* The nursery jingle which had baffled us by its senselessness was senseless no longer. The red rose and the white rose were two men called Ludwig and Bruno Rose—and they were out of prison.

Iris was saying: "Page eighty-four at last! Peter, this is it. Turn to page eighty-four."

I turned the pages feverishly. I passed the study of the Hall-Mills case which I had glanced at the night before. I paid it no attention. I was holding everything for page eighty-four. In a second now we might learn the facts for which we had been hungering ever since our first fatal interview with Emmanuel Catt.

From the distant arena I could just hear the strains of the brass band blaring out "Yankee Doodle." That remote, rollicking music made the immediate silence even deeper.

I reached page eighty-four. It was the first page of a

new essay, entitled: "Murder Among the Roses," by
Emmanuel Catt.

Beneath the title was a brief paragraph giving the bur-
den of the article to come. With Iris hovering at my
elbow, I read:

> A study of a little-known but fascinating murder
> case in which the Rose brothers, two circus aerial-
> ists, caused the death of their partner, Gino
> Forelli, during a public performance of their tra-
> peze act, and were finally brought to justice by the
> courageous efforts of three women and an ele-
> phant.

"Gino Forelli!" exclaimed Iris. "They were all aerialists, and Ludwig and Bruno Rose murdered Gino Forelli."

"And Eulalia and Lina and Zelide and Edwina somehow brought them to justice for it." I stared at those short
sentences which managed to pack such a wallop for us.
"That's what we've been playing around with, honey. The
man with the lisp and the other man who wore my uniform are the Rose brothers. They're out of prison and
gunning for the ladies who sent them up the river."

"Darling, this is too wonderful for words. We're going to
know the whole truth. We don't even need the Beard or
anyone. We can just take this book to the police and then
. . . Come on, let's read it. Quick."

We both took a plunge into the first page of Mr. Emmanuel Catt's essay. It was quite a page, I'm sure, full of
leisurely charm and psychology and mellow references to
intimacy with the late Mr. Alexander Woollcott. It was
just the thing for a quiet evening at home with a pipe and
a fire and a spaniel. But it was exasperatingly short on
facts.

As we struggled on, waiting for Mr. Catt to come to the
point, I was dimly conscious that another sound had mingled with the distant strains of "Yankee Doodle." At first
it was merely an indistinguishable blur of human voices.
Then I caught snatches of laughter and singing.

The literary Beard, still evading facts as if they were
the black death, was describing a scintillating dinner

party in Philadelphia. Suddenly Iris put her hand on my arm and said: "Listen, Peter."

The noise outside was much louder. It was obvious now that a group of people were coming down the corridor toward us. The laughter echoed uproariously. The singing drowned out the band. It was a raucous rendition of Mendelssohn's "Wedding March."

Iris's face was radiant. "The 'Wedding March,' darling. The 'Wedding March.' Zelide."

She ran to the dressing-room door and pulled it open. I followed her, tucking Mr. Catt's book under my arm. As my wife and I hurried into the corridor, we were just in time to see a procession of people sweep around the corner into full view.

It was as motley a congregation of people as I had ever seen. All crowded together, I made out the tallest man in the world, the fat woman, a couple of flaxen-haired midgets, the tattooed lady, the snake lady, a plump, important ringmaster in top hat and tails, youths in green tumbler uniforms, and a bevy of young blond aerialists in feathery tights and capes—doubtless the "Birds" of Madame Zelide's world-famous Bird Ballet. Gambolling around them like a group of excited poodles was a garish fringe of clowns.

Everyone was in a state of jubilation, dancing and slapping each other on the back. The fat lady carried a bottle of wine. Most of the aerialists were brandishing bottles, too. And all of them, with various degrees of musical success, were bellowing out the "Wedding March."

While they swarmed toward us, I saw that the gala parade was focused around two central characters. One of them was a swarthy Greek gentleman with a huge gardenia in his buttonhole. The other was a woman whose arm was looped through his—a solid blonde with an exotic mauve creation perched on her massive curls.

As I saw them, I could have joined in the joyous chorus myself from sheer relief.

There, on the arm of her grinning groom, was Madame Zelide Rose Annapoppaulos.

This was the end. Everything was going to be all right now.

Zelide had miraculously survived her wedding night.

The procession was almost upon us now. The voice of the ringmaster boomed above the cacophony. "Ah, Madame Zelide, you scared us. You are not at your hotel. You do not come for the performance. No one knows where you are. Something terrible has happened to Madame, we say. And now it is this—this happy event. A bride. Madame Zelide Rose no longer." He kissed his own plump forefinger. "From now on, Mrs. Zelide Annapoppaulos." He bowed at the bridgeroom. "The bride of a ringmaster in his day of a great distinction."

"Madame Annapoppaulos," chorused the crowd in happy unison.

"Yes," announced Madame Zelide coyly. "Yesterday we meet by chance in San Francisco, my old friend and I —and in a minute it ees love which springs up again and we fly to Nevada to be married." Her laughter burst refreshingly. "But the circus steel come first. I say to Dmitrios, my career she always come first. I say to Dmitrios, even in the marriage bed, that I must be here for the Bird Ballet. I do not desert my dear friends."

"Madame Zelide is here for the Bird Ballet," chanted the blond aerialists in well-trained reverence.

I grinned at Iris. Iris grinned at me. They had flown to Nevada to be married. Unwittingly they had eluded the Roses, and now they were back.

The wedding procession surged past us like a tidal wave, sweeping Zelide and Mr. Annapoppaulos into the dressing room. We joined the tag end of the procession. In a few seconds, the whole party was safely inside except for a couple of clowns who stood in the door with their backs to us.

I prodded one and said: "Let us get by, please. We've got to see Madame Zelide."

Inside the room I could hear Zelide's gusty laughter and the popping of corks. The two clowns turned. One was dressed in a costume of blue and white diamonds. The other was in red and white diamonds. They stood, blocking the doorway. Above the chalked white faces and the bulbous red false noses, they stared at us intently.

I said: "Let us get by, will you? We have to see Madame Zelide at once."

The eyes of the white and red clown flickered. Suddenly he swung round and shut the door of the dressing room so that we were barricaded from the people inside. We and the clowns were the only people in the corridor then.

I said: "Don't you understand English? We want to get into that room."

Very slowly, the white and red clown put his hand into the floppy pocket of his costume. Very slowly he brought it out again. Iris gave a gasp because his fingers were closed around a shining revolver.

"Lieutenant and Mithuth Duluth," he lisped. "How very thilly of you to come here."

The blue and white clown laughed. The revolver was aimed directly at my wife.

"One peep out of either of you," continued the clown with a lisp, "and Mithuth Duluth getth it in the belly."

CHAPTER XIII

Fate seemed to have a diabolic weakness for the turn-about device. One moment everything was going fine. The next moment everything was awful. This moment was awful. I put my arm around Iris. The clowns stared. The revolver gleamed. I could still hear Zelide's lusty laugh booming in the dressing room beyond the closed door.

What was the use of hearing her laughter when the Red Rose and the White Rose made an insuperable barrier between us?

Because that is how it was. There was no question that those two unattractive clowns were Ludwig and Bruno Rose.

I looked at the two strangers who had given me the worst twenty-four hours of my life. The loose clowns' costumes concealed their figures. Conical clowns' caps covered their hair. The false noses, the chalked cheeks, the grotesque lipstick mouths deprived their faces of any individuality. They were just clowns' faces.

All I could see was their eyes. I didn't trust those bright fanatical eyes any more than I trusted the revolver.

The red clown slipped the hand that held the gun into his capacious pocket. The bulge showed that it still had Iris covered. He jerked his head to the left.

"Get moving," he said. "Down the pathage. Get moving."

I could have yelled and people would have poured out from Zelide's wedding celebration. But before they reached us, my wife would be dead. I felt I knew enough now about Ludwig and Bruno Rose to be sure of that.

I still kept my arm around Iris. Trying to sound casual and succeeding merely in sounding asinine, I said: "Baby, the kind gentlemen want us to go with them."

"How sweet of them," said Iris.

"Make it thnappy," lisped the red clown.

We started to move to the left, away from the arena it-self deeper into the network of corridors. The passage which should have had some kind of traffic was empty. The two clowns fell in behind us. The red clown's revolver was pressed against Iris's back.

"If we path anyone and you bat an eye even, Mithuth Duluth getth it," he said.

I knew something about judo. If I had been alone, I would have gambled on grappling for the gun, but I did not dare risk it with Iris there. I still had Emmanuel Catt's book under my arm. It was probable that the Rose broth-ers knew it by sight. If they did, they would suppose that we had read it and gone even further than we had toward ferreting out the truth. Until now, we had merely been harmless puppets for them to maneuver. But now knowl-edge, or at least the appearance of it, had made us dan-gerous to them, and they weren't the type to think twice about adding a couple of extra murders to their schedule.

Even so, I had a feeling they weren't going to shoot us. Zelide was their primary objective. They weren't likely to jeopardize their plan against her by killing us first unless it could be done discreetly, without the betraying sound of a revolver shot.

The faint thud of the brass band playing in the arena was growing even fainter as we moved toward the end of the corridor.

"Left here," said the red clown. "Turn to the left."

Iris was pale, but her arm, against mine, was steady. I said: "What are you going to do with us?"

"You'll find out thoon enough," said the red clown. "Turn left."

We turned into the new passage, with the two clowns after us. It was narrower than the one we had left. Its walls were bleak and unpainted. It came to a dead end in front of us at a single steel door. There was complete silence now. We had reached the most deserted part of the Stadium. The Roses obviously knew their way about. Perhaps, in their days as aerialists, they had played here.

I wasn't liking it at all.

We reached the steel door at the end of the passage. There was a key hanging on a hook next to an electric-light switch. The blue clown stepped forward, took down the key, and swung the heavy door outward. Inside, stone steps stretched down into the darkness of a cellar.

"Turn around," said the red clown.

Iris and I turned around. We stared straight into the revolver. Above it, the red clown's eyes were gimlet sharp.

"Back down the thtairth," he said.

If he was going to shoot, we would be helpless from him backing down the stairs. Now or never was the moment to grapple for the gun. I glanced at my wife. I winced at the thought of what would happen if I grappled and failed.

As if reading my thoughts, the red clown said: "Move over in front of your huthband, Mithuth Duluth."

Iris stepped in front of me. She made a screen between me and the red clown. That put an end to any attempt to struggle for the gun.

The blue clown was hovering silently at the other's side, still without speaking.

The red clown said: "Back down the thtairth."

I gripped Iris's elbows, and began to draw her backwards down the steps into the darkness below. The two clowns were framed by the open door—one figure in red and white diamonds, one in blue and white diamonds. Each downward step, giving a low angle view, made them loom larger and larger. The muzzle of the revolver gleamed evilly.

If they stayed at the door, that meant they would not shoot, for the explosion from the gun would echo along the corridors. If they started down the steps after us, then they were going to try to kill us, and it would be a question of a battle to the death in the darkness.

Under my moist hands, Iris's elbows were trembling. That slow, backward journey seemed interminable.

Suddenly the door above us swung shut and we were

in total darkness. I heard the key turn in the lock and then the heavy tread of the Rose brothers' footsteps hurrying away down the corridor above us.

I relaxed my grip on Iris's elbow. I didn't feel much of anything except relief that she was unharmed. *Crimes of Our Times* was uncomfortable under my arm. I stuffed it into my pocket. Iris twisted around to face me. A nervous laugh came out of the darkness.

"It's really true about your past life racing through your mind. When I was sure he was going to shoot, I even remembered how I was locked up in my room when I was five because I called Aunt Susan a pig."

"Was she a pig?" I said.

"Yes." My wife's hand found mine. "Peter," she said with sudden desperation, "isn't it awful? We were so near to Zelide, and now . . ."

"Exactly."

"Couldn't we have done something? I felt so stupid being held up right in front of her dressing room."

"We could have done something, but we'd be too dead right now to remember what it was."

A musky odor floated up from the cellar below us. Now that the danger to Iris was past, I was getting jittery about Zelide.

"We've got to get out of here quickly," I said. "There's no one to warn Zelide now. We even took Catt's book from the dressing room. Any minute they'll try and kill her."

"But they can't kill her now—not with all those people in her room. And if I know anything about wedding celebrations, it'll go right on till it's time for the Bird Ballet."

A thought made my spine tingle. "The Bird Ballet. That's it, of course."

"Why?"

I gripped my wife's arm in the darkness. "How did Gino Forelli die?"

During an actual performance of the circus, it said. Peter, you can't think . . ."

"Sure. You're right that they can't get at her while she's in the dressing room. But they're clowns. Clowns can go anywhere in the ring while the other acts are in progress. They're aerialists, too. We know that. They could climb up on the trapezes right in front of the audience and people would think it was just a gag. With the ringmaster suspecting nothing and Zelide suspecting nothing, they could cut through a rope—anything. Baby, if I know the Roses, that's what they're planning to do, to kill Zelide in the ring."

"Peter!"

"What else can they do? They've got to kill her quickly. They'd have killed her last night if they could. Now that the police have found the other two bodies, it's just a question of time before the truth about this old murder comes to light. They've been working against time. That's why they used me as a red herring to keep the police off the scent while they made their getaway. They're probably all set for it right now. Once they've killed Zelide, they can slip away, duck their clowns' costumes, and scram. That's why they didn't bother to kill us just now. They're planning to be on their way to safety before we get out of here."

"Yes, Peter. But what are we going to do? Break down the door?"

"We couldn't break it down. No use banging either. We're too far from anyone. We could scream ourselves blue in the face before people heard. There's only one thing to do. We've got to find another way out of this damn cellar—and quickly."

I peered into the darkness. "There must be a light somewhere."

"Have you got any matches?"

"A few."

"Try up by the door. There should be a switch there."

"There isn't. It's outside in the passage. I noticed it when they were locking us in."

I struck a match. Its feeble light illuminated the part of the cellar floor below us. It was strewn with old pipes, slats, broken poles, a moldering gym horse, all the useless junk that ends up in the cellar of a sports stadium. The cellar itself stretched indefinitely away into the darkness.

Before the match went out, we hurried down the last of the stone steps. I lit another match. As it flickered, we started picking our way through the rubbish. The air was bad. The silence was absolute. There was a feeling of desolation, as if no human being had passed through for months. A rat bolted out from an old ice-hockey goal and scuttled across our track. Iris gave a little cry and the match went out.

Match by match we wound our way deeper into the bowels of the cellar. The Lawrence Stadium went in for cellars in a big way. A couple of dozen Phantoms of the Opera could have lived in this one without intruding upon each other's privacy. I had hoped to find some furnaces, for where there were furnaces there would also have to be some sort of exit. But we didn't find them.

There must have been a special section for the heating system. This vast area was nothing but a graveyard for abandoned sporting accessories.

My supply of matches was growing dangerously low. Before the one I held burned out, I lit two cigarettes and gave one to Iris. A small army of empty crates was stacked against the wall. We sat down on one dispiritedly.

The tip of Iris's cigarette glowed in the darkness. "We're going to be a sensation ten years from now," she said. "The skeletons in the Stadium cellar."

"There must be another exit somewhere."

"But where? Maybe we ought to start a fire."

"And roast ourselves to death?"

"Oh, darling, it's so discouraging. We know Zelide's going to be killed and we can't save her. We've got the whole solution to the mystery in that essay and we can't even read the darn thing. It's enough to drive a girl nuts. It's . . ."

Iris stopped. Her hand crept to my knee and clutched it.

"Listen," she breathed.

I listened. From somewhere at some distance to our left in the impenetrable darkness had come a sound— the cautious, blundering sound of something moving.

It wasn't the sort of noise a rat could make, unless it was vastly larger than any rat I had ever met. The sound came again—a scuffle, then a sharp, explosive swear word.

That settled it.

We were not the only people in the cellar.

While Iris's fingers pressed into my knee, I sat very still. The Rose brothers could easily have returned and come down to the cellar without our hearing the door open. We were that far away from the steps. But if the Rose brothers had returned, their only object would be to kill us. They certainly would not warn us of their approach by blundering around and swearing.

The chances were good that the third person beyond us in the darkness was a potential friend.

I whispered to Iris. "Wait here. I'll go see."

My wife's hair brushed against my cheek. "Let's both go. It can't be the Roses."

Off to our left, there was a splintering crash as something toppled to the ground. It was followed by a bellow of indignation.

"That certainly isn't the Roses," said Iris.

We slipped from the overturned crate. Hand in hand, to keep contact, we started cautiously through the blackness. There was some more grunting and cursing ahead.

I called: "Who's there?"

The grunting and cursing stopped. My voice echoed eerily and faded away.

Iris called: "Please, who is it?"

A woman's voice seemed to reassure that invisible person, for a reply came: "Where are you? I'm lost and I unfortunately have no matches."

"Stick right there," I said. "We'll come to you."

I lit one of my few remaining matches. By its light Iris and I threaded our way through a forest of stacked wooden chairs, relics, presumably, from remote political meetings. We emerged at the other end. The match burned down to my finger and I shook it out.

I could hear the unknown man quite close to us. To save matches. I started to grope toward him. I stretched one hand ahead of me to guide me. Suddenly, my fingers gripped something soft and hairy, and an irascible voice said: "Pah!"

I pulled back my hand, struck a match, and held it up. The fluttering light played on a man who stood squarely in front of us between an ancient upright piano, of all things, and a pile of threadbare tennis nets.

He was a large man in a meticulous grey suit with a

sprightly white carnation in his buttonhole. Dignity en-
veloped him like an opera cloak. And below a pair of
dark, outraged eyes sprouted a magnificent growth of
black beard.

For a second I felt this must be some hallucination
born of the poisonous cellar vapors. But the vision was
real enough.

There we were, lost in the Stadium's catacombs, face
to-face with Mr. Emmanuel Catt.

CHAPTER XIV

Mr. Emmanuel Catt stared straight at us. He obviously didn't recognize us in the uncertain matchlight. Obviously, too, he had recovered his sobriety, although patches of grimy dust stained his immaculate pants and a curl of straw peeped rakishly from behind his left ear.

He said in a voice of thunderous admonition: "Sir, you pulled my beard."

"I'm sorry," I said meekly.

A regal gesture of the head accepted my apology. He turned to Iris, giving her a formal bow. "You must excuse me, young lady. A misadventure has—ah—locked me in this cellar. I would be most grateful if you would direct me to an exit. I have pressing business that requires my immediate attention."

He spoke as if it were perfectly natural to find a naval lieutenant and a girl in the cellar. Presumably he thought we lived there.

Iris, who seemed to have been stunned into speechlessness, gave a little gasp. The match went out. Then in unison my wife and I said: "Mr. Catt."

He r'rumphed in the darkness. "You—ah—have the advantage of me. I do not believe I have the pleasure . . ."

"You certainly have the pleasure," said Iris. "You slept in our bathtub last night."

137

"Your bathtub, madam?" He gave a pained cough as if Iris had been guilty of a hideous impropriety. Then, with the faintest tinge of embarrassment, he added: "I regret to say that I—ah—was not quite myself last night. A slight indisposition. It is a malady which—ah—affects me periodically. Most tiresome. If I caused you any inconvenience, I take this opportunity to extend my apologies. And now, if you will be so kind . . ."

I had never heard an orgy of drunkenness and goatishness called a slight indisposition before.

Sarcastically I remarked: "Don't think for a moment that you inconvenienced us, Mr. Catt. You just threw us headlong into a couple of murders. That's all."

"Murders!" echoed the Beard. "You—ah—surely you are not this Lieutenant Duluth and his wife of whom I have read in my afternoon newspaper?"

"Of course we are," said Iris. "You've got to remember us. Hatch and Bill—our friends have been searching for you all over the city. *The red rose . . . the white rose . . . the elephant . . . page eighty-four . . . buriful girl . . . pussy.* Oh, what does it matter if you remember us or not? You know about everything and we knew just enough to drive us crazy. You must help us save Zelide."

"Well, well. Lieutenant and Mrs. Duluth!" Emmanuel Catt's voice had lost its frigid formality and was purring now with satisfaction. "I must confess that I recall nothing of making your acquaintance last night. My malady frequently brings slight lapses of memory. If I slept in your—ah—suite, I must have been sufficiently well to return to my own hotel, for I distinctly awoke there this afternoon."

So all the time that Hatch and Bill were chasing false beards to Oakland, Mr. Catt had been sleeping off the champagne in his own bed.

Emmanuel Catt purred on: "What a happy accident to come upon you, Lieutenant. I have as yet only the sketchiest knowledge of these terrible tragedies. Poor Eulalia; poor Lina. I foresaw such an event and warned them of their danger in a most specific manner with roses and a copy of my essay. I even made a special trip from my work in Hollywood as psychological consultant at Continental Studios to make sure they came to no harm

—a trip which, unfortunately, was rendered ineffective by my indisposition. You seem to have taken a prominent part in the drama. Perhaps you would be so kind as to tell me . . ."

I could see his mind working. America's foremost criminologist was already thinking in terms of his second essay on the Rose brothers. So far as he was concerned, the Roses and the mortal danger to Zelide were forgotten. Ludwig and Bruno could merrily go on making data for the end of the essay while Mr. Catt took time out for a cosy little chat plumbing the depths of Lieutenant Duluth's psychology in the cellar under the circus. (*A delicious locale.* I could see it in print already.)

I said: "Right now, Mr. Catt, I'm going to be so kind as to tell you exactly one simple fact. The Rose brothers are here at the circus. They're planning to murder Zelide, probably during the Bird Ballet. Heaven knows how you got into this cellar. That doesn't matter either. The only thing that matters is—how to get out."

"Yes, yes." The Beard sounded a trifle crestfallen. "You are indeed right. How thoughtless of me. I was so stimulated by meeting you that for a moment . . . But it was with the very intention of aiding Madame Zelide that I hurried from my hotel the moment I read of the tragedies. Since the other two ladies seemed so imprudently to have ignored my warning, I was determined to see that Madame Zelide—an admirable woman—should be safe. I arrived at the circus a short time ago and made my way to Madame Zelide's dressing room. I was about to enter when a pair of clowns with—ah—a revolver . . ."

"So that's it," I said. I might have guessed that the Beard, who seemed to know so much, was an even graver menace to the Roses' plan than we. It was only natural that they should have committed him to our exclusive cellar concentration camp.

"A most colorful and ingenious disguise," he was saying. "I must confess I would not have recognized either brother, although, of course, they recognized me." Mr. Catt, after having denied all knowledge of us, was now talking as if we were intimate friends and fellow crime experts with all the facts at our finger tips. "A rather titillating sensation to be held up at the point of a pistol, Lieutenant. Although I was alarmed at the time, I am most gratified now to have had the experience." He giggled. I could imagine the beard bobbing up and down in the darkness. "I have always had a great partiality for this case and to have encountered the protagonists in so —well, so intimate a way. Most absorbing!"

I tried to stem that tide of words. I knew how the little Dutch boy must have felt with his finger in the broken dam wall.

Mr. Catt went on: "And I feel you are correct in your assumption that the Rose brothers will attempt to murder Zelide in some fashion which approximates to the death of the Purple Rose. You have interpreted their psychology with penetration. Revenge is sweeter when it can conform to an aesthetic pattern. And with their particular type of monomania . . . dear me, I am off again, am I not? Yes, you are perfectly right. We must think out some method of escaping from this somewhat malodorous cellar."

I said: "Did the Rose brothers bring you here down a passage and through a steel door?"

"Yes. A most solid door. They also took the precaution of locking it. I am afraid we shall not be able to break our way through it. Dear, dear, time is short. I could wish that I had sought aid from the police instead of coming so impetuously to warn Zelide myself. This is vexing, most vexing."

Vexing was at least one word for it. While Emmanuel Catt chattered on, I ran my fingers over the remaining matches in the book. I had five left. We could still go back and try banging on the door, with the slender chance of attracting attention. Or we could use up the matches investigating the rest of the cellar. I decided to gamble on finding a second exit. Iris agreed. Emmanuel Catt was too busy telling us how he differed with the late Alexander Woollcott on some nice point of criminal psychology to express an opinion.

I stood for a moment, remembering the layout of the cellar as I had seen it in the light from the last struck match. Behind us stretched the way back to the steel door. In front of us was the part of the cellar which Iris and I had already explored. There was an unpromising-looking wall on our left. I decided to strike boldly out to the right into the unknown.

I led the way with Iris behind me and Mr. Catt volubly bringing up the rear. The matches had to be saved for an emergency. I kept my hands stretched in front of me and progressed cautiously through the darkness with a kind of slow-motion goose step to avoid tripping over any invisible hazard.

We had gone some distance when Iris's voice broke into Mr. Catt's learned monologue with a sharp: "Hush, Mr. Catt!"

America's foremost criminologist obediently broke off in the middle of a sentence.

"Listen, Peter," said Iris.

Until then the cellar had been completely silent except for the sounds we made ourselves. But now, as I listened, I heard a vague, rumbling noise from the darkness ahead. It came from somewhere above us and sounded like the throb of heavy traffic.

"What is it?" said Iris.

I didn't know. I started forward again toward the sound. It grew more distinct—a ponderous, rhythmic thumping. It certainly wasn't traffic. There were no automobile noises. It was as if gigantic dancers were pounding out a saraband above us. Even the boards of the invisible ceiling creaked and groaned.

As I strained my ears, the Beard suddenly exclaimed: "Ha! We know now where we are."

"What do you mean by ha?" said Iris.

"Surely, Mrs. Duluth, you are enough of a circus lover to recognize the nimble footfall of the elephant."

"The elephants!" echoed Iris excitedly. "You're right. We're under the elephant pens. They must have just come back in from the ring."

While she was speaking, a faint, new smell trailed to my nostrils. It was quite unlike the sour odors that had so far dominated the atmosphere. It was a sweet, nostalgic smell, a country smell, and I recognized it at once.

It was the smell of hay.

I said: "Wait here a minute. I'll be back."

Following my nose like a hound-dog, I groped toward

the unlikely fragrance. After several steps, my hands, extended in front of me, made contact with something that was unmistakably hay.

Above us, the confused rumble of moving elephants continued. I called: "Iris, Mr. Catt. Come over here. It's O.K. Nothing in the way."

In a few moments, they were at my side.

"What is it, Peter?" said Iris.

"Hay," I said. "Fresh hay. Elephants upstairs. Hay here. Elephants eat hay."

"Hay has to be got to elephants," broke in Iris enthusiastically. "There must be an exit. Strike a match—quick."

I lit a match. The hay was there all right, a great stack of it reaching to the ceiling. I swivelled around, holding the little flame out. To our right a ladder stretched from the floor and was attached to hooks in the ceiling.

With a most undignified whoop, Mr. Emmanuel Catt ran toward it. I saw his broad figure scramble on to the lowest rung. Then the match went out.

Iris and I hurried to the ladder. By the wheezing grunts that issued from the darkness I could tell that the Beard was climbing. I stared up to the ceiling and made out faint cracks of light.

Iris saw them too and called: "There's a trap door up there, Mr. Catt. Right above you."

Mr. Catt's majestic voice boomed down to us. "I had already observed the chinks of light, Mrs. Duluth. I trust I will find it unlocked."

The elephants were having themselves a time above our heads. The prospects of escape from that abominable cellar made me lightheaded. It suddenly seemed quite absurd that America's foremost criminologist, beard and all, should be scaling a ladder into a pen full of elephants.

A particularly emphatic grunt came from the darkness above us. Then, slowly, the cracks widened. Light streamed in, revealing Mr. Catt's hands clutching a wooden trap door and pushing it upward. His face came into view, peering through the aperture he had made in the ceiling. Straw was on his hair and in the beard. He looked like Pluto about to issue from his subterranean palace.

Suddenly an expression of alarm spread over his face. He dropped the trap door shut, exclaiming: "Mercy!"

With incongruous agility he scrambled down the ladder again and was at our side.

Iris said: "What's the trouble?"

Mr. Emmanuel Catt was panting from his exertion. "The trap door seems to be in perfect order, Mrs. Duluth. But it is unhappily situated. When I peered into the stall above, I found myself staring straight into the —ah—rump of a large elephant with a pink ribbon around her neck. I am virtually convinced that this elephant is Edwina. As I pointed out in my essay, her temper is notoriously uncertain. I do not feel she would relish strangers suddenly appearing from the bowels of the earth, as it were. Before we proceed, I suggest that we attract the attention of a keeper to—ah—restrain her."

"Oh, we don't want to call a keeper," said Iris. "We'll have to explain what we're doing in the cellar. There'd be delays. He'd be suspicious. We've got to get to Zelide quickly. I'm not afraid of Edwina. I think she's sweet. Let me go first, seeing we're both ladies."

The Beard clucked in alarm. I said: "No, baby. I agree about not getting a keeper. But I'm going first."

I moved to the ladder and started up it.

Mr. Catt's voice broke into anxious life: "But, Lieutenant, Edwina has a career of violence behind her. As you may know, she—ah—broke the collar-bone of Bruno Rose."

I didn't know, of course. Half of what he said was gibberish, anyway. "Maybe she didn't like Bruno Rose," I said. "And, if she didn't, I don't blame her. She's got nothing against me."

I felt above my head for the trap door and pushed it forward. I climbed another rung of the ladder. Blinking at the unaccustomed light, I stared into the stall. Edwina was there, all right. She was standing very close to the trap door. This time it was not her—ah—rump that confronted me. She was head on, gazing directly at me from small, unblinking eyes. The ribbon had slipped around her neck and the large pink bow dangled behind one ear.

"Hello, Edwina," I said feebly. "That's a good girl. How's tricks, Edwina?"

I didn't know how to talk to elephants. I could only assume that you treated them like dogs. She flapped her ears and, picking up hay with her trunk, showered it over her head. She still watched me.

Feeling self-conscious, I wriggled up out of the trap door on to the hay-scattered floor of the stall. Edwina suddenly whistled. I jumped. I wondered whether elephants were like dogs and smelled the adrenalin or whatever it is that glands give off in moments of crisis. Edwina didn't seem interested in my glands or my collarbone. She merely picked up more hay and tossed it over her shoulder.

"Good Edwina," I said sycophantically. "Good girl, Edwina."

The bars around the stall were not high. They would be easy enough to scale. No keeper was in sight. In the other stalls the rest of the elephants, relaxing after their act in the ring, thumped and weaved about. I took a step closer to Edwina. She didn't appear to mind.

I called back over my shoulder then: "O.K., Iris."

In a few seconds, my wife emerged from the trap door. Although there was hay in her hair, too, she was very beautiful. She was holding a wisp of hay in her hand. She joined me, giving Edwina a bright, social smile.

"Good afternoon, Edwina."

She held out the hay as if it had been a Boston teacup. Edwina looked at it and then half turned away, immeasurably bored. She watched Iris, though, out of the corner of her eye with the tolerant intolerance of a very old lady.

Soon Mr. Emmanuel Catt progressed through the trap door and closed it. He cast Edwina an uneasy glance and said: "The sooner we leave this stall, I feel, the wiser it would be."

I said: "Come on, then. We have to climb."

I pushed Iris up and she scrambled over the bars. It

was more difficult to maneuver Mr. Catt, but I managed. Then I vaulted up myself.

Throughout the entire proceedings, Edwina retained her composure. She was too old and too wise to concern herself aobut the unorthodox behavior of a naval lieutenant and a girl and a bearded gentleman.

The three of us stood a moment outside the stall, confronting each other. Iris's silver-fox wrap and the Beard's carnation didn't go with the dust and the hay. I didn't look exactly G.I. myself. But I didn't mind. We were free at last.

The pendulum had swung our way again.

CHAPTER XV

A glance at my watch sobered me somewhat. It was almost four-thirty. The circus had already been under way for an hour and a half. The time cue for the Bird Ballet must be perilously near.

"Come on," I said. "This has got to be quick."

We all three started to scurry past the elephants towards the arch which led backstage to the dressing rooms and Zelide's wedding celebration. A couple of nondescript men, presumably the valets of the elephants, were loitering in a corner. They stared but were not curious enough to follow us.

We ran through the arch. Ahead was the performers' entrance to the ring. Out in the arena, the band was blaring a martial air. People were milling around the entrance in a confused crowd. We elbowed forward. Iris wormed her way ahead of me. Suddenly she swung round, clutching my arm and pointing over heads towards the actual arena.

"Look, Peter," she gasped.

At the very mouth of the arena, near enough almost to touch and yet infinitely inaccessible, I saw a serried rank of feathered blondes marching out into the red, white and blue sawdust. They progressed in military rhythm to the pounding of the band. A rumble of applause rose to greet them. And, moving grandiosely at their head, was a single, even more feathered blonde.

Madame Zelide herself.

We were too late by the fraction of a minute.

The world famous Bird Ballet was on its way out for the dazzling finale of the circus's gala opening.

I stared hopelessly. The pendulum had swung back. Then I saw something else that set my blood racing with despair.

Leaping, running, tumbling and dancing around the bevy of aerialists were two clowns.

A red and white clown and a blue and white clown.

"The Roses," I cried.

Recklessly I barged through the hangers-on to the brink of the arena. Iris and Mr. Catt battled after me.

"Zelide!" I shouted to the colorful parade. "Madame Zelide."

Arms grabbed me instantly from behind and pulled me back. The group of stagehands had closed in on Iris and Mr. Catt, too. One of them said to me: "Buddy, are you nuts? There's a show on. You can't get out there."

I tugged myself free. "But I've got to get to Madame Zelide. We've got to stop the act."

The men were crowding around us.

"You can't stop the act, bud. Surely you got enough sense to see that."

"But Madame Zelide—she's in terrible danger," said Iris.

I could see the procession moving closer and closer to the centre of the ring. I could see the tangle of trapeze ropes hanging from the vault of the ceiling and the tall pink platforms which were to be part of the Bird Ballet. The band went on with a boom of tubas. And the two clowns, turning sensational handsprings, were weaving in and out of the aerialists.

Iris and Mr. Catt were arguing with the stagehands. They were getting nowhere. Everything they said only convinced their listeners that we were harmless lunatics. The men had regrouped themselves so that they made a solid wedge between us and the entrance to the arena. It was no use. By the time we explained, it would be too late.

I saw what we had to do.

"O.K.," I called to the men. "Sorry we bothered you. Forget it."

I grabbed Iris by one arm and Mr. Catt by the other.

"We've got ringside seats. That's our only chance. Get down to the ringside and then over the barrier into the ring."

"Of course," said Iris, panting. "Come on, Mr. Catt."

With the stagehands smirking incredulously, we turned tail and started to run back to the animal pens. We passed the elephants, the bored caged animals, and the sidehows where the tallest man and the fat lady and the tattooed lady and the snake lady, all refreshed by Zelide's wedding celebration wine, were preparing to cope with the custom that would soon be inundating their booths. As we ran up the stairs which led to the audience entrances to the Stadium, I pulled the tickets out of my pocket. We only had two. But there was nothing we could do about that.

We tumbled into the first aisle we reached. No one was at the entrance checking tickets. We started down through the audience.

The Stadium was enormous, with thousands of people jammed into crowded tiers. The noise they made was deafening, and that vast oval seemed nothing but a white sea of faces.

In the ring below, the trapezes were being lowered from the nest of ropes above. The band had finished its march and was sliding into a honeyed version of "Chiribiribin." The feathered blondes, taking little tripping steps, fanned out to their individual trapezes. In the very center of the ring, beneath a slowly descending pink trapeze, was Madame Zelide herself, monumentally pink, bowing and kissing her hand to the crowd.

But it was the clowns who kept my attention riveted. They were both swarming up guide ropes which flopped down from the ceiling on either side of Zelide. They climbed with the agility of monkeys, gibbering and making faces at the audience as they climbed. I saw the ringmaster who stood to one side, resplendent in his top hat and tails. He was gazing up at the clowns as if he had not expected them in the act. After a moment, however, he looked away. Obviously the crowd was approving of the clowns; obviously, too, the ringmaster supposed either that Zelide herself had added them to the Bird Ballet or that, with the license extended to clowns, they were merely putting on an extemporary show which heightened the effect.

We hurried through the audience towards the ring. I didn't know exactly what we were going to do any more than I knew exactly what the Rose brothers were going to do. I only knew that the danger was extreme and that somehow Zelide had to be warned.

Suddenly, as I passed one particular row, I felt my arm seized. I swung round and with a sinking heart found myself staring straight into the watery eyes of Cecil Grey. The actor who had driven me to Lina's the night before was sitting on the extreme end of a bench. His hand was still on my arm and there was nothing friendly about his grip. There was nothing friendly about his expression either. He had clearly read the afternoon papers and was quivering all over with the excitement of a righteous citizen about to expose a double murderer.

Iris and Mr. Catt had gone on ahead. If I stopped to explain to Cecil Grey—what could I say? On the other hand, if I broke away from him, he would certainly rush for the nearest policeman and give chase.

After a moment's indecision, it occurred to me that the time had come when a couple of policemen would be very handy. It would mean my certain arrest, and Hatch would probably have had a far better idea. But Hatch wasn't there and we needed help. I tugged my arm from Grey's grasp and sent him slumping sideways against his neighbor.

As I clattered away down the aisle after Iris and Mr. Catt, I heard Grey's actorish voice crying: "Quick. Quick. That's Lieutenant Duluth. The man wanted in the murder case. Quick."

A mild commotion broke out behind me. I didn't care. In the ring the subsidiary aerialists had all jumped up onto their trapezes. To the lilting strains of "Chiribiri-bin," they were slowly ascending, swinging their pink-sheathed legs coquettishly. But, with a mastery of suspense, Madame Zelide herself was still on the ground, bowing in front of her capacious pink trapeze.

The two clowns had climbed now to the very vault of the Stadium. Absorbed with what was going on below, the crowd had no more interest in them. They were in full view of thousands of people, and yet they were virtually unobserved. I felt grudging admiration for their brazenness.

But what were they going to do?

The commotion behind me was growing more ominous. Iris and Mr. Catt were at the foot of the aisle, clutching the rail that separated them from the ring and staring upwards. I joined them. As I did so, Iris gave a little cry.

"Peter, up there . . . something flashed in the spotlight. The red clown has a knife."

That, then, was the Roses' plan. They were going to cut through part of one of Zelide's trapeze ropes. They wouldn't completely sever the threads. Nothing as crude as that. They would merely weaken the strands so that once Madame Zelide was hanging high above the sawdust and swinging through her aerial pirouettes the rope would gradually fray and eventually send her crashing to an "accidental" death.

Suddenly "Chiribiribin" broke off, giving way to a stirring drum roll. Madame Zelide blew a final kiss to her public and, reaching upwards for the ropes, sprang daintily onto the trapeze.

Iris's fingers on my arm tightened. "Look, Peter. They've done it. They're swarming down the ropes. They're going to slip away before it happens."

I looked up. The two clowns were sliding down the guide ropes towards the ground. In a few minutes, the Roses would be safe out of the ring, safe out of the circus, safe on their way to a hideout which they had almost certainly prepared by now.

The clamor from the audience behind us was gathering strength. I glanced over my shoulder to see Cecil Grey and two policemen lumbering down the aisle.

This, if ever, was the moment.

"Tallyho," I said. "View halloo."

I jumped over the barrier and down on to the sawdust

of the ring. Iris came tumbling after me. With unexpected dexterity, Mr. Emmanuel Catt vaulted down to join us.

Shouts and screams rose behind us. The buzz of curiosity and alarm swelled to an uproar. From all corners of the ring, attendants, horrified at the sight of trespassers in the arena, were closing in on us. Dimly I saw that the two clowns had almost reached the earth.

The drum roll still went on. Ahead of us, in the center of the ring, Madame Zelide sat on her pink trapeze, rising slowly, inexorably to her doom.

Emmanuel Catt, putting on a superb burst of speed, passed me and plunged towards the trapeze—a bearded Jupiter with the fleetness of Mercury. Iris and I dashed in pursuit. Pandemonium had the Stadium in its grip. The two clowns jumped from the ropes and started gamboling and somersaulting inconspicuously towards the exit. The ringmaster, flourishing his whip, was bearing down on us.

It was Mr. Emmanuel Catt who reached the trapeze first. Zelide was dangling now above our heads. Her pink, muscular legs were swinging. Although she was staring down at the Beard in stark amazement, her lips were still stretched in a broad, professional smile.

The ringmaster raised his whip. I threw myself at him. At the same instant, Mr. Catt crouched like a massive, bearded pard and hurled himself upwards. It was a mad, March Hare moment. I saw his large hands grab Zelide's ankles. The ringmaster and I were locked in a fierce embrace.

And then, in a farcical heap, America's foremost criminologist and the world-famous Madame Zelide tumbled together into the red, white, and blue sawdust at our feet—an inextricable confusion of blonde hair, black beard, and pink tights.

Attendants and policemen were surrounding us. The ringmaster was struggling ineffectually in my arms. The chaos that was Emmanuel Catt and Madame Zelide squirmed in the patriotic sawdust.

But I felt nothing but triumph. I still had only the shadowiest notion of what everything was about, but I didn't mind.

Impossibly comic and sensational as the climax had become, we had won. There was to be no backward swing of the pendulum this time.

Against all odds, we had saved Madame Zelide Rose Annapoppaulos at last.

CHAPTER XVI

From that moment on, so many things happened at once that the memory of them is confused. Someone was blaring through the public-address system in a futile attempt to quench the flaming excitement of the audience. The ringmaster broke away from me, threw one despairing glance at his star aerialist writhing in the sawdust, and grabbed a microphone that must have connected with some headquarters backstage. Above the general clamor, I heard him moaning into the mike: "Bring the elephants. Quick. The act is ruined. Bring something for the crowd to look at. The elephants."

Zelide, gabbling indignantly, was stumbling to her feet. Mr. Catt was getting up, too. People were pressing around, shouting and jostling each other. Iris and I were forgotten. No one seemed to remember exactly who had started what. I stretched on tiptoe, staring over the bobbing heads. I could just catch a glimpse of the two clowns making their unobtrusive way against the stream of people towards the exit.

"Those clowns!" I shouted. "Get them. Get after those clowns."

No one paid any attention. I was just someone else shouting. With Iris behind me, I started to beat my way through the mob. I had gone a few paces when a hand settled on my shoulder and swung me around. Two policemen were standing there with Cecil Grey dramatically at their side.

"That's the man," the actor was saying. "That's Lieutenant Duluth." He pointed at Iris. "And that's his wife."

The second policeman took Iris's arm. Both officials looked dazed. The one who had me by the shoulder muttered: "Lieutenant Duluth, you're under arrest."

In the midst of that bedlam, the remark sounded on the anticlimactic side.

"O.K., Officer," I said. "I'll go with you. But there's something you've got to do first."

I swept into an incoherent rush of words about the two clowns, pointing and gesticulating. Iris joined me.

In feverish counterpoint with our voices, I could hear Emmanuel Catt nearby booming down Madame Zelide's incensed Italian.

". . . Madame, I am deeply sorry to spoil your performance . . . but you must listen to me. . . . The Roses, I say . . . Ludwig and Bruno . . . they are here . . . they were going to murder you . . ."

The audience was still seething. The public-address system was still blaring.

"The Roses!" echoed Zelide sharply.

"Yes, yes," came Mr. Catt again, warring with my passionate plea to the policeman. "They are here, I say. Those clowns. Didn't you receive my warning flowers? Haven't you read in the paper that Eulalia and Lina are dead?"

"Dead!" screamed Madame Zelide. "I see the flowers, yes. But I read no papers. Eulalia and Lina—dead. Oh, oh, so it ees true. It . . ."

She broke off. One second later she had rushed up to my policeman, her blonde curls awry, her feathered tights spattered with sawdust.

"Queeck, queeck," she said panting. "Those clowns. Murderers. After the clowns. Murderers. Roses."

Between us, Madame Zelide and I had reduced the policemen to a state of almost imbecile confusion. While they stuttered at the aerialist, I seized my opportunity and broke away through the crowd, rushing after the fast-disappearing figures of the two clowns.

That action of mine shattered the spell. To a man, the random throng around Madame Zelide's trapeze began to tumble in pursuit. At first, I think, they were chasing me. But soon Madame Zelide herself caught up to me. Her tights were wrinkled; her blonde hair streamed out behind her. But she was as formidable as the Spirit of Liberty leading a revolutionary mob and she was shouting, like some lunatic Victory slogan: "Clowns. Murderers. Roses. Clowns. Murderers. Roses."

From then on, Zelide and I were the acknowledged leaders of the troop. Mr. Catt and Iris stumbled to join us. I don't think any of the others knew what they were chasing, but mob hysteria carried them forward and they too began to shout in meaningless echo of Zelide: "Clowns. Murderers. Roses."

The audience went completely crazy then. I didn't blame them. They had come to see a circus. Now they had a demented track race on their hands. The roar from the packed tiers surged over us like a titanic wave.

Ahead, the clowns had almost reached the exit from the arena. A little knot of people was grouped around the gap in the rail, watching our approach. They did not seem to connect the clowns with anything. I yelled my lungs out to them to stop the clowns, but the din was so great that I could scarcely hear my own voice.

The clowns reached the exit and ducked through the watchers out of sight backstage. Zelide, the Beard, Iris, and I surged forward at the head of our cohorts. Zelide and I arrived at the exit simultaneously.

Zelide, her eyes ablaze, grabbed the nearest man. "The clowns. Queeck. Which way they go?"

"Clowns?" echoed the man. Understanding dawning, he turned and pointed down the corridor towards the elephant pens. "You mean that couple of clowns? Just went down there."

"Thees way!" screamed Zelide, beckoning over her shoulder. "Thees way. Queeck."

We started down the passage. The others pressed behind, crammed together as close as herrings in a can. I knew that at least one of the Rose brothers had a gun. I knew they would be as dangerous to meet up with as trapped tigers. But the crowd pushing us on was beyond anyone's control.

The passage took a turn to the right. Zelide and I were hurtled toward the corner. We reached it. And, as we did so, sounds of tumult even greater than those behind us suddenly roared from the passage ahead. There were gigantic crashings and prancings and the hoarse cries of men. But one sound soared above all the rest. It was a jungle noise unbridled enough to chill the blood in the warmest veins. I recognized it at once.

It was the furious trumpeting of an elephant.

With the others pounding behind, Zelide and I shot around the corner. I shall never forget the sight which confronted us.

The Rose brothers were there, all right. They stood at the end of the passage with their clowns' backs to us. They stood perfectly still, staring at what was in front of them.

And the thing in front of them was Edwina. She loomed across the passage, blocking their path of retreat completely. Her great wrinkled head was held low. Her trunk was curved menacingly forward, and the huge pink ribbon flapped behind her left ear like a monster butterfly.

In the passage behind Edwina, I caught glimpses of the other elephants, patient and bored, and of the men who had been ordered to bring them out into the arena to quiet the audience. The men were yelling at Edwina, who was holding up the whole parade. But she paid no attention.

She just stood there, perfectly still, staring at the clowns while the clowns stared back at her.

As we surged around the corner, the blue clown glanced over his shoulder at us and whispered something in his brother's ear. The red clown was still staring at Edwina. Suddenly he took a step toward her, and the sound of a revolver shot echoed down the corridor.

Instantly Edwina sprang into life. With a scream, she reared up on her huge hind legs. She plunged forward.

A swift blow from the side of her head sent the blue clown sprawling to the floor. She trumpeted. The red clown fired again. Edwina's trunk lunged at him, knocking the gun from his hand. It coiled around his waist and jerked him up into the air.

We were all streaming forward. Zelide, with a courage that impressed me, ran straight up to Edwina, shouting: "No, no, Edwina. Do not keel him. Put heem down, Edwina. Do not keel him."

Even in her frenzy of pain and fury, the elephant seemed to recognize Zelide's voice. With a great shake of her head, she lowered her trunk and dropped the limp body of the red clown at the aerialist's feet. She stood quite still then, the blood seeping from her thick, grey hide.

The crowd poured around me and leaped on the clowns. Two men picked up the dazed blue clown and pinioned his arms behind him. Two others jumped at the panting red clown. Someone grabbed up the gun.

Everyone was shouting. Someone had seized my arm. I turned around. It was my policeman. The look of stunned incomprehension was still on his face, but this time he pulled out a pair of handcuffs and snapped them over my wrist.

"I said you're under arrest," he spluttered. "All this craziness . . . clowns, roses. To hell with it. I'm here to get Lieutenant Duluth and his wife and I'm going to get you."

I grinned at him. The other policeman and Mr. Emmanuel Catt had the two Roses safely under control. I was certain of that. I was perfectly ready to be arrested now.

It was all over but the shouting and a couple of explanations.

As the policeman started leading Iris and me away, I took one last glance over my shoulder at Edwina.

She had relapsed into her ancient, tolerant apathy. Although the blood still trickled from her side, she seemed no more worried by the two revolver shots than I would have been by two gnat bites. Zelide was patting her trunk. Very gently, Edwina lifted its tip and curled it around the world-famous aerialist's wrist.

I had no idea what Edwina had against the Rose brothers or what they had against her. But one thing was only too clear. In this last round of their remarkable battle, Edwina, the elephant, was very definitely—the winnah!

CHAPTER XVII

We never knew how Madden's circus managed to restore order after the havoc we had wrought with its gala opening. While the Stadium was still rocking to its foundations, the policeman hustled Iris and me out through a side exit into a waiting police car. He wasn't trusting us at all. With me handcuffed to his left wrist, he sat in the middle of the back seat and tucked Iris in on his right. He ordered the driver to take us to headquarters.

My elation at having seen the Rose brothers captured was beginning to subside. It was pleasant to know that Right had triumphed, even though the issues at stake were still so vague, but our road to victory, paved as it was with good intentions, had been constructed in a most unorthodox manner. I had walked out on a couple of corpses; I had held back vital information; I had posed as a civilian; I had broken virtually every canon of an officer and a gentleman. I had also exhibited myself on the front pages of the newspapers.

Even with Mr. Catt, Hatch, and Bill as my champions, I doubted whether the police were going to be fond of me. My commanding officer loomed large in my thoughts, too. In the light of my week-end activities, would I strike him as the serious-minded type of lieutenant junior grade who merited promotion?

As our car reached headquarters, another automobile had just drawn up in front of us. Out of it emerged one policeman handcuffed to the red clown and another handcuffed to the blue clown. The Rose brothers, apparently, had received no serious injuries at the trunk of Edwina. Trailing out of the car after them came Mr. Catt and Madame Zelide, whose unseemly feathered tights were partly concealed under a theatrical cape. They all progressed, chattering, up the steps into the building. A more subdued group, we followed. As we entered the bleak vestibule, we were in time to see the others disappearing through a swing door.

Our policeman, swaggering, presented us to another man in uniform behind a high desk and said: "Lieutenant and Mrs. Duluth. Murder suspects. I got 'em."

From his expression I could tell that I was not the only one thinking about promotion. He conducted us into a small, empty room where he unhandcuffed me.

"The Inspector'll send for you when he's good and ready," he said. "Got to turn in my report."

"O.K.," I said. "Listen, do something for me. Know Williams and Dagget, a firm of private detectives here?"

The policeman nodded suspiciously. "Sure. Why?"

"Call them. Tell them what's happened. They know all the dope. Get them to come right around."

The policeman was reluctant but finally consented. He left us then, locking the door behind him.

It was a horrible little room with a single bench running along one wall and with barred windows. Iris and I sat down on the bench. Iris slipped her hand through my arm.

"Give me a cigarette, darling."

I lit two with one of my last three matches. My wife inhaled dreamily. "Clowns. Murderers. Roses," she quoted. "Darling, wasn't it fun?"

"I suppose so," I said, thinking of the way my commanding officer's nostrils dilated when he was mad.

"And Edwina routing the Roses like that. Peter, we've got the laugh on Hatch. We saved Zelide." She paused. "Exactly what did we save Zelide from?"

"The Rose brothers," I said. "Remember?"

"Oh, I know that," said my wife testily. "I mean what

was it really that the Rose brothers had against Zelide and Linda and Eulalia? And how did Edwina fit in? And what was poor Eulalia doing mixed up in a circus murder? And who actually was Gino Forelli? And . . . I'm bursting to know what it's all about and here we are locked up in this miserable room and . . . Peter!"

That last word came out in an explosive cry.

"What's the matter?" I said, my commanding officer's nostrils still busy dilating in my mind.

"Mr. Catt's essay." My wife was pulling the forgotten *Crimes of Our Times* out of my pocket. "We may be arrested for murder, but at least we can find out who we murdered and why. Page eighty-four. Quick."

Iris's enthusiasm infected me. She reached page eighty-four. We started to read. Now that Zelide was safe and the Roses were under lock and key, Mr. Catt's leisurely style was no longer exasperating. In fact, it cast a queer spell of its own.

As we read on, I even forgot the dilating nostrils.

From: *Crimes of Our Times,* edited by John L. Weatherby, copyright, 1943, by Featherstone Press, N.Y.C. Reprinted by permission of the author and publisher

MURDER AMONG THE ROSES*

by

Emmanuel Catt

* I am presenting here—and I think this is the most logical place for it—the unabridged text of Mr. Emmanuel Catt's illuminating essay on the Rose murder. Perhaps I should advise the reader that Mr. Catt is at present working on a sequel to his study which covers the final phases of this remarkable case. Serious students of crime will doubtless find in Mr. Catt's treatment far more psychological penetration and literary distinction than in my own highly personalized narrative: P.D.

MURDER AMONG THE ROSES

BY

Emmanuel Catt

I am obsessed by this crime. I feel about it very much the way the late Mr. Edmund Pearson must have felt about the butcheries in the Borden household. Probably even more so, for, whereas Mr. Pearson could study his divine Lizzie only obliquely and from afar, I had literally a ringside seat at the Rose murder and I was close enough to the people involved to obtain intimate peeps behind the scenes such as are seldom vouchsafed to theorists in crime.

And, apart from my personal obsession, there are other reasons why I feel it my special duty to keep this affair constantly before the public eye. For the Roses are veritable *fleurs de mal* whose evil shoots have by no means withered, but will—if one dare look into the crystal of the future—one day burgeon again into poisonous blossoms of deeper and bloodier red.

I hereby serve warning on an apathetic public—and on certain individuals to be specified later—that we have not heard the last of the Roses. Their account with society is by no means settled.

Though not altogether surprised, I have been disappointed by the almost universal indifference to my favorite murder. Though it has been written up, with the usual gross exaggerations and inaccuracies, by the sensational magazines and Sunday supplements; though the original tragedy was accorded a headline in the Philadelphia papers, the final apprehension and sentencing of the criminals rated only a few brief paragraphs, while the psychological undercurrents of the story—fraught as it was with the whole gamut of human emotions—have never attracted the pen of any serious analyst except myself.

The public has remained listless. The intellectuals have yawned. Even my late friend, Mr. Alexander Woollcott, self-confessed connoisseur in the nicer points of murder, would have none of my Roses. He insisted that the case was too flamboyant; that it lacked light and shade; that the characters in the drama were wholly wanting in contrast and subtlety. Bluntly, he attributed my own excessive preoccupation (and here one may snatch a faint whiff of professional jealousy) to the fact that I myself was present when the murder was committed.

That is true. I was present—and surely this is the very apogee in the career of any criminologist—I was an actual eyewitness to what I myself consider one of the most interesting and one of the most cunningly conceived murders of the past century.

I was a witness, in company with some three thousand other persons, when the handsome young aerialist, Gino Forelli, professionally known as the Purple Rose, crashed to his death in the Circus Arena in Philadelphia, on June 4, 1936.

That there were so many witnesses to his death—so many thousands who could think and talk of it as their own individual tragedy—might be superficially assumed to have secured for the case a wide and lively public interest. But here we run into a peculiar quirk in mass psychology. When people, even children, go to a circus to witness spectacular and dangerous feats, there is in their subconscious minds a thrilling expectation, nay, almost a hope, that they will witness some spectacular disaster. So, when Gino Forelli, by his spectacular death, gratified the latent expectation in those thousands of people, he gave them a thrill, certainly, but it was only the exaggerated and yet quite logical intensification of the thrill they had expected when they paid their entrance money. And, even if they had read later that their own private accident was, in fact, a murder, it would not have excited or titillated them as such because it had failed to stimulate those peculiar cerebral reflexes which are normally stimulated by murder.

Also, the locale itself militated against its popular acceptance as a memorable murder. The circus, unlike the stage and screen, is not a mirror of normal life or normal people. It sets out to provide the abnormal spectacle, the abnormal thrill. Consequently, murder in a circus, where anything outrageous may be expected, is far less piquant than murder in, say, a country vicarage.

Again, the circus is a world peopled with puppets and grotesqueries. Its "uglies," such as the clowns, the dwarfs, the freaks, are too ugly to approximate even the least favored of our neighbors. The "beauties," as typified by the fair equestriennes, the pard-skinned lion tamer, the dazzling aerialist, are deliberately presented as too heroic, too fair and good for human nature's daily food. They are embodiments, not people, and their personalities are definitely subordinated to their acts. The private life of the actors, unlike those of screen and stage stars, are not an object of curiosity even to the most avid circus-goers. Who cares about the man or woman behind the tinsel? All of us, young and old alike, know that they are mere marionettes, here today and tomorrow jerked relentlessly away.

Some of my more snobbish friends have suggested another reason why the Rose case has never—to descend to a vulgarism—"caught on." While they condescendingly concede to the circus a certain entertainment value, they insist that its artistes are neither socially nor temperamentally interesting as murderers or murderees. They shrug aside the circus folk as little better than vagrants whose lives are so squalorous and vulgar anyhow that no one cares if they murder each other any more than one cared about the mutual massacrings among the Chicago bootleg gangs.

I must remind these snobs, who think that murder, to be interesting, must confine itself to the upper-income brackets or the social register, that blue blood—and Boston's best blue blood at that—was represented in this affair by one of the persons most deeply involved. Miss Eulalia Crawford, had she not been what newspapers repulsively refer to as an "elegant socialite," might have made any case memorable by her beauty, her outstanding personality, and her talent as a puppet designer. In this field she has achieved a reputation second only to that of the admirable Tony Sarg. Miss Crawford provided more than a mere snob appeal.

But, a truce to these ratiocinations. There is at least one quite definite reason why the Rose homicide never obtained the attention it merited. It is a sort of unfinished

symphony. Nor is it unfinished in the same sense as those
great unsolved mysteries such as the Ross kidnapping or
the Elwell murder which have always captivated popular
imagination. For, in the case of the Roses, the actual
criminals were known and apprehended. They were even
sentenced, albeit inadequately. But they never faced trial
in the accepted sense of the word. And they certainly
were never tried for murder. A murder trial, with its
wide publicity, its fanfare of photographers and reporters,
stamps the lineaments of a case, and of its participants,
indelibly on people's minds. It lifts even a minor killing
out of the humdrum rut and, whatever the verdict, it
manages to catch up the threads and tidy off a case to the
public satisfaction.

The Roses were never tidied off. One day, as I have
already hinted, they may themselves gather up the loose
threads of the case, and do a little tidying off on their
own account.

Now, to my story. And since I was an eyewitness to the
first act in the grim drama of Gino Forelli's death, I ask
the reader to pardon undue egotism and to allow me to
narrate the events as I saw them.

I shall never forget the evening of June 4, 1936. I was
staying in Philadelphia, where I had the good fortune to
dine with that eminent bibliophile, the late Mr. A. Edward
Newton, who was one of the few men in America—and
certainly the only one in Philadelphia—who knew how to
serve a dinner worthy of the name. The meal was the
more pleasant in that it was to be followed by a visit to
the circus, a form of entertainment for which I retain my
childish passion. An abundance of Pol Roger 1926 also
played its part, and I recalled the fact that a clairvoyant
gypsy once told me that three words beginning in C—
which is incidentally the first letter of my name—were
to prove important in the shaping of my destiny. The
words were: Crime, Champagne, and Circus.

This was indeed the night for my three C's—the night
when they were to convolute around me and finally to
coalesce in a weird and dramatic pattern.

My gypsy might—for I am notoriously susceptible—
have added a fourth fatal C: Charmer. And there was
one present that night in the person of Mrs. Phoebe

Gilkyson, a delightful Philadelphian whose *emballement* for the circus was almost equal to my own.

As the car purred through the mellow summer evening towards the Arena in North Philadelphia, my host's daughter, a gifted psychoanalyst, raised the interesting point as to whether adult enjoyment of the circus is merely a relic of atavistic infantilism or whether it springs from the sadistic impulse, latent in all of us, which makes us relish dangerous and spectacular feats because subconsciously we hope to see injury and suffering. Since I have already touched on this latter point, I reintroduce it merely to show that Miss Newton, like my gypsy, was gifted with a certain clairvoyance.

There is no need for me to describe the circus arena with its tawny jungle sights and sounds; its garish lights; its freaks; its frolics. The very smell of the sawdust was as exhilarating as the Pol Roger which I had enjoyed at dinner.

Nor need I describe the earlier acts which were, as I remember, in the old tradition, and neither better nor worse than usual. Let me hasten to my climax.

The finale of the evening was the aerialist act known as The Flying Roses. Though it was a three-ring circus, their trapezes were set up in the center only. However, in order to avoid the appearance of emptiness, each of the two side rings was left with a circle of elephants, sitting immobile on inverted tubs. But all eyes, side and center, were strained towards The Flying Roses. The two girls in the act were billed as Mesdames Lina and Zelide. The three men—named for the color of their scanty tights—were the White Rose, the Red Rose and the Purple Rose, the last-named (Gino Forelli) being the star.

There is always a thrill when the aerialists climb up to the dizzy heights whence their performance emanates. And all good aerialist acts are so arranged that the thrill is a mounting one, a steady crescendo of excitement. At first, while the net beneath is still spread, the two girls give graceful exhibitions whose chief appeal is to the aesthetic senses. Then they perform more difficult feats in conjunction with the White and the Red Rose. Meanwhile our star, the Purple Rose, keeps discreetly in the background.

Then the two girls, Zelide and Lina, retire to the subsidiary role of "feeding," or merely swinging out the trapeze as it is required, and the three males get to work in earnest. First the safety net is removed, which lends to the act the spice of real danger. The Red Rose and the White Rose go through a routine which, though more spectacular, is only really the hors d'oeuvre to whet the appetite for the rich fare which is now to be provided by the stellar Purple.

And from the moment that he starts his first easy swing from his trapeze, one is conscious of being in the presence of genius. Gino Forelli is a Nijinsky among aerialists and his performance is so expert, so dazzling, that his partners, by comparison, seem as clumsy and as heavy as the elephants sitting solemnly below on their inverted tubs. And to the act the Purple rose brings not only the physical perfection of his face and body, but also that smiling, indefinable something that can only be called charm.

I am no connoisseur of male pulchritude. A fanatical concentration on the female form divine has left me little talent in that direction. In another age, perhaps, young Forelli, with his broad shoulders and narrow hips, might have attracted the chisel of a Praxiteles. His *élan* and virility must have made him particularly attractive to women. He was, in short, that traditional captivator of female hearts—the handsome young man on the flying trapeze.

After he has flashed, like a purple dragonfly, through a few more numbers, there comes the final announcement from the ringmaster:

"Ladies and gentlemen, you are about to witness the most difficult, the most dangerous feat ever performed by any aerialist in the world—the famous Two and a Half. In short, ladies and gentlemen, the Purple Rose will turn two and one-half somersaults in the air during the time that he is being swung from one of his partners to the other."

The band starts up an important rat-tat-tat. The White Rose and the Red Rose, hanging by their knees from their trapezes, start to toss the Purple Rose from one to the other in what might pass for limbering-up exercises. Then the White Rose takes him and swings him higher and higher until, when he has reached the highest possible point, he will release him for the somersaults, after which the Red Rose, swinging out from below at exactly the right moment, will catch him as he descends.

The swinging is prolonged, for hours it seems, while the audience watches, heads moving in the rhythm of the trapeze, eyes wide with the pleasurable horror of anticipation.

The rat-tat-tat of the band grows louder. The moment of release comes at last, right up against the roof of the arena, more than sixty feet above the ground. We watch, breathless, as the Purple Rose curves gracefully, cutting the air cleanly in two and one-half circles. We watch as the Red Rose swings out from his side, hands outstretched to catch him, to break his downward flight.

The suspense is agonizing as the Purple Rose, righting himself from his final somersault, throws out his hands for his partner's, clings for a brief instant and then—convulsively the fingers open and close, feverishly struggling to obtain a grip, but—they are one millionth of a second too early or—too late.

From the total height of over sixty feet the Purple Rose plummets sickeningly downward—down to the sawdust-strewn floor below.

No one could ever forget the cry, half gasp, half scream, which broke from that packed arena. I can well believe that, as I read next day, it was audible in City Hall, several miles away, above the roar of Philadelphia's night traffic.

It was followed by a long moment of the deepest silence. One was vaguely conscious that a female figure, young, dark, and beautiful, had run forward and was bending over the body of Gino Forelli.

Nothing else stirred. The band had broken off to a man. During those terrifying half seconds of utter silence it seemed that the whole scene had frozen into complete immobility. As on a brightly painted canvas one saw the two Rose brothers, idle on their trapeze above; the foolish elephants sitting still on their inverted tubs; the red-coated ringmaster staring motionless at the dark young woman who crouched in the sawdust over the body of Gino

Forelli. And all around the multitude was shocked into
the vast silence of death.

Silence. . . .

Then, suddenly, the silence was broken by a sound
more weird, more primitive even than the cry which had
just risen from the shocked spectators. It was the harsh,
angry trumpeting of an elephant.

I was aware of rapid movement. One of the elephants,
a hideously wrinkled pachyderm known as Edwina, had
abandoned her tub in the side ring and, bellowing through
a raised trunk, was rushing across the arena towards the
prostrate aerialist.

Now everybody started to move at once. The ringmaster hurried forward, his hand raised in a vain effort to
check the front-seat spectators who were surging blindly
forward. The Rose brothers slid down from their lofty
perches. Everyone was milling around like ants, seem-
ingly unconscious of the danger from Edwina, who had
gone berserk. I saw her, still bellowing as she moved
purposefully forward, bring down her raised trunk on the
shoulder of the White Rose, throwing him to the ground.

Then the other elephants started to get excited, and
pandemonium reigned. Our party was near the front and
things were getting dangerous. It became my patent duty
to ease my fair companions out as expeditiously as possible.

Before leaving for home we learned that Gino Forelli
was dead. His fall had broken his neck and he had died
instantaneously.

The inquest was held the next day. Through the in-
fluence of Mr. Newton I was fortunately enabled to at-
tend it.

It was a drab, pedestrian affair. First the circus authorities gave evidence that the act was performed as usual;
that it had been rehearsed and shown to the public on
literally hundreds of occasions; that the perfection of the
performers was such that no safety net had been considered necessary. Mesdames Zelide and Lina were called
next. They corroborated that the act had been performed
as usual. They added—and here I fancied that I detected
a slight reluctance—that there had been no failure or
negligence on the part of the surviving partners.

Then it was the turn of the Rose brothers. Dressed in subdued black and echoing each other's words, they testified that their dear comrade had been a fine aerialist, a great artist. Never had he shown signs of slipping until—well, recently. Pressed by the coroner, they sorrowfully admitted that recently he had seemed to be losing his nerve. In short, Gino had confided in them that he had been resorting to a certain drug which, taken shortly before a performance, seemed to bolster up his flagging courage. That was all they knew; all they had to say, except that they had both seen him taking pills of some sort before coming into the ring.

Mr. Annapoppaulos, the ringmaster, and a man of obvious probity, bore out their testimony that the young man was in the habit of "taking something." He, too, had seen Gino slipping tablets into his mouth on several occasions. He had been told that they were to settle a queasy stomach.

Medical evidence more or less clinched their statements. Post-mortem analysis had revealed the presence in the body of a considerable quantity of a drug known as benzedrine, or amphetamine, which at that time was easily obtainable without benefit of a physician's prescription. Likewise a supply of the tablets had been found in Gino's dressing room.

Expert medical testimony was then brought forward with regard to the nature of this drug. The experts stated that, while relatively harmless in the usual way, benzedrine had a marked effect not only on ocular accommodation, but also on nervous and muscular co-ordination. In short, while it gave a feeling of courage or confidence, it was an extremely dangerous drug if taken inadvisedly by anyone (an aerialist in particular) engaged in the performance of an act where split-second timing and complete co-ordination of all reflexes meant the difference between success or failure. Or, in this particular instance, the difference between life and death.

The verdict, as expected, was death by misadventure.

Throughout the proceedings I found myself watching with considerable fascination a beautiful young woman whom I had recognized at once as the girl who had first run out into the ring the night before. Her expression during most of the testimony was one of indignation or frustrated anger rather than sorrow. I noticed also that, on several occasions, she opened her mouth to speak or to utter some protest. But each time she apparently decided against it.

I seized the opportunity of following her and introducing myself as soon as the inquest was over. Miss Eulalia Crawford, who seemed never even to have heard of me, refused at first to pay me any heed. But when I mentioned that I was a well-known criminologist she paused in her headlong stride and, wheeling round to face me, exclaimed: "Criminologist? That's a sort of private detective, isn't it?"

Overlooking this insult in view of her overwrought condition, I urged her to come with me to some quiet place where we could talk. Abstractedly she followed me to the cocktail lounge of the Bellevue-Stratford. But she volunteered no remark, not even after we were seated and I had ordered a bottle of their finest champagne.

Nonetheless, some instinct told me that she was eager to unburden herself of those remarks which she had left unspoken at the inquest.

Finally, I said gently: "You were fond of poor Gino, weren't you?"

And quietly, but with that flaming candor which was so characteristic, she replied: "He was my lover."

For a moment neither of us spoke, and then, with sudden intensity, she flared: "Those were lies, all lies you heard this morning. Gino wasn't losing his nerve. He didn't take that damned drug."

"But, my dear young lady, the medical evidence . . ."

"Damn the medical evidence," she broke in. "I know. I tell you I know those two devils were trying to kill Gino. I know why. And you"—she turned on me almost accusingly—"you're supposed to be a crime expert. Well, figure this one out and see what you think."

Miss Crawford's story was told me passionately and excitedly. I was under the spell of her beauty, and of the champagne, as I listened. Recollected in sobriety, her tale was somewhat as follows:

Eulalia Crawford had joined Welland's Circus about a year previously, as much—I imagine—to escape the inanities of postdebutantism in Boston as to gain experience in her chosen field. Being already a skillful maker and manipulator of puppets, she had no difficulty in obtaining a position in one of the sideshows. The Bohemian life appealed to her and she found her fellow artists —the male element especially—refreshing and invigorating. Though by no means a *femme galante,* Eulalia was certainly no prude. She was frank to admit that at first she had been vaguely attracted by the sulky masculinity of Ludwig Rose (the Red Rose). She had even toyed with the idea of accepting him as a sort of casual lover, in spite of the fact that he was married to Madame Zelide. But Ludwig, though violently attracted to her, was only one of a two-man team. He and his older brother Bruno (the White Rose) were as inseparable in their amours as in their trapeze act. When Ludwig hinted at this unnatural state of affairs to her, Miss Crawford was utterly disgusted, the more so because she found Bruno as physically repulsive as he was mentally cunning and crooked.

She sent Ludwig about his business (and I can well picture her doing it) in no uncertain terms.

But Nature, who abhors a vacuum, was quick to compensate Eulalia with one of Her own children. For Gino Forelli was a veritable child of Nature and he loved Eulalia with a natural unihibited passion which was utterly satisfying to them both, and which left no room for the outside world. They were both young, both physically beautiful, and both exceptionally talented. Small wonder if they aroused the envy, and often the jealousy, of those around them.

And smaller wonder that they aroused the jealousy of the Rose brothers. Ludwig had taken his dismissal with the worst possible grace and, on several occasions, ignoring the unwritten code of the circus, had forced his attentions upon Eulalia. Once Gino caught him and a fight ensued. Let me give the sequel in Miss Crawford's own colorful phraseology:

"Gino was as strong as a lion and he fought like one. But as soon as he had knocked Ludwig down he changed in a twinkling. The poor darling couldn't really bear to hurt a fly. He picked Ludwig up; wiped his bloody nose with his own handkerchief and fussed over him with all the tenderness of a woman. He even apologized for losing his temper; said it must all have been a mistake and actually embraced Ludwig, calling him his 'good comrade' and 'friend.' Then he made us shake hands all round and got out a bottle of Orvieto. Ludwig drank with us, but I shall never forget the look on his face. Now I know that when Gino knocked him down he was actually signing his own death warrant."

Miss Crawford's fine dark eyes flashed dangerously as she continued her story. From that very day, she asserted, things began to go mysteriously wrong with Gino. He complained of vague stomach pains after meals, especially after meals eaten in company with the Rose brothers. This magnificently healthy young animal, who had never known a day's illness, was obliged to go to a doctor. The physician poohpoohed his ailment as heartburn and prescribed sodamint tablets. The trouble ended as mysteriously as it had begun.

Next, Gino was the victim of an assault one night just as he was coming from a visit to Edwina, the elephant who was a special pet of his. A cloak was thrown over his face and he felt himself being dragged backwards. The location of the attack, however, was unfortunate for the assailants, since Edwina, hearing Gino's smothered cries for help, broke loose from her pen and routed his adversaries. Though no physical damage was suffered by anyone, it was noticeable that the Rose brothers thereafter carefully avoided the proximity of Edwina, who had developed for them a most embarrassing dislike.

But the guileless Gino never dreamed of suspecting his "comrades," his two partners. Not even when Zelide, Ludwig's own wife, came to him secretly and begged him to leave Welland's Circus. She would give no definite reason for her request, but it was obvious to Eulalia that she had overheard her husband say, or half say, something that made her fear for the young man's safety. Miss Crawford had added her own pleas at the time, voiced her own suspicions, but Gino had merely laughed at her, insisting that the Roses were his good friends who loved him like a brother!

"And so," Eulalia concluded, "he stayed on and let himself be murdered. Yes, deliberately murdered."

For a while we sat there in the Bellevue-Stratford lounge without speaking. I filled the champagne glasses. Hers was practically untouched.

At length, as tactfully as possible, I suggested that if her suspicions were as strong as all that, she ought to take them to the police. Unless, of course, her reputation . . .

"Damn my reputation," she snapped. "But if I really could prove—"

She broke off with a jerk and sat staring stonily in front of her. Then, speaking to herself rather than to me, she murmured: "Perhaps I could. Perhaps Zelide and Lina would help me. Perhaps . . ."

Once again she broke off. Then, suddenly, and without another word, she got up and left me—left me, incidentally, to finish the better part of a quart of lukewarm champagne by myself.

I have never seen Eulalia Crawford since that day.

Two or three weeks later I happened to notice the following small paragraph on one of the inside pages of *The New York Times*.

FLYING ROSES ARRESTED

Today the police are holding Bruno and Ludwig Rose, known to the circus world as the White Rose and the Red Rose, and famous for their trapeze act styled The Flying Roses. The brothers were held on charges of assault and battery preferred by their wives, Lina and Zelide Rose, and by Miss Eulalia Crawford, puppeteer in Welland's Circus. Police authorities refused to comment on the rumors that the two acrobats [*sic*] are also being questioned with regard to the recent death of their partner, Gino Forelli (the Purple Rose), who broke his neck in a fatal fall in the Circus Stadium in Philadelphia on June 4 last. Prisoners were remanded without bail.

It looked, I reflected, as if Nemesis, or Miss Crawford, were catching up with the two Rose brothers.

But while Nemesis presses relentlessly forward, let us

turn our minds backward awhile for a glimpse at the events which led up to our catastrophe.

Somewhere in Italy, some time in the late eighties, were born two brothers Rosa who developed uncommon gifts as trapeze artists. When or how they came to America I do not pretend to know. I can state positively however, that by 1908 the two of them, together with the women they had trained and lawfully married, were part and parcel of Welland's Circus, their act being known, even then, as The Flying Roses. My boyhood impressions recall two thin-legged young men with heavy mustachios and two plump, smiling women who swung from the trapezes in permutations and combinations more dazzling and exciting than anything I had witnessed before.

They were a popular feature until the late twenties, by which time their wives, the original Mesdames Rose, were growing a trifle too plump and too varicose, and the mustachioed signors a little too stiff and too lean in the shanks.

But The Flying Roses were an act. And in the circus an established act must never die.

Fortune had endowed the Rosa (now known as Rose) brothers with talent and industry. It had crowned their efforts with success. But it had denied them one thing necessary to perpetuate that talent and that success in their own family. They had no sons to carry on the tradition. Each brother did, however, have a daughter. The two cousins, Lina and Zelide, had been cradled, weaned, and reared on the trapeze. Consequently as soon as they were old enough, they were called upon to supplant their mammas in the act.

But their papas were getting tired too, and perhaps a trifle arthritic. While zealous for the act which they had established, they were sensible men who knew the handwriting on the wall when they saw it. They knew that middle-aged aerialists, even though partnered by graceful young girls, were not aesthetically pleasing to a finicky public. They knew that the best act grows anemic unless young blood is pumped into its veins. And since this could not be their own blood, they had agreed that it must come from another source.

Consequently, some time before their actual retirement, they had undertaken to supervise the training of the two young apprentices who were eventually to supplant them.

Their choice had rested on two youths of Prussian birth who played clowns, tumblers, and other odd parts in the circus. These two showed some natural ability coupled with the application and patience necessary for their tedious training as aerialists. The 'prentices, Bruno and Ludwig Kramer—and they also were brothers—were not brilliant or colorful, but they were good specimens physically and they had stamina and doggedness, together with a marked oneness of mind and purpose which made them function excellently as a team. At this period they seem to have been serious, self-effacing youths who kept themselves to themselves and bided their time.

Finally, and I think the date was about 1932, their plodding was rewarded and they were officially signed on as principals in the Flying Roses Act. Immediately Bruno and Ludwig signalized their adoption into the family by changing their names by letters patent to Rose and by marrying the two Rose girls, Zelide and Lina, who were to be their partners. That these unions were entered into cynically and for motives of ambition rather than affection is evidenced by the fact that the brothers matched each other with coins (as they later openly boasted) as to which of them should take which girl.

And so, while the original Rosa brothers betook their arthritic limbs off to grateful retirement, the two Kramers (now the White and the Red Rose) took the act over and started to fly the trapezes in their own sweet way.

It has always been a matter of surprise to me that Lina and Zelide (especially Zelide, who has the more positive personality) should have been willing to marry these two unprepossessing young Prussians. But who am I to analyze the subtleties of the female heart? Perhaps they felt it their duty towards the act. Perhaps they had a genuine affection for their husbands at first. Disillusionment, however, must have come quickly, for the two brothers soon began to show themselves in their true colors. The quiet, self-effacing youths had disappeared and their place was taken by a pair of tyrannical, arrogant knaves.

Ludwig, the younger of the two, was not without some

pretension to good looks, but his surly disposition and moronic viciousness of temper had made him an object of almost universal dislike in the circus world. Bruno, the White Rose, was more plausible and far more intelligent. He assumed a brusque, hearty manner, which, while it aped rugged sincerity, actually concealed a low form of patient cunning similar to that exhibited by his more notorious namesake, Bruno Hauptmann, the kidnapper. One characteristic they had in common. Both brothers showed, if not actual affection, at least a blind, unswerving loyalty to each other which was worthy of a better object. This was more than mere devotion; it was a *unanimity* of idea and desire which extended far beyond their teamwork on the trapezes. They shared everything—their ambitions, their pleasures, their hatreds. They would even have shared their wives had not the two women objected. Miss Crawford hinted that they tried to share their amours and it was common knowledge that, when they went on extramarital sprees, they pimped and procured for each other in a manner that must have shocked even the most hardened trollop.

But, most important of all, each took on the animosities and petty spites of the other. A slight to Ludwig was repaid by some act of vicious retaliation from Bruno. And if anyone offended Bruno, he was apt to trip over some shin-barking obstacle as he left his dressing room in the dark, or to find some messy or malodorous object in his bed—a gift from Ludwig, whose moronic predilection ran to practical jokes.

Their attitude towards women betrayed the Prussian in them. Women were chattels and each considered that he—or his brother—had a sort of divine right to enjoy any female who happened to take his fancy. They further showed their scorn of women, as soon as they obtained control of the act, by relegating their wives, whenever possible, to subsidiary roles while they themselves "hogged" the spotlight more and more.

This was as unwise as it was unwarranted. Though efficient aerialists, the Rose brothers lacked that something which for want of a better word is called color. Applause dwindled to almost nothing. Rival shows such as Ringling's and Barnum's had better, more colorful trapeze

artists. It soon became obvious to the circus management
—if not to the principals—that The Flying Roses once
again needed new blood if they were to survive.

And new blood was soon forced upon them in the person of Gino Forelli, the brilliant and unfortunate youth
who was later to be known as the Purple Rose. Bruno and
Ludwig tolerated him at first because they felt that his
training period, like their own, would take years of slog-
ging work. He was no immediate challenge to their
fading laurels. But here they reckoned without Gino.

For Gino was something quite out of the ordinary even
in a circus. Born of Italian parents, literally within the
circus enclosure, the boy knew no other life and cared for
little else. His mother was an equestrienne, his father one
of the keepers in charge of the elephants. From earliest
infancy Gino was the joy and pride of Welland's Circus.
Everyone loved this laughing, dark-eyed boy—including
Edwina, the oldest and most hideous of the circus elephants. He adopted her as his special pet. There is a
story, none too well authenticated, that once, when the
animal's ugliness of appearance and disposition made her
destruction advisable, Gino went to the authorities and
pleaded for her life. With a cunning prompted by affection
and desperation the boy suggested that the pachyderm's
gnarled appearance might be turned to profitable account.
She might be billed—and heaven knows how this could be
proved or disproved—as "Edwina, the Oldest Elephant
in Captivity." Gino had his way; the slogan captivated the
public and Edwina became the most celebrated elephant
since Barnum's Jumbo. After being the outcast of the herd,
Edwina knew the joys of a stellar role with all its com-
forts and perquisites. One reason the more for gratitude
and devotion to her young patron.

Edwina is a digression but not an unimportant one.

Gino's ability in the circus did not end with the animals.
He appears to have been a youthful prodigy with a ver-
satility equal in his own humble sphere to Mozart's in the
world of music. At the age of ten he was able, so I am
credibly informed, to fill in expertly in almost any given
act. He was a champion tumbler, a juggler, a funambulist,
an intrepid rider, and an adequate performer on most
instruments in the band. One story, which for obvious

reasons is frowned upon by the circus authorities, relates how sixteen-year-old Gino once took the place of Tito, the Fearless Lion Tamer, when that worthy was suffering from an infected hand and could not enter the cages. Gino controlled the big cats so nonchalantly and gave such a courageous performance that Tito almost sent in his resignation immediately.

And Gino was just as anxious to conquer the air as he had conquered the ground. To be an aerialist had always been one of his ambitions. Madame Zelide has told me how, after the performance was over, he was often to be found swinging from trapeze to trapeze, trying out difficult figures and utterly indifferent to the fact that there was no safety net below him. Zelide also told me—and here she must be regarded as an expert—that when Gino started to train with the Rose brothers, he mastered in a few weeks routines which normally took years to perfect. His timing, she said, was perfect; his technique flawless. In an incredibly short while he was taking his place, not only as a principal, but as a star among the Flying Roses.

From his first public performance the applause was terrific. Soon the act was receiving top billing again and it was restored, as the *pièce de résistance,* to the final place on the program.

Since we know their characters, it is not difficult for us to guess how the Rose brothers must have felt about the success of their brilliant colleague. They were scrupulous in observing all the principles of teamwork during the training period, in rehearsals, and throughout actual performances. They pretended to welcome the "comrade" who had raised the act to such dizzy heights. Perhaps only their wives really knew what was going on in those warped, patient minds. Indeed, Zelide has since told me that, in her opinion, the brothers would have eventually eliminated Gino even if Eulalia had never entered the picture at all.

But Eulalia Crawford did enter the picture and Gino died.

We know the manner of his death and the events which led up to it. Now let us turn to the events which followed it. Or, rather, let us shuttle back to the point where Miss Crawford left me so abruptly in the Bellevue-Stratford cocktail lounge and consider the steps that were taken to bring about the eventual arrest and punishment of the two Roses.

Although I have not seen Miss Crawford since the day she voiced to me her more than embryonic suspicions, I do not have to rely upon guesswork as to her subsequent actions. For soon afterwards I had the pleasure of meeting Madame Zelide, and from her somewhat fragmentary account I can piece together the story.

Zelide is a strange mixture, as outstanding artistes so often are, of sense and sensibility. And, at the time of Gino's death, she must have been tugged to emotional ribbons. She had loved the young Italian with the affection of a warmhearted woman and the appreciation of a fellow artist. They were, in a sense, compatriots. She had no love for her husband and he had aroused her suspicions sufficiently to make her warn Gino of his danger. But it is one thing to warn a man while he is alive and safe and quite another thing to accuse someone else of wilful murder after his death.

And—on what exactly could she found her accusations? Zelide had testified at the inquest and she had testified what she believed to be the turth. The act had been performed as usual. Both the brothers had fulfilled their parts with their usual precision. With tears in her eyes she told me that, even if she had been looking for it, she could not have noticed anything wrong. The fault, as far as *perceptibility* was concerned, must have rested with Gino. But a dozen or more *imperceptible* things might have been done by the Red Rose as he swung out from below to catch his descending partner. Zelide knew—and who could know better?—that a millionth of a second's error in timing, an invisible closing, a tiny withdrawal of a hand, a contraction even of a finger at the moment of contact— any one of these might have passed unnoticed by Zelide, yet anyone might have had a fatal termination.

In short, the Rose brothers had been in a perfect position to commit a perfect murder in full view of thousands, and to commit it in such a way that it would look like an accident—an accident for which only the dead man could be held responsible.

Zelide, being a sensible woman, realized all this. Lina

realized it, too. They had both liked Gino and they were further outraged by the desecration of their beloved act. But they both agreed that there was nothing they could do.

And then Eulalia came to them, outraged on her own account and fulminating suspicions that, to her, were certainties. At first she must have run up against a stone wall, for neither Zelide nor Lina liked Eulalia. Brought up themselves in the closely knit world of the circus, they regarded this society girl as an interloper. They had resented her intimacy with Gino and felt that she had been bad for him, both as a man and as an artist. Probably they also resented the fact that their husbands found her attractive.

One can picture the first conference between the three women, who were united only in their common sense of outrage. One can savor its atmosphere of secrecy—for that was essential to them all—of warring emotions, common dislikes and distrusts. One can picture the swift glances that pass between Lina and Zelide as they silently ask each other whether they care, or dare, to confide in this alien girl their own dark suspicions of their husbands. One can feel their dislike and distrust mounting as Eulalia crashes on with her own story. One can realize how hopeless it must have seemed to them ever to work together in full co-operation.

But there was another female who had been outraged by Gino's untimely death. Her suspicions were stronger even than Eulalia's certainties, for they were based on even keener instincts—an animal's. I refer, of course, to Edwina, the elephant. She had been swift to avenge the death of her beloved. She had rushed out to attack the White Rose immediately after the disaster and had succeeded in breaking his collar-bone. A few days later she hurled herself at the Red Rose as he passed near her pen, and only his agility in swarming up a nearby post saved him from annihilation.

Edwina was convinced, and she had the courage of her convictions. Zelide assured me quite positively that it was Edwina's certitude (and perhaps fortitude) that strengthened the hand of the three wavering women and somehow consolidated them into unity.

Finally, after several more conferences, they conceived a plan.

And here I should point out that it took considerable courage and determination to do what they did, for the obstacles in their paths must have seemed almost insurmountable.

They really had nothing to go on except their female intuitions. Tangible evidence was out of the question. Even to show that the brothers had entertained feelings of malice towards Gino was well-nigh impossible. The two Roses had never committed any overt act against their younger partner. They had always been outwardly friendly during his lifetime and they acted with sorrowful decorum after his death. The stomach pains suffered by Gino, the mysterious night assault, proved nothing at all. Even the fight, which might have been adduced as malice-making, had ended in handshakes all around and renewed professions of comradeship. Ludwig and Bruno, industrious, assiduous Prussians that they were, had covered their tracks perfectly. As for Edwina and her trumpetings—those could be laughed off as the senile acts of a crotchety and unpredictable pachyderm.

There was only one way—and that the most difficult—to prove that the Roses had acted deliberately and with malice. This was to obtain from one, or both, of them a confession.

But the close-mouthed Ludwig, the cunning Bruno, having attained their desired end, were hardly likely to oblige with an admission of guilt. It had to be tricked out of them somehow.

And there was one weak spot, one chink in the Roses' armorplating; and it was here that the three women decided to attack. This point, or Achilles' heel as we might call it, was Ludwig's infatuation for Eulalia, which, since it was unsatisfied, smoldered with ever-intenser heat. The leading role fell to Eulalia, therefore, and a very unpleasant one it must have been.

She faced it squarely and with fortitude. First of all she abandoned any appearance of grief for the dead Gino. She was gay and inviting, letting it be known that she was by no means inconsolable. She even hinted publicly in front of Zelide, who whispered it to her husband, that the young Italian's virility was not all it might have been.

One does not care to speculate on the exact lengths to which Miss Crawford was obliged to go. Let it suffice that she soon had Ludwig eating out of her hand. Whether, when it finally came to the point, she relied on the tongue-loosening effect of passion to gain her desired ends, or whether—and there would be poetic justice in this—she preferred the tongue-loosening effect of benzedrine, we will not inquire. Anyhow, by flattery, cajolery, and subtle denigrations of Gino, she gained Ludwig's confidence completely and finally managed to maneuver him into a situation where, with Lina and Zelide concealed within hearing range, she induced him to confess, nay to boast, about the measures that he and Bruno had taken to eliminate their unfortunate partner. Once having started to talk, Ludwig said enough to put a rope around both his own neck and his brother's. And Lina and Zelide were in a position to hear every word.

He bragged—and here I have Zelide's positive testimony—that he and his brother first experimented with mixing ground glass into Gino's food, but this was abandoned as being too "sissy" [sic]. The night attack, which was made on the impulse of an intoxicated moment, was more manly according to Ludwig's standards, but too imprudent according to Bruno's. It was Bruno who thought of substituting benzedrine pills for the sodamint which Gino had been taking ever since the glass experiments. The idea had come to him from a newspaper article describing how benzedrine affected muscular control and accuracy of aim in certain forms of athletics. And then, during the act, Ludwig was to make certain by . . .

Unfortunately Zelide never heard exactly what they had planned for Ludwig to do during the act. She could bear it no longer. Trembling with indignation, she burst from her hiding place, dragging Lina after her. As she faced her husband, he must have realized at once how he had been trapped.

"Never, never I forget his face," cried Zelide as she recounted the story to me. "It was black like Satan and snarling like a tiger. His eyes were bloody . . ."

His actions, too, were bloody. With the savagery of a tiger he launched an attack upon the girls. He crashed his fist into Zelide's face, knocked Lina down, and plunged murderous fingers into Eulalia's throat. The screams of the women, ironically enough, brought not the help they needed, but an ally for Ludwig in Bruno, who was never far absent. Sensing what had happened and, infected by his brother's fury (here, perhaps, we have a true case of a *folie à deux*), he joined in the cowardly attack. Unable to use his hands because of his broken collar-bone, he availed himself of his feet and kicked his prostrate wife so brutally that she sustained an injury to the hipbone which has prevented her from ever performing again.

Help came at last, but only just in time. When the Roses had been finally overpowered, it was found that, in addition to Lina's damaged hip, Zelide had a fractured jaw and Eulalia was within a hair's breadth of death from strangulation.

These injuries, shocking as they were, served at least one useful purpose. They enabled the police to hold the Rose brothers in custody until the three women were recovered enough to bring charges against them for conspiracy to murder Gino Forelli.

And, in due time, they did.

I now come to the least satisfactory part of this history. It is unsatisfactory because legal details are, by their very nature, uninteresting. Also, it is unsatisfactory to me because it is the only part of my narrative where I have neither full understanding nor complete documentation. The ethics of the legal profession prevented me from questioning the attorneys, for either the prosecution or the defense. Consequently, since I am unversed in the niceties of the law, I can only offer a layman's interpretation of the concepts which underlay the legal actions of both parties.

The case against the Roses for assault and battery was clear. But the more serious charge of murder presented obvious difficulties from the beginning.

That the Roses had deliberately conspired, maliciously and feloniously, to kill Gino Forelli there was probably no doubt in the minds of the prosecuting attorneys. The evidence, however, was of a most unsatisfactory nature, being pure hearsay and dependent on the words of three women who were palpably biased against the accused. Then there was the eternal difficulty with regard to wives giving testimony against their husbands, and the fact that no disinterested party had overheard the "confession."

The defence attorneys doubtless realized that all this was in favor of their clients. But they had their difficulties, too. They knew that, at a public murder trial, the appearance of Lina and Zelide, bruised and damaged as they were, would be hopelessly prejudicial to their two husbands. They were probably even more afraid of Eulalia Crawford, who would be fearless in using her money and in exploiting her social prominence to any degree that might encompass the downfall of the brothers.

Finally the defense hit upon a compromise—and a wise one from the point of view of their clients. They persuaded the two Roses to try to bypass the assault charges by the offer of heavy compensation to the injured women and, in the case of Forelli's death, to plead guilty to involuntary manslaughter. There was a question, of course, as to whether this latter plea would be permitted. That was for the court and for the prosecution to decide. And the prosecution knew their difficulties only too well. The abortive poison attempt and the ill-considered night attack would, they felt certain, be inadmissible as evidence at any murder trial. They were not proved at the time and they did not result in serious injury to the victim. Only the benzedrine remained as a peg for obtaining a murder verdict. And the court may well have pointed out the weakness of this peg, since benzedrine is not a poison in the ordinary sense of the word and it was only made lethal by the extraordinary nature of the circumstances under which it was administered. All of which would be extremely difficult to present convincingly to a hard-headed jury.

Consequently the plea was allowed.

And so the Rose brothers pleaded guilty to involuntary manslaughter and admitted that they had substituted benzedrine for Gino's sodamint tablets. They gave as their ridiculous reason: "They hoped thereby to break off relations between their partner and Miss Crawford, which relations they considered undesirable and against the interest of their act." Their claim was apparently based on a belief that benzedrine is a sort of *an*aphrodisiac—

and there is some vague medical evidence to support this. Of course they feigned ignorance of any properties in the drug which might have been disastrous to an aerialist, and they expressed surprise and sorrow that, by their relatively innocent action, they had *involuntarily* brought about their partner's death.

Since the maximum penalty allowed by law for involuntary manslaughter is comparatively mild, the Roses had good reason to congratulate themselves.

But their exultation was short-lived. The women were not through with them yet. Captained by Eulalia, who had grimly insisted on paying all their hospital bills out of her own pocket, the three Indomitables now moved in solid phalanx against the Rose brothers. Knowing that they could never exact adequate retribution on the score of Gino's murder—for man cannot be brought into legal jeopardy twice for the same crime—they concentrated on their own injuries.

Scorning all offers of compensation, they pressed their charges relentlessly, adding assault with intent to kill to their earlier charges of assault and battery. And here they had evidence aplenty. Their gaping wounds cried out with mute mouths against the brutality of the Roses.

And they won, of course. The net result of their victory was a sentence—or rather a series of sentences—for the Rose brothers which totalled approximately ten years at penal servitude. Even so, they should have been grateful, for they deserved a far heavier punishment.

They should have been grateful, as I said before, that they escaped the publicity of a murder trial and all the unpleasant notoriety which is the inevitable concomitant of a *cause célèbre*. Their photographs were not published in the press and I doubt if more than a handful of the spectators who saw Gino perish in that crowded arena ever bothered to follow the fate of his murderers. Even so, the public memory is short, and Ludwig and Bruno will be unrecognized and unremembered when they come out of prison.

When they come out. . . . What will their thoughts be then? What will be their plans?

Perhaps I can answer my own questions.

Last year, when I was preparing this review of their

case, I managed to obtain an interview with the Rose brothers in Philadelphia, were they are at present confined at the Eastern Penitentiary and where, incidentally, their behavior is said to be exemplary.

Exemplary their behavior may be, but I will stake my reputation as a psychologist and physiognomist that their hearts are still unchastened. When I told them that I was anxious to include a history of their case in this present series, their reaction was extraordinary. They were not flattered and elated as hardened criminals usually are to hear that their exploits are to be given to the public. They were not indignant as innocent men would have been. Nor did they exhibit the silent shame that betokens true penitence. They talked to me and they talked volubly. Bruno's somber eyes lit up with fanatic light as he spoke, while Ludwig lisped enough venom to poison a family of rattlesnakes. Why were they so articulate? Because they saw in me, a writer, someone whom they might persuade to excoriate the "women who had betrayed them." Themselves impotent and imprisoned, they wanted me only as a vehicle for their pent-up spite. I listened in shocked horror as they vied with each other in pouring out obscenities against Eulalia Crawford and their wives (now ex-wives, I am glad to say). Their words are unprintable, nor would I corrode my pen with such filth. But they were impressive and they impressed me with one unshatterable conviction. The Rose brothers are monomaniacs and their psychopathic vindictiveness must one day find some *out*let.

*Out*let! When they come *out!* And, as they say in the vernacular, it won't be long now. Ten years, with time off for good behavior, have almost slipped by and soon—unrecognized and unremembered—the prison will spew forth two vicious killers burning with blood lust for revenge.

What will they find in the great world outside the prison walls? Welland's Circus in no more, its stock-in-trade having been taken over by the Madden interests. The Flying Roses no longer fly. The act died with Gino Forelli.

But the people concerned in the drama of the Roses are still alive. Eulalia Crawford has left the East and is patriotically donating her talents to wartime America in San Francisco. Lina, happily remarried, is living there in retirement also. Zelide, alone of the Roses, remains in harness, delighting visitors to Madden's Circus with her troupe of all-female aerialists known as the Bird Ballet. Edwina, at this present writing, is in harness too and still "The Oldest Elephant in Captivity."

Beware, Edwina, if your longevity shall have extended to the day when your two enemies are released from prison.

Beware, Zelide; though you are a bird, you cannot soar high enough to escape the crooked arm of vengeance.

Beware, Lina; the drab plumage of happy domesticity will not shelter you when the day of reckoning comes.

Beware, Eulalia; your fame will make you an easy mark and the police, overtaxed by war duties, will be too busy to protect you.

And to myself, self-elected interpreter and prophet in this tragic case, I say, Beware, Emmanuel Catt!

When they come out! . . .

For the Roses will come out into a world preoccupied with a grim holocaust which dwarfs even the most lurid fancies of their twisted minds. The mass murder of war will be a giant camouflage net, lending them cover, anonymity, protection for the lesser murders that will be in their hearts. They will strike silently, swiftly, and then, swiftly, silently, they will disappear—back into the shadows . . remorseless . . . unregenerate.

CHAPTER XVIII

I closed *Crimes of Our Times*. Our polite equivalent of a prison cell was very quiet and the rousing *Bewares* which had brought the essay to its dramatic close still rang in my ears. Whatever his shortcomings, Emmanuel Catt had at least proved himself a true prophet. The red rose and the white rose had indeed meant blood and, although we had saved Zelide, both Eulalia and Lina had fallen before the brothers' bloody, prison-fostered revenge.

Eulalia, Lina, Zelide, Edwina, those four females, who had figured only as names or corpses in our life until then, had been kindled into vivid reality for me by Emmanuel Catt. Eulalia, the beautiful Boston Fury bent upon the destruction of her lover's murderers; Lina, the brow-beaten little wife who had had her one moment of courage; Zelide, the warmhearted artiste who, for justice, had risked her life against two formidable killers; Edwina, the ancient elephant who had loved a man and fought for him like a warrior.

They had been a valiant quartet.

"Poor Eulalia," Iris's voice cut into my thoughts. "She was wonderful, so brave. And all the family ever did was to snoot her because she'd had an affair with an Italian! And what an affair! Darling, if only I'd heard about Gino

Forelli's death, some little thing about it, we might have been able to save her."

I looked around the small, musty room. I was remembering where we were and not liking it.

"The essay says the Red Rose had a lisp, Peter," Iris was saying. "Then it was the Red Rose who killed Eulalia and the White Rose who killed Lina. The Red Rose killed the girl who'd tricked him, and the White Rose killed the wife who'd betrayed him. Mr. Catt even had that figured out beforehand. That's why he sent Eulalia red roses and Lina white roses."

"And they both wore my uniform," I said. "That's another fancy use they made of me. They put Lieutenant Duluth on the scene of both crimes to make them look like the work of one man. That way each of them could get an alibi for one of the murders." I shrugged. "They're smart, all right."

"Smart. They're more than smart." Iris gave a shiver. "If I'd ever known who we were up against, I'd have given in before we started." A faintly smug smile crept over her face. "But we fixed them, didn't we, darling?"

I was feeling a little smug myself. "Yes, baby," I said. "We fixed them."

"And won't Hatch be proud of us?"

"Yes," I said, remembering with some satisfaction how low Hatch's opinion of my intelligence had been.

A key scraped in the lock and the door opened. Our policeman came in. The I've-caught-a-murderer expression was wiped off his face. He looked confused and irritable. That, I felt, was a good omen.

"The Inspector's ready to see you," he said.

We got up. "Did you call Williams and Dagget?" I asked.

"Yeah. They've been contacted. They're coming over."

That news gave me the extra fillup I needed. I felt quite jaunty as Iris and I followed the policeman through the drafty central office and through a door marked: INSPECTOR ROBERT WEBB.

We entered a large, private office. At one end of it, a police inspector, presumably Inspector Webb, sat behind a desk. He was a slight man with white hair and dark, world-weary eyes. At his side, brandishing a copy of *Crimes of Our Times* and talking emphatically, stood Mr. Emmanuel Catt. Zelide was sitting in a chair by the window next to the solid, amiable figure of Mr. Annapoppaulos. Cecil Grey was there, too, self-important among a group of policemen. They were all paying respectful attention to Mr. Catt and did not notice our entrance.

". . . and so I must impress upon you . . ."

"All right, all right, Mr. Catt." The Inspector's mild voice broke into the Beard's monologue. "You have convinced me, and we have already contacted Philadelphia. Soon we will have the complete files on the Rose brothers and we'll be able to make positive identification."

Cecil Grey saw us then. He spun around, pointing at us, getting all he could out of his moment in the lime-light.

"There they are. And he was wearing a civilian suit when he made me drive him to Sloat Boulevard last night. He's the one who . . ."

Mr. Catt turned from the desk and fixed a thunderous gaze upon the actor. "You are an ignorant young man and will be so kind as to keep your opinions to yourself," he boomed. As Grey wilted, he progressed towards us, his hands outstretched, a smile beaming through his beard. "Lieutenant Duluth and Mrs. Duluth, let me be the first to congratulate you. As I have been impressing upon the Inspector, although my own—ah—indisposition prevented me from aiding the ladies, you two seem to have acted with great courage and daring. I am most anxious to hear your account of what happened."

"Yes, yes." Madame Zelide was upon us in a flurry of feathers and cape. "The manager, he just telephone from the circus. My ropes are indeed cut almost through. I should have gone boom to my death like poor Gino if eet ees not for you. I thank, I thank. Such courage, such skeel."

With Italian ardor, she threw herself at Iris, kissing her and then started kissing me. I hadn't been prepared for so much enthusiasm. Sheepishly, I disentangled myself from the world-famous aerialist and muttered: "Any little thing we did, I'm sure . . ."

A discreet cough from Inspector Webb put an end to the love fest.

He said: "Lieutenant and Mrs. Duluth, will you please step over here? The Rose brothers will soon be brought in. They're removing their clown costumes and cleaning them up. Before that, I want to hear your story."

He waved Zelide and Mr. Catt away. They took up their places on chairs next to Mr. Annapoppaulos. A police stenographer sat by the Inspector, his pencil poised over a notebook.

"Firstly," said the Inspector, who was nothing if not G.I., "you will please give us your full names."

I gave him our names. Then, while his alert eyes studied my face and the stenographer scribbled, I started our story. I told them of Mrs. Rose giving us her room at the St. Anton, of the man with the lisp who telephoned us to ask if Iris was Eulalia, of the theft of my uniform in the Turkish bath, and of our first, dramatic meeting with Mr. Catt in the St. Anton ballroom. It was rather difficult to disguise the extent of Mr. Catt's unfortunate "indisposition," but I did my best. After that, I explained our actions up to the point where we had found Eulalia Crawford dead in her apartment.

Inspector Webb interrupted me there for the first time to murmur: "You realize, of course, that in failing to report the murder you were breaking the law?"

"Yes," I said meekly.

But Iris, her spirit roused, cut in: "What else could you expect him to do? He'd been framed. If he'd called the police then, he'd have been arrested. There'd have been no chance to save Lina . . ."

"Perhaps, but . . ." The Inspector gestured with his hands. "Continue, Lieutenant."

I continued. Throwing a handsome and merited bouquet to Hatch for his contributions, I reviewed our search for the Beard, my disastrous trip to Wawona Avenue, the mysterious return of my stolen uniform, and the second disappearance of the Beard from our hotel room.

I realized that my narrative was not presenting either myself or America's foremost criminologist in a very flattering light. I shot him a furtive glance. He was staring with immense dignity out of the window. If he heard my references to his "malady," he was magnificently ignoring them.

It did not take long to tell of our flight to Hatch's apartment and the sensational trip to the circus that ensued.

"That's everything," I concluded. "We never exactly knew what it was all about. We just blundered on, I guess, and tried to do what we could. Hatch Williams and Bill Dagget will be able to check on it all when they show up. I suppose they're O.K.?"

"A most reputable firm," murmured Inspector Webb. "Always on the side of the law." He glanced at the stenographer, who stopped scribbling and then gazed up at us. "Well, as a police officer, I can hardly commend your behavior, but I have to admit that you acted with courage and resourcefulness in a most awkward situation. You also were responsible for saving Madame Zelide's life." He paused. "You will be in San Francisco for a while?"

"No," I said. "I've got to get back to the base tonight."

Although I'd known that all along, saying it came as a shock. I had only a few more hours with Iris. We'd frittered my whole precious leave away with those unspeakable Rose brothers.

Inspector Webb was looking grave. "I'm afraid I will need you for the inquests and the arrangements. If you give me the name of your commanding officer, I will see whether we cannot arrange an extension of leave."

He said that completely dead-pan. For a moment I didn't take it in. Then I grinned. Then Iris grinned.

"That would be swell," I began. "I—that is, I think it might be arranged."

The Inspector shrugged. "I will do my best. We'll need Mrs. Duluth too, of course. And now, perhaps, if you'll take a seat over there . . ."

Iris and I found seats together at the back of the room. We sat down. I took Iris's hand. I had stopped thinking about the Rose brothers. I was thinking more intimately again, in terms of the cupids' behinds.

Inspector Webb had called Mr. Catt and Zelide back to his desk. They were all gabbling together. I didn't listen. Then, from a door behind the desk, a policeman came in with two men. One of them was thin and greying, in a dark suit; the other was big and chunky. One wore a green tie; the other wore a red tie.

Iris nudged me. "Peter, there they are at last. The Red Rose and the White Rose."

After all they had done to us, I expected to see two monsters sinister enough to co-star with Boris Karloff. But at first glance the two men looked disappointingly like any other two respectable citizens.

I had only a brief glimpse of them, however, for at the same moment the door from the outside office opened and Hatch and Bill came in with another policeman. I waved enthusiastically at Hatch, and Iris and I hurried to join the group around the Inspector's desk.

Hatch and Bill and their policeman stood on the right. The two newcomers and their policeman stood on the left. Zelide and Mr. Catt were in the middle.

As we came up, Inspector Webb said: "Lieutenant Duluth, are you able to identify these two men?"

I stared at them. The one with the green tie lowered his eyes. The one with the red tie stared back at me stolidly.

"No," I said. "We only saw them in clowns' costumes. You couldn't tell. You . . ."

"I can identify them positively." It was Mr. Catt who spoke. He swung round with majestic dignity and pointed. "That is Bruno Rose—and that is Ludwig Rose."

"Yes, yes," added Zelide intensely. "That ees Bruno Rose and that ees Ludwig Rose, he who was my husband who keel Gino, who keel Eulalia and Lina and try to keel me. Those are them, the peegs."

Zelide was pointing in the same direction as Mr. Catt.

As I followed their pointing fingers, everything was suddenly as topsy-turvy as a torpedoed destroyer. I heard myself gasp. I saw Iris's mouth drop open in astonished horror.

Dimly I heard a voice. It was the voice of the newcomer with the green tie. "Yes, those are the men who came into our office Wednesday to make inquiries about Mrs. Lina Brown. The one on the left said he was her brother and wanted to locate her. My partner, Mr. Dagget, will corroborate."

"Yes," said the red tie. "Williams is right. Those are the men."

Both of them were pointing. Mr. Catt and Zelide were still pointing, too. And they were all pointing in the same direction.

They were pointing at the men whom I had known as Hatch Williams and Bill Dagget.

For a moment I was incapable of speech. Then I spluttered: "But it isn't possible. They're Hatch and Bill. They were with all the time."

"They helped us," peeped Iris.

"They—they even showed me their card," I said. "They must be Dagget and Williams."

Stiffly the red tie said: "I am Mr. Dagget and this"—indicating the green tie—"is Mr. Williams. If these two men showed you one of our cards, they obtained it when they visited our office last Wednesday."

"But . . ."

The Beard broke in: "And as for being with you all the time, Lieutenant—the whole picture is perfectly plain to me now. Posing as private detectives, they made you virtually prisoners from the very beginning. As their —ah—scapegoat, they could not afford to let you out of their sight. This is most interesting, most ingenious. I am afraid that you and your wife were thoroughly hoodwinked."

Hoodwinked!

Obviously, relishing my confusion, the Beard gestured at "Hatch." "Allow me to present Bruno Rose." He nodded at "Bill." "And permit me to present Ludwig Rose."

I stared glassily at our old "friends." They returned my stare. "Hatch's" melancholy eyes, whose pessimism had inspired me with such respect, were narrowed now in crafty contempt. "Bill's" handsome ox face was heavy with sullen, thwarted fury.

Realization of my own folly was flooding through me like sea water through an open porthole. Puppets! Iris and I had called ourselves puppets. But we hadn't known the half of it. The Rose brothers, with a brazenness that was staggering, had won our confidence and, even while they were murdering, had had time to oversee our every movement and direct us deeper and deeper into the pit they were digging for us.

Bruno and Ludwig Rose hadn't been just puppeteers. Nothing plain and simple about them.

They had been supercolossal puppeteers de luxe.

CHAPTER XIX

Mr. Catt's large—ah—rump was planted firmly between mine and Iris's on the sitting-room davenport of his suite at the St. Francis. He had just opened the fifth bottle of champagne and there was foam on his beard. He was very merry.

We should have been merry, too. Everything had worked out to perfection. Inspector Webb had contacted my commanding officer by telephone, and his extravagant praise had won me not only a five-day extension of leave but also a broad hint that the promotion would go through. Iris's studio, sensing her publicity value as a heroine-starlet, had consented to let her remain with me while they shot the movie around her. And, to cap it all, Mr. Catt, who was due to leave at midnight for Hollywood, where he was acting as technical adviser to a cinematized biography of *Lucrezia Borgia,* had gallantly signed his suite over to us. Everybody loved us; we had five full days ahead of us; we had the plushiest hotel suite of any married couple in San Francisco; we were full of champagne.

We should have been in an eighth or ninth heaven, but we weren't.

It was Mr. Catt himself who was being the rub. We admired him; we were grateful to him; we would probably erect a simple cenotaph to him if he died. But it was ten-thirty and he showed no signs of leaving and even less signs of stopping his monologue.

With his projected essay on the reappearance of the Rose brothers firmly in mind, he had made a painstaking reconstruction of our every movement and emotion. The more champagne he consumed, the more deeply he plunged into the intricacies of psychology. He was on the Rose brothers now.

"Most ingenious, most resourceful." He gulped his champagne and gave Iris the suggestion of a wink. "I spoke to one of the policemen who had searched their car. Everything was prepared for their getaway, even to bankbooks of deposits made in Mexico City under assumed names. If their plan of using you as their temporary—ah—red herring had worked, Lieutenant, they would almost certainly have been safe across the border by now, with their twisted lust for vengeance fulfilled."

"Yes," I said mechanically. I was looking at Iris. She was wearing her black evening gown again with virtually nothing above the hips. We had redeemed it along with the rest of our things from the Rose brothers' apartment on Fillmore. I was thinking about something that could only happen when we were alone.

"I have rarely if ever heard of murderers with such deftness, such genius for improvisation." America's foremost criminologist poured himself another glass of champagne. He still spoke in the rolling phrases of his literary style, but every now and then a slight clumsiness was slipping into his speech. "Let us review once more in its entirety their intricate method of exploiting you two to your uttermost."

Iris arranged her face into a bright smile. I tried to look intelligent. This would make the fourth time we had heard this routine and, even though every detail of it was familiar by now, the saga of our own gullibility still embarrassed me.

"Let us commence," said Mr. Catt, "with the two Rose brothers in the lobby of the St. Anton. They have learned that Madame Zelide has a room there and they are looking over the ground with a view to making an attack upon her. It should be clear that Madame Zelide's arrival in town was the signal for their crimes to begin because it was essential, if they were to fulfill their purpose and escape before the deaths were linked with the Forelli case, that all three women should be killed on the same night. Very well. By a most interesting coincidence they happened to observe your encounter with Madame Zelide—Mrs. Rose, as she was to you—at the desk, and they naturally believe Mrs. Duluth to be the Eulalia whom they have not seen for eight years. Here, they feel, may be a most fortunate opportunity to kill Eulalia, for they have certainly prospected at her apartment and discovered that she has rendered herself inaccessible there. In consequence, Bruno calls you on the house telephone only to discover that they have been mistaken and that the girl they saw in the lobby was merely Eulalia's cousin."

Iris yawned. She was very good about it. No one but me would have noticed the slight constriction of her jaw muscles.

"Very good." Mr. Catt passed a hand over the champagne-sprayed beard. "A pair of lesser criminals would have lost interest at that point, but not the Rose brothers. With a swiftness of thought which, I feel, we must attribute to Bruno, the cleverer of the two, they see at once how valuable Lieutenant Duluth could be to them as a means of gaining entrance to Eulalia's—ah—fortress. Ludwig is sent ahead to the Turkish bath. Bruno follows. It is simple for Bruno to take his brother's locker key, substitute it for Lieutenant Duluth's and slip Lieutenant Duluth's key to Ludwig. While Bruno keeps an eye on Lieutenant Duluth's progress through the baths, Ludwig can slip back to the lockers, dress himself in Lieutenant Duluth's uniform, and betake himself away. Now, were they to stop the grim little comedy there, Lieutenant Duluth might well have created a disturbance and reported the theft of his uniform to the police, which would have seriously jeopardized their plans for murdering Eulalia. Once again Bruno improvises a safeguard against this. Making use of the card which he has taken from Williams' and Dagget's office, he seizes an innocent-seeming opportunity to acquaint himself with Lieutenant Duluth and wins his confidence sufficiently to assure the fact that Lieutenant Duluth will not call in police aid for the stolen uniform. In this way, Ludwig's road to Eulalia is protected."

Iris looked at her watch and exchanged a rather wild glance with me. I fidgeted, but I still felt it would be impolite to remind Mr. Catt of the time. After all, it was his suite. What sort of gratitude would it be to evict him forcibly?

"Now here again, a lessher . . . exchush me, a lesser criminal might have felt his work was done, but not so Bruno. There was still the risk, slight, of course, but real, that Lieutenant Duluth and Mrs. Duluth would change their minds and pay a visit to Mrs. Duluth's cousin, after all. This had to be guarded against at all costs since their visit might well coincide with Ludwig's murderous one. So what does Bruno do? In character as Hatch Williams, the private detective, he strolls over to the St. Anton around nine, ostensibly to report on the stolen uniform, but in fact to keep Lieutenant and Mrs. Duluth under observation."

He hiccuped, put a large hand to his beard, bowed gravely to Iris, and continued: "Here, indeed, his genius for improvisation was put to a serious test because I appeared in the picture. Of course, he knew me by sight although I flatter myself that, until that moment, I had managed to conceal the fact from him that I was in San Francisco. The moment, however, that you told him of my warning message erroneously given to Mrs. Duluth on the assumption that she was Eulalia, he realized that my presence represented a grave menace to their plans. Bruno Rose also realized that if you two were to learn the whole story of Gino Forelli from me, you could no longer be cat's-paws—a slight pun there, I believe—but would also become grave menaces. But having heard from you of my—ah—indisposition, he appreciated the fact that there was no immediate danger of that. I had naturally aroused your interest and anxiety for Eulalia, and Bruno Rose could not dissuade you from telephoning to her without stirring your suspicions. Therefore, what did he do?" He looked at us rather blearily over his refilled glass of champagne. "What did he do?"

Iris and I said we didn't know. We knew perfectly well, but he liked it better that way.

With a broad smile of satisfaction, he continued: "Once again, he made a virtue of nesheshity. And it is here that Ludwig, the less perspicacious of the brothers, added his brilliant contribution to the scheme. Mrs. Duluth had telephoned Eulalia's apartment just at the moment when Ludwig, having killed her, was going to slip away. He realized in a flash that, having arrived at the apartment posing as Lieutenant Duluth, all he had to do was to persuade you two to come over and you would be hopelessly compromised with the death." He paused. "This phase will be paid most particular attention to in my eshay. It'sh . . ."

He hesitated, looking a little vague as if the threads of his argument were slipping. He drank some more champagne and his face brightened.

"Ah, yes, let us return to Bruno. While you were on your way to Eulalia's apartment and Ludwig was speeding away from it to their hideout, Bruno remained at the St. Anton to keep an eye on me. As I have said, so long as my—ah—indisposition continued, I was no danger to them. But the moment I was restored to health, I would naturally constitute the gravest possible menace, for I would either warn the ladies myself or go to the police. However, at that juncture, it was shafe enough merely to watch me. After some time, having become weary of the St. Anton, I proceeded to the Green Kinomo—ah—Kimono, where Bruno followed me. By that time he judged that Ludwig had returned to their apartment. In consequence, he telephoned him, informed him of my presence in San Francisco, and advised him to change from the uniform into a civilian suit and hurry to the Green Kim—to the bar and keep an eye on me. Bruno himself, meanwhile, returned to the St. Anton to see whether or not you would come back."

Iris gave another yearning look at her watch and murmured: "It's getting a little late, Mr. Catt. I think perhaps if . . ."

"And here"—Mr. Emmanuel Catt lifted a large hand, almost overturning an empty champagne bottle—"and here comesh a good part. Bruno was smart, very smart.

He knew you would have to do one of two things. You could call the police from Eulalia's and thereby get seriously involved in a murder charge which would give them ample time to kill Lina and Zelide and escape. Or, realizing the dangers of this step, you might return to the St. Anton in search of me. Bruno was ready for either exigency. You chose the second course, returned to the St. Anton, and Bruno was awaiting you."

I glanced over my shoulder. The bedroom door was open. I could see the bed. It was almost more than I could bear.

"With what dexshterity," exclaimed Mr. Catt, "did he walk on thin ishe—ice. Bent upon clearing yourselves of Eulalia's murder, you were naturally determined to pursue me and learn more of the Roses. As your announced friend, Bruno could not dissuade you. In fact, he welcomed any move that delayed your going to the police and had no fears of me in consequence of any indishposhishion. Therefore he led you both to the Green Nikomo and there introduced you to Ludwig as his partner, Dagget. If you look back you will doubtless recall that Ludwig, when he was known to you as Dagget, spoke very little and then only used words without shibilants so that you would not realize he lishped."

Mr. Catt smiled rather foolishly. "Now, neither Bruno nor Ludwig obviously dared to be seen by me, for fear that I would recognize them. Therefore, they remained in the bar while you two came into the back room to talk to me. There Mrs. Duluth was successful in obtaining Lina's address from me. Mrs. Duluth brought the news back to you at the bar and instantly Bruno had his plan for the murder of Lina perfect. It was as simple as it was daring and, if successful, would have disastrously incriminated Lieutenant Duluth."

Mr. Catt poured all that was left of the champagne into his glass. "When Bruno saw that the Lieutenant was determined to visit Lina and warn her of her danger, he appeared to encourage this step, merely persuading him to go first to the St. Anton and change into the civilian suit. This, of course, was to gain time for himself. For his own plan was to leave Ludwig in charge of Mrs. Duluth and me, to hurry back to their apartment, change into the uniform, send a telephone message to the drug-store which his investigations had told him was across the street from Lina, drive his car to Wawona Avenue, and murder Lina before Lieutenant Duluth, travelling by trolley, could arrive. It was his plan to have Lieutenant Duluth arrive at Wawona Avenue only to find Lina dead as Eulalia had been dead. However, thanks to his chance encounter with Mr. Grey, Lieutenant Duluth got there before Bruno. It was only a lucky accident for Bruno that kept Lieutenant Duluth from saving Lina then and seeing through the whole intricate web of—of desheet."

My head was spinning. I would have given a great deal for the opportunity to let out a loud, piercing scream.

"Having murdered Lina," continued Mr. Catt emphatically, "hish plan works according to schedule. He drivesh back to his—ah—base of operations, changes out of the uniform, and then, before you have time to return in the trolley, slips up to your room at the St. Anton and puts your uniform back in the closet. Key in pocket. Easy. Now why did he do that? Do you ashk me why?"

Iris looked at me. I looked at Iris.

In a dreadful, croaking voice, I said: "Why?"

America's foremost criminologist giggled. "I'll tell you why. Because tha' wash hish plan. Hish plan was t'put Lieutenant D'luth into so unlikely a position tha' no polishman on earth would ever believe hish story. An unknown gentleman with beard who warned about roses; two private detectives who didn't exist; and finally a uniform that had been stolen and yet hadn't been stolen. Young man, tha' wash his plan. And it succeeded. Sho unli'ly—no one would'v' b'lieved."

It seemed to me that, for the first time, the faintest suspicion had come to Mr. Catt that his—ah—indisposition might be returning. He drew himself up with imposing solemnity, shot a furtive glance at me out of the corner of his eye, and then continued:

"After that—shimple. Mrs. Duluth brought me to your room. You were there. Mrs. Duluth was there. Wha' hish plan? Leave ush all there! Shay he'll come back in morning to pick us all up and go to polishe. No intenshun going to pleesh really. Plan to arrive in morning, take ush all into hish car, pretend to take ush to pleesh, make some excushe, take ush to—ah—bashe 'f operationsh, lock ush in, maybe even kill ush, then go to shircush kill Zelide. But wha' happened? I—ashk—you. Wha' happened?"

He was weaving very slowly back and forth now. Something about him reminded me of Edwina.

"Wha' happened wash thish!" He leaned towards Iris. "I woke up in mi'l ni'. Left your room, bathtub, wen' back t' my roo'. Eshcaped. Put different complexshun enti'ly. Bruno furioush when he found I'd gone. I wash at liberty. Anything mi' happen. Got to find me before I came out of my indishposh . . . Wha' he do? Take you and Misush Duluth to hish 'partment, pershuaded you to wait there for him, tried to loca' me, failed, went to shircush, thinking you were shafe out of picture in 'partment. Went to shircush, hope kill Zelide, didn't work . . . you . . . me . . . Shtadium shellar . . . elephant . . . Edwina . . . th' elephan' . . ."

He was leaning over more heavily against Iris now. His eyes closed. His beard bobbed up and down.

Iris, shaking him sharply, said: "Mr. Catt, it's eleven. You've got to hurry or you'll miss your train."

Mr. Catt nestled against her. He half opened one eye and then closed it again.

I threw a despairing glance at the bedroom. I went over to him and started shaking him, too.

"Mr. Catt. Wake up. You're due in Hollywood. You've got to wake up."

Very slowly Emmanuel Catt opened his eyes. He twisted his head around so that his face was six inches from Iris's. His beard was tickling her cheek. He grinned last night's broad, goatish grin.

"Buriful girl," he said.

Iris looked at me hopelessly. "Peter . . ." And then, shaking him: "Mr. Catt . . . Mr. Catt, I say . . ."

"Mr. Catt," I bellowed.

Slowly, very slowly, Mr. Catt moved his head so that he was staring at me. He half raised a hand, trying to point.

"Nashty man," he said. "Go 'way. Nashty man. Boo!"

His eyes came up again, fixing on Iris's face. He gave a seraphic smile.

"Buriful girl," he muttered, "Nashty man. Buriful gi . . ."

He collapsed then with a thud into Iris's lap. His snores started to swell into their symphonic crescendo.

Iris stared at me over his beard. I stared at her.

With a sigh of resignation, she said: "Well, darling, what shall it be—the davenport or the bathtub?"

"He liked the bathtub last night," I said. "But this time—the davenport, I think."

"Why?" asked my wife.

I glanced into the bedroom.

"It's farther from our—ah—base of operations."

Birdy

"AN AMAZEMENT . . . ENCHANTING
. . . ELECTRIFYING."
The New York Times

Birdy

"MAY BE A CLASSIC FOR READERS
NOT YET BORN."
Philadelphia Inquirer

Birdy

"TO READ IT IS TO FLY"
People Magazine

Birdy

THE NATIONALLY ACCLAIMED NOVEL BY
WILLIAM WHARTON